MAYBE A WRITER
My Life In Threshold

Richard West

KINGMAKER PUBLISHING
First published in Great Britain by Kingmaker Publishing Limited in 2022
© 2022 Kingmaker Publishing Limited
www.kingmakerpublishing.com

Copyright © Richard West

Richard West has asserted his moral right under the
Copyright, Designs and Patents Act, 1988, to be identified
as the author of this work.

ISBN 978-1-8384918-3-3

Printed in Great Britain by
Biddles Books Limited, King's Lynn, Norfolk

MAYBE A WRITER

My Life In

Richard West

Now it's time for you to forget your distant glory
Now it's time for you to fulfil another story
Maybe a painter, a guide, a clerk, a maker
Or maybe a writer...

Threshold – *Lost In Translation*
from the album *Legends Of The Shires* (2017)

Contents

Prologue		xi
Chapter 1	To Somewhere I Belong	1
Chapter 2	Just Another Dream	9
Chapter 3	You Hoped And You Prayed	19
Chapter 4	Get Your Mind-Set Altered Here	31
Chapter 5	Control Is Hanging By A Thread	41
Chapter 6	No Straight Lines, No Simple Answers	51
Chapter 7	Goodbye Mother Earth	63
Chapter 8	The Storm That Won't Be Calmed	75
Chapter 9	There's Purpose In The Sky	87
Chapter 10	Can We Go On?	99
Chapter 11	There's A Storm Outside	111
Chapter 12	The Dust Of The Afterglow	123
Chapter 13	And So We Carry On	137
Chapter 14	A Faded Photograph	147
Chapter 15	The Moon Goes Round The World	155
Chapter 16	Greater Stories Still	165
Chapter 17	Stopped By Unrelenting Forces	173
Chapter 18	Don't Know What The Future Brings	181
Acknowledgements		191
Photography Acknowledgements		193

In loving memory of my father Anthony Templar West (1930-2022)

Prologue

As I drove into the muddy car park of Longcross village hall in my beloved, rusty Alfa Romeo 33, the band had already started rehearsing. It was a damp, neglected building surrounded by woodland, which made it feel like it was in the middle of nowhere, despite being only a stone's throw from the M3 motorway into nearby London. It was the perfect place to make a lot of noise.

I stepped out of the car, unloaded my keyboards from the boot and weaved my way between large puddles of rainwater towards the front door. As I walked into the building, I was immediately confronted by an immense wall of sound – drums, bass and heavy twin guitars – performing a monstrous riff that sounded like the most powerful thing I had ever heard. It was my first Threshold rehearsal, and I was suddenly nervous about how my keyboards would sound against such a huge sonic onslaught. Up until now I had only heard the songs within the controlled confines of the recording studio. Experiencing them performed live and loud was something else entirely.

So let me introduce you to the band…

On lead guitar was Karl Groom, the reason that I was becoming part of this massive soundscape. Cool, calm and softly spoken, his long hair offered the only clue that he was in a metal band. Karl had formed Threshold five years earlier in 1988, performing covers of songs like Def Leppard's *Animal* and Whitesnake's *Here I Go Again* in local pubs and student venues alongside original early compositions such as *Mother Earth* and *Paradox*. I had met him a couple of years earlier and this was now our third band together. We had instantly clicked over our mutual passion for music production and computer games, and had got to know each other quite well during long studio sessions and even longer road trips touring across Europe the year before. He was a phenomenal guitarist and had become a good friend. However, at this point the rest of the band members were less known to me.

MAYBE A WRITER

Behind the drums was Tony Grinham. I had met him briefly at the studio, and had spent many hours glued to his Amiga games console playing Sensible Soccer and Skid Marks with Karl after some late night recording sessions the year before. Tony was a lovely character, always ready with a funny comment or a joke. He adored being in Threshold, seeming to be not only the band's drummer but also its greatest fan. He had a roadie called Scott whose tasks appeared to involve setting up the drums and ensuring that Tony kept cool courtesy of a large fan and a seemingly endless supply of soft drinks. There was always a two-litre bottle of Coca Cola to hand, and the words 'Scott, Coke!' would become one the band's regular catchphrases.

On bass was Jon Jeary, the band's original vocalist, who had once famously fainted on stage while singing the high notes of *Mother Earth*. He looked like a perfect frontman too, with shoulder-length blonde hair and a constant sense of purpose about him. He was also an excellent wordsmith and was the lyric writer for the band. On guitar duties alongside Karl was Nick Midson, a quiet, shy figure with long bleached hair and a black leather jacket. He seemed oblivious to the fact that he looked like the coolest, most rock-star-like member of the band. He and Karl could riff together as one and the result sounded awesome.

And on vocals was Damian Wilson, who at that moment came bounding out of the hall's dingy kitchen and pounced on Jon like a tiger. Damian had the longest hair I had ever seen. He was highly gregarious and always bursting with energy. He had only joined the band the year before, having shown up at the studio one day with an acoustic guitar and a powerful voice while Karl was producing music for a mutual friend. Since then Threshold had released one song, the dark and brooding *Intervention*, before signing a record deal with a small independent label for their debut album *Wounded Land*. Damian greeted me warmly and I prepared to set up my keyboards.

At that moment in time, I had no idea that Threshold would become a major part of my life for the following three decades. I had only joined as a session player to record a few parts on the album, and I had no plans to immerse myself in the world of heavy metal. A year earlier I had been writing pop music for Simon Cowell and I was sure that was where my future lay. But, as I was soon to learn, the path you choose doesn't always lead where you expect. This particular journey would result in us producing 12 studio albums, performing in over 20 countries and getting ourselves in the charts along the way.

Prologue

But, right now, all I was worried about was how on earth I was going to hear what I was doing over the tremendous explosion of sound going on around me.

Tony counted us in and we launched into the opening bars of *Consume To Live*, as I hastily warmed up my fingers for the rather frantic lead solo that would be coming up in a few moments. This was a world away from how I thought music would be, growing up in rural England watching *Top Of The Pops* and writing songs on the family piano.

So, before I say anything more about where I found myself, let me say a little about how I got there…

Chapter 1

To Somewhere I Belong

I WAS BORN AT THE RATHER unsociable hour of 2:30am on 27th November 1967 at Redhill General Hospital in Surrey, England. I was given the name Richard Lansdowne West, the middle of these being an old family name which was just unusual enough for me to be embarrassed about as a young child and proud of as an older one.

Our family home for the first two years of my life was in the small, picturesque Surrey village of Abinger Common, from where my Dad would commute every day to London for his job as a management consultant. However, Dad found the long hours exhausting and both he and Mum yearned for the country life, so in 1970 they sold the house and headed west to the other side of the country and another small, picturesque village, this time located in south Devon. This village was called Newton Ferrers and it would be our home for the rest of my childhood.

Newton Ferrers was an idyllic place to grow up. Nestled on the estuary of the River Yealm, it is surrounded by farmland and served by half a dozen small shops, a church and a waterside pub. At low tide you can cross over to the neighbouring village of Noss Mayo by traversing one of two walkways (known as 'vosses') which are set deep into the riverbed. Rather coincidentally, the vosses are perfectly located to connect the village pub to two other drinking establishments in Noss Mayo. The vosses are best crossed on foot at low tide, not on a bicycle when the tide is coming in, as I would come to discover more than once when I was older.

Our house was called Steps Cottage and it was located half way up the river valley, surrounded by fields and seemingly endless woodland. At the foot of the valley below, the dark turquoise river flowed lazily towards the sea and was dotted with fishing boats, dinghies and yachts. For those familiar with her children's books, I can safely say that I enjoyed a proper Enid Blyton childhood, playing in the woods and messing about on the river with my two sisters, Caroline and Jo. Dad started an engineering company with a friend in the nearby village of South Brent before later moving into reproduction antique furniture. Mum set up a part-time business baking home-made cakes and biscuits, which she sold at a weekly market stall in the town of Totnes.

Dad bought a boat, so on Saturday mornings we would often carry packed lunches, life jackets and fishing equipment down the 30 steps to the lane in front of our house, followed by another 70 steps down the valley to a small quay on the riverside. From there we would row a wooden dinghy out to the boat and then set sail for the open sea, running fishing lines to catch pollock for dinner or stopping to have our lunch on a secret local beach that was only accessible by water. If we were lucky, we were allowed to hold the rudder, but only if there were no other boats nearby. When we returned to our mooring at the end of the trip, it was usually my job to clamber to the front of the boat and use a hook to catch the buoy where the boat was moored. This was the scariest part of our outings and I once fell overboard, but fortunately my life jacket did its job and I just bobbed up and down in the water until Dad fished me out.

Apart from having a picture-postcard view of the river and valley below, the house itself was rather less impressive. Steps Cottage was a tumbledown, timber-framed two-bedroom bungalow with no central heating. When we moved in, Dad had put up some panel walls to divide the two bedrooms into four smaller ones, providing us with sufficient sleeping areas but little in terms of space or soundproofing. We relied on log fires to heat the main living areas, and there was nothing better than warming up in front of a glowing fire after a long boat trip.

Steps Cottage was always filled with the sound of classical music. According to family history, when I was about two years old, I approached one of Dad's huge hi-fi loudspeakers and pressed my body, hands and face against it to absorb the sound. I don't recall what piece of music was playing but evidently the experience made a significant impression on me. My whole family is very musical and growing up we always had two pianos in the house so we could play duets together. In his younger days my Dad had won the annual music prize at King's School Bruton. He was a keen chorister and had toured Italy with the Bach Choir, sung with the London Symphony Chorus and performed at one of my favourite venues, the majestic Royal Albert Hall in London. By the age of five, I was enrolled in piano lessons, and after a few years I had started writing some basic compositions of my own.

When I was eight years old, I was taken out of the local primary school in Newton Ferrers and moved to Plymouth College Preparatory School, a private school 11 miles from home. On my first day I was moved up a year because I was considered to be a smart pupil, so I found myself surrounded by boys who were much older than me. Preparatory school was a blur of black, red and green school uniforms, scary disciplinarian teachers who would call you to the front of the class to whack your hands with wooden rulers if you couldn't remember something, trading Star Wars cards in the playground between lessons and trying to offload the worst elements of school dinners such as liver, swede or strange grey gooseberry puddings to anyone who would have them.

There was very little to enjoy about preparatory school, and my abiding memory is of standing in the playground shivering, wondering why we were forced to wear short trousers in the middle of winter. One day, I attempted to break the monotony by supergluing my best friend Mark to his seat during Mathematics. It didn't help at all, and we both got in a lot of trouble. Thankfully, a couple of years later I successfully graduated to Plymouth College senior school and life improved considerably.

Although most of the music at home was classical, the exception was on Thursday nights when we would watch *Top Of The Pops*, a weekly BBC TV show that featured the latest pop and rock music. Mum noticed which songs I liked and one day she bought me a couple of 7" singles, Billy Joel's *My Life* and Queen's *Don't Stop Me Now*. I was utterly captivated by them. I had yet to discover the wonders of record stores and had no idea that the songs I saw on TV could be bought and played on a record player. I listened to them endlessly, and when I had heard them enough times I started working out how to play them on the piano, first the melodies and then the bass notes and basic chords. I had been starting to find piano practice rather dull, but this gave me a whole new love for the instrument. It wouldn't necessarily help with my classical exams, but it was invaluable for learning how to play music by ear.

I wasn't the only boy from Newton Ferrers to attend Plymouth College. Another was Brendan Hansford and he was like an older brother to me. We spent many weekends and school holidays playing tennis together at the courts across the river in Noss Mayo, or skateboarding down the village's many hills. Most of them were too steep for skateboarding and were more suitable for tobogganing during the winter, but Court Road was perfect. It was a downhill stretch of road about half a mile long which started near my house and ended close to Brendan's house. We would spend hours racing down that hill, peddling back up and racing down again, sometimes marking chalk slalom courses on the tarmac to make it more challenging. There were very few cars on the road, so it was a wonderful place to while away an afternoon.

We also enjoyed making music together. Every household seemed to have an upright piano in those days and there was one at Brendan's house. There was also an old acoustic guitar and Brendan had recently bought an electric guitar and a small practice amplifier. Armed with these weapons we would sit and jam for hours. One moment we would be working out how to play something from his record collection such as *Paranoid* by Black Sabbath, with Brendan riffing away on his electric guitar while I played the bass part on the acoustic, and the next moment we would be trying out something I had written on the piano.

It was Brendan who introduced me to albums. One day he lent me his copy of *...And Then There Were Three...* by Genesis. He told me it would take a few spins to get used to, and suggested I tried the song *Say It's Alright Joe* first as he thought it was the most accessible. So that evening, I carefully placed the LP onto Dad's turntable, dimmed the living room lights, sat on the floor in front of the huge loudspeakers and had my mind blown. It was love at first listen, and it has remained one of my favourite albums for my whole life. When I hear it, I'm instantly transported back to that moment, absorbing those soaring melodies, the beautiful keyboards and the complexity of the music so far beyond the pop singles that I had heard up until that point. I know everybody has their favourite Genesis album and nobody agrees with each other, but this one changed my world forever and will always be my first love. This was my introduction to progressive rock.

* * *

Towards the end of 1979 I discovered that there was also pop music on the radio. I started tuning in to the Top 40 singles chart countdown on BBC

Radio 1 every Sunday night, and this would become my main source of new music for the next few years.

In fact, it would become my obsession. I was captivated by the assortment of rock and pop music moving up and down the charts every week from acts such as The Police, Status Quo, Rainbow and Gary Numan. Every weekend I would join countless other kids across the nation who recorded their favourite songs from the radio onto cassette tapes, hoping that the disc jockey wouldn't talk too much over the start or end of the song and spoil the recording. Taking the obsession one step further, I also wrote down the chart countdown every week and re-ordered the songs into my own personal chart. I knew that one day I wanted to be in the Top 40. Little did I know how long it would take for that to happen, or that it would taste so bittersweet when the moment finally came to pass.

I gave my first live performance when I was around 12 years old. I had been selected to play a short classical piano piece at a rather sombre school recital. It all started fine, but then went horribly wrong in the middle when I forgot how the piece went. I tended to memorise pieces rather than relying on the sheet music, but in front of an audience my nerves got the better of me and I couldn't remember how it went. There was a painfully awkward silence which felt as if it lasted a lifetime but was probably only a few seconds. I wanted the ground to swallow me up. I looked desperately up at the sheet music and tried to work out where I was. Finally, I found my place and finished the piece, earning myself a rather hesitant and awkward round of applause from the numerous parents, teachers and fellow students who were in the audience. I knew one thing: I had absolutely no interest in doing that again.

I was a socially awkward child, unable to sit still or concentrate, and usually on the verge of getting into trouble for one thing or another. Unsure of what to do with me, my parents took me to see a child psychologist in the hope of understanding what was going on in my head. After a few sessions I was diagnosed as hyperactive, and it was eventually concluded that this was caused by an allergy to artificial food colouring.

Nowadays such allergies are well understood, but when I was a child this knowledge was only just starting to emerge. Artificial food colouring was everywhere; not just in brightly coloured sweets, but also in sausages to make them look more appetising, in margarine to make it more yellow, and even in oranges to make them more, well, orange. It seemed as though it was impossible to avoid. As a result, I was given special school lunches and banned from eating colourful sweets. Sadly, the change of diet didn't make me any less socially awkward. The social habits you learn as a child are hard to shake off, and joining a separate queue each day for a special school lunch only made me feel more cut off from my classmates.

By now I had written a few songs and made recordings of myself singing them at the piano. I had no idea how professional records were made, but I knew that, if I wanted to produce music of my own, I needed a way of capturing more than just the piano and vocals. I needed a way to add more layers to make them sound more like the songs I heard on the radio. There were two portable cassette recorders in our house, so I experimented by recording the piano and vocal onto one cassette and then playing it back at the same time as performing another instrument, capturing the result on the second cassette recorder.

The results were quite poor, mainly because the process relied on a low-quality microphone in one machine picking up the sound from a low-quality loudspeaker in the other one. The more parts I added, the worse the sound quality became. However, I wasn't too concerned at the time; the important thing was that I now had a rudimentary way of making multi-track recordings.

I had recently started cello lessons after being enthralled by a solo cello recital in our local village hall. We also had a ukulele in the house which I could play to a reasonable standard, so both of these instruments started to feature on my early recordings. I didn't have any drums, so I made do with hitting large empty cardboard boxes with pieces of wood. One of my drumsticks was a curved wooden slat from the back of a broken dining chair. The songs I was writing were a fairly varied assortment, mostly pop-rock in style but with the occasional piano ballad or tentative foray into the more complex world of progressive rock.

At the age of 13 I started my fourth year at Plymouth College. This was an important moment, because fourth year pupils were allowed to leave the school grounds during lunch break. Our free time was between 12:45pm and 2:00pm, so a hastily swallowed lunch meant there was just over an hour to explore the city. For me, that meant one of two things: video arcade games or record shops.

Quite close to the school were a café and a snooker club, both of which had arcade games. The school strictly banned us from entering either establishment, so visiting was risky but a few of us always managed to get in. For some of my friends it was just a place to smoke cigarettes, an activity that was also forbidden. But I wasn't interested in smoking; I was just there for the games. The café had a space shooter game called *Gyruss* and the snooker club had an athletics game called *Track & Field*. Both of these were highly addictive, and many ten pence pieces were surrendered in the pursuit of high scores and bragging rights.

Slightly further afield was Plymouth city centre, a brisk 15-minute walk for an eager teenager. And this gave me access to record shops. My first stop would be in Plymouth's main music store, HMV on New George Street. However, while it was fun to browse all of the latest releases, most albums cost at least £4.99, which was more than my pocket money would allow. A few doors down from HMV there was a Woolworths convenience store which had a 'Reduced' section, selling older 7" singles that were no longer in the charts, so this would be my second port of call. Although it was rare to find something I wanted, the price of 29p instead of the usual 99p meant it was always worth a visit.

Once I had finished browsing in Woolworths, I would head a little further down the street to the south entrance of Plymouth's indoor market. This consisted of a huge array of booths and stalls selling food, clothing, jewellery and antiques, and, most importantly of all, second-hand records. There were usually two or three sellers at the market who offered an assortment of singles and LPs, and I could browse forever, checking back every week for new additions in their seductive wooden crates.

My final destination was my favourite store of all. It was called Wants and it was located in Market Way, just along from the north exit of the market. Wants was a second-hand store specialising in records, electronic equipment and musical instruments. And it was my heaven. The selection of records was fairly small compared to the indoor market, but the store owner was clearly a progressive rock fan. His crates were full of mysterious looking record sleeves by the likes of Genesis, Yes and Emerson Lake & Palmer, and often I would be drawn to records just because of their artwork. But the most alluring part of the shop was at the far end of the room, beyond the record displays and the shelves of used hi-fi equipment and loudspeakers. It was the synthesizer section.

Nestled amongst an assortment of used electric guitars, amplifiers and home organs was a wondrous collection of monophonic synthesizers. Made by exotic sounding companies such as Moog, Korg, Roland and SIEL, these beautiful creations looked like they had just arrived from outer space. They were covered in flashing lights and had knobs and sliders for adjusting oscillators, filters and a multitude of other parameters that I had never heard of. If the shop was quiet, I would try them out, experimenting with the controls and trying to recreate the sounds on my favourite records.

One day I would eventually buy my first proper synthesizer from this coveted collection, a SIEL Mono synthesizer, but for the moment I could only dream.

Chapter 2

Just Another Dream

APART FROM MUSIC, my other great passion was computing. It was 1982 and arcade games were now everywhere, transporting players into space battles for a few glorious minutes with *Defender*, *Phoenix* and *Galaxian*, or losing them in the pixelated worlds of *Pac-Man* and *Donkey Kong*. That year my parents bought me my first home computer, a Sinclair ZX81. It was a small black box with a miniature keyboard, no screen and no hard drive. You had to plug it into the TV to see what you were doing, and any computer code that you wrote had to be saved onto cassette tape. It was incredibly basic and boasted a mind-bogglingly tiny 1 kB of memory. But I was hooked.

I learned to write simple programs, such as making a blocky-looking ship move across the screen and a submarine that could shoot at it. But the 1 kB memory was a serious limitation. The later addition of a 16 kB memory pack transformed everything, because now I could recreate basic versions of some of my favourite arcade games like *Space Invaders* or *Frogger*, although anything more complex wasn't possible because the computer's processor was too slow. I would sit for hours writing code while I listened to recordings of my latest compositions on repeat.

The following year I got an Acorn Electron, a more powerful computer with better graphics, larger memory and a much faster processor. It came with a few games, but my passion was to code them myself, and with this new machine I was able to tackle more complex games like *Pac-Man* and the challenging final level of *Phoenix*, something that hadn't been possible on the ZX81. I also tried my hand at programming strategy games such as *Connect 4* that could play against me. Dad had first bought me the ZX81 in the hope that it would provide me with some useful skills for my future career, and although programming arcade games wasn't exactly what he had in mind, the coding skills I acquired proved very useful later in life.

However, while my computer skills were thriving and my songwriting skills were starting to develop, my school work was suffering. Despite my special diet, artificial food colouring was hard to avoid completely, especially with the temptations of sweet shops and school tuck shops, so I continued to be a hyperactive and disruptive pupil. Because of this, as the final term of my fourth year at Plymouth College drew to a close, I was told that I would have to repeat the year.

Over the summer my Mum enrolled me onto a week-long church camp. I was slightly apprehensive, but I was told that I would spend most of the time playing football, so I agreed to go along. The campsite was set in a large field in the countryside, and during the evenings we would all gather in a marquee to hear about God. On the last morning the organisers asked if they could pray for me to be healed of my food colouring allergy. After a moment's hesitation I accepted, so everyone closed their eyes and started to pray. When I got home later that day I rushed into the house and jumped up and down excitedly, trying to explain to my Mum that I was no longer hyperactive! It must have been rather hard for her to believe as she watched me bouncing around the room, but from that moment on I no longer had a problem with food colouring.

For the rest of the summer holidays I busied myself with my music. The quality of my productions had improved thanks to the addition of two pieces of equipment from my parents. The first was a Teleton dual cassette music centre, which replicated my previous multi-track recording process but without so much loss of sound quality. The second was my first electronic keyboard, a cheap and cheerful Casiotone CT101 with 15 built-in sounds. I am forever grateful to Mum and Dad for these two gifts. Although they were a long way from being professional studio equipment, they cost far more than anything we were given for birthday and Christmas presents, and were way beyond the reach of my pocket money. But they knew how much I wanted to progress with music, and this new gear helped to shape the next stage of my development.

In September 1982 I returned to Plymouth College to retake my fourth year and joined a new class of boys my own age. Most of them had been together for years and had already formed close friendships and groups, so I was a bit of an outsider. But they gave me a warm welcome and one by one I started to get to know some of them and make friends. However, it wouldn't be long before something happened that stopped me getting too close to anyone for a while.

One school lunchtime, I was browsing the reduced-price singles in Woolworths as usual when I noticed a dark shadow fall over me. Suddenly, before I knew what was happening, I felt a large hand groping me from behind and I heard the low voice of a man offering me £50 to go with him. I was absolutely terrified. In a blind panic I managed to escape his grasp and bolted for the exit. I ran down the road towards the indoor market as fast as my legs could carry me, convinced that he was following me and desperate to lose him in the maze of market stalls. I exited the market on the opposite side, ducked up a small alley beside Wants and finally stopped to catch my breath. There was no sign of him.

I headed back to school, constantly looking behind me to make sure I wasn't being followed. The whole experience left me very shaken and had a profound effect on my behaviour. I started to avoid crowded spaces, preferring the safety of solitude to the fear of not knowing who was around me. I couldn't bear to be followed and I would cross the street or change direction so that nobody was walking behind me. The events of that lunchtime changed my personality completely, making me slow to trust other people and turning me into something of a loner.

I stopped visiting the record shops after that, preferring to stay in the safety of the school grounds. One of my classmates discovered I was a Queen fan and offered to sell me five of their albums for £12 as he had grown bored of them. It was an absolute steal and I listened to them endlessly, devouring every detail from the experimental echo-laden guitar solo on *Brighton Rock* through to the sophisticated balladry and vocal harmonies of *Play the Game*. Queen was now officially my favourite band.

* * *

As 1983 came around, the world looked bright and sumptuous. Huge blockbuster movies like *Star Wars: Return of the Jedi*, *Octopussy* and *Flashdance* filled our local cinema screens, and the UK music charts were dominated by the equally glamorous synth pop of bands like Duran Duran, Spandau Ballet and Depeche Mode. My schoolmates were starting to make music too, and before long my class boasted three guitarists, a bassist and a drummer.

MAYBE A WRITER

Simon Rees and Bruce McCarthy were two cheeky best friends who had bought electric guitars. They called themselves The Undesirables and had written a catchy punk song called *Beat In Time*. Another boy called Richard Turner was learning bass, and one day the four of us assembled at his parents' house for our first jam. His parents had a home organ, which made every sound you could possibly wish for as long as you wanted something that sounded like a church organ. We jammed our way through *Beat In Time*, with me adding very non-punk organ parts in the background, and so our first attempt at a school band was born. Occasionally we would be joined by Paul Hawkins, who had an electronic drum unit with four pressure-sensitive pads. I don't think we ever settled on a band name and we never played any gigs, but we got together quite a few times to practise. I had written a rather dreary ballad called *Blue Forest* and we spent many sessions running through that, but eventually our enthusiasm waned, and the band disappeared as fast as it had begun.

The following year my music production quality took another step forward thanks to a surprising gift from some neighbours. The musical theatre writing duo George Stiles and Anthony Drewe had rented the cottage next door while they were preparing for one of their musicals to be staged in Plymouth. They were great guys and became good friends with our family. They had recently upgraded their recording set-up from a four-track recorder to an eight-track machine, and they very kindly decided to give me their four-track recorder. I was blown away; it was incredibly kind of them. It meant I could now record more tracks layer on layer, moving me another small step towards a professional recording set-up.

I had now started compiling my finished home recordings onto cassette tapes to make my own albums. I began sharing copies with my classmates, and this was when I experienced my first reviews. The general tone was encouraging but that the vocals could use some improvement. I remedied this by enlisting my younger sister Jo, whose voice sounded a lot nicer than mine, and we gave ourselves the name Pink Noise. The subsequent tapes were much better received by my classmates, although looking back I think they were probably more interested in my sister than the music.

By the age of 16 my best subjects at school were Mathematics and French. I had benefitted from being taught the basics of French three times: once at the primary school in Newton Ferrers, then at the preparatory school and a third time when I started at Plymouth College. However, as my class prepared to take our French O Level exams, I was annoyed to discover that we had a new teacher who couldn't control the classroom and was unlikely to help me progress further. He was actually a lovely chap, and I suspect he would have made a great teacher for older, more mature students. But in a school where most teachers ruled the class with strict authority, his class became one of the few places where we could misbehave and cause chaos. I suspect I was one of the worst offenders.

It all started innocently enough. We used to fold up pieces of paper to make small V-shaped pellets that we could flick across the room at high speed using elastic bands. At first, we would just flick them at each other, but after a while we started firing them at the teacher while he was writing on the board. He would invariably spin around in a fury and slam his hands on his table, before slowly marching towards whoever was sitting at the front of the classroom and placing his hands on the corners of their desk. From here he would peer around the room and try to locate the culprit. He would hurl a volley of insults at us, using a variety of choice phrases such as 'insolent morons' and 'blithering idiots'. Always one to love a chart, I would keep a tally of his most used phrases in the back of my exercise book. 'Insolent morons' topped the charts for most of the year.

Once I had learned his behaviour patterns, I hatched a cunning plan. One day before class began I decided to sit at the desk nearest the front. I squeezed out some ink from a cartridge pen onto the corners of the desk. Then I went to the front of the classroom and moved the teacher's table so that it was balanced precariously on the edge of its podium. I took my seat and watched the scene unfold. It worked beautifully. After firing a few painful pellets into the teacher's hind quarters, he spun around furiously and slammed his hands on the table. The table slipped off the podium with a loud clatter, sending his briefcase and books flying. He looked up in a rage, his face turning a deep shade of purple. He marched slowly forwards and placed his hands on the corners of my desk. They landed perfectly in the ink. Bullseye! I tried to keep calm. I wanted to run for cover and burst out laughing at the same time. He leaned towards me and stared furiously into my eyes. "Did you do that?" he growled in a low, menacing voice. "Of course not," I replied. "Do you think I would be stupid enough to sit at the front if it had been me?" I don't think he believed me.

MAYBE A WRITER

Corporal punishment was common at Plymouth College in the 1980s. I was once caned for being disruptive during English class, and 'slippered' (repeatedly whacked with a training shoe) during Physical Education for no apparent reason whatsoever. Our deputy headmaster Frank 'Judge' Jeffries could often be spotted patrolling the school grounds, menacingly flexing a long cane in search of troublemakers. One boy who was more regularly on the receiving end of this cane than most was Geoff Warren, a mischievous character who sat at the back of our classroom. He was also a budding guitarist and one day he invited me to his house to jam. We got on well and started to meet up regularly, sometimes at his house and sometimes at mine. We gave ourselves the name Emergency Exit. We were both aspiring songwriters and before long we had a number of original songs in our repertoire. The culmination of our efforts would be two gigs, one at a house party and one at the school.

The house party was at Jeremy King's house. Jeremy was one of Geoff's neighbours and a keen model maker, who would go on to have a successful career creating special effects and models for the film industry. But that night he was the host of my first ever live gig. Up first that evening was Simon Rees, performing a selection of covers by the likes of The Jam, Pat Benatar and The Waterboys, alongside a few original songs of his own, with me occasionally accompanying him on the keyboards. And then it was the turn of Emergency Exit, with special guest vocals by our host Jeremy on a track that Geoff had written about school called *Alphabet Rap*, as well as a few more of our own compositions and covers of songs by Dire Straits, Re-Flex and Spandau Ballet. I loved every second and wished it could go on all night. It couldn't have been more different to my sombre piano recital experience.

The second gig was at the end of year concert at Plymouth College, an evening of music, comedy, sketches and speeches. A group of us performed three tracks, consisting of Geoff's *Alphabet Rap* and two cover songs. The first of these was Pink Floyd's *Another Brick in the Wall (Pt. 2)*. We had practised it in the school music room, but Geoff wasn't confident playing David Gilmour's soaring guitar solo, so it was decided that I would play it on my Casiotone CT101 through a home-made fuzz box that Geoff had made for me. David Gilmour, please forgive me. I'm sure there have been many renditions of this song over the years to varying degrees of competence, but I can only imagine what our version sounded like!

The final song of our set was a cover of *Hey Jude* by The Beatles, except with the words rewritten and the title changed to *Hey Judge* in honour of our much-feared deputy headmaster. By now Geoff and Judge had become good friends, and it was decided that during our rendition of *Hey Judge* he would march into the school hall holding his cane and looking furious. It was the perfect climax to the concert, and some of the younger boys in the audience looked truly petrified as Judge threw open the door at the back of the hall and walked grimly towards the stage. The effect was only slightly lessened by the fact that Judge was finding it very hard not to smile, an expression that none of the pupils at Plymouth College had ever seen on his usually stern and frightening face.

* * *

Once I had passed my driving test, Dad bought an old Fiat 126 from a neighbour so that my older sister Caroline and I could drive ourselves to school. It was an absolutely tiny machine with a 650cc two-cylinder engine, an official top speed of 65 miles an hour and the ability to crawl from 0 to 60 mph in a soporifically slow 47 seconds. It seemed like a suitably powerless car to keep us safe and stop us getting into trouble. However, the flipside was that the only way to get anywhere was to treat the accelerator as an on-off switch, so later when I started driving more powerful cars I always tended to go too fast.

I only crashed the Fiat twice. I came very close a third time, but thankfully stopped a few centimetres short of the dry-stone wall after my handbrake turn had sent me skidding out of control. I had quickly got to know the car, constantly pushing it to its limits to learn every subtlety of its handling and behaviour. At least, that was what I thought.

One Saturday I was driving along a single-track country lane to a local beach with four friends, which to be honest was a bit of a squash. Suddenly another car came around the corner and the road was too narrow for both of us. I slammed on the brakes, but the extra weight of my passengers was too much for the poor little car and it wouldn't stop. I felt very sorry for the driver of the other vehicle, who had accidentally taken a wrong turn and had not meant to be on that road at all. I felt quite sorry for myself too.

The second collision took place late at night as I was driving home, very carefully I thought, from an evening out at Fiestas nightclub in Plymouth.

MAYBE A WRITER

Suddenly I hit some black ice and skidded gracefully, almost in slow motion, into the car coming the other way. My parents weren't very happy. Fortunately, they didn't know about the handbrake turns. I had recently discovered that if you pulled on the handbrake and span the steering wheel you could do a 180 degree turn and race off in the opposite direction. It was particularly satisfying on wet, country roads and I became somewhat of an expert. It didn't work so well on grass though, as the lack of grip sent you skidding off in the wrong direction, and that was when I had narrowly missed the dry-stone wall. As an aside, the Fiat could definitely go above 65 mph, especially down a long hill such as the A38 towards Buckfastleigh where I once reached 80 mph, as the local policeman would readily attest.

On my 18th birthday I was given some money towards my dream purchase, the SIEL Mono synthesizer which had been lurking seductively in the far left-hand corner of Wants for the lofty price of £175. Armed with this wondrous new machine, the old family piano, a cheap electric guitar and a Roland TR606 drum machine that I had bought for £100 by selling my childhood train set, the quality of my recordings rose a little higher. However, any dreams of producing a professional recording would have to stay on hold. I knew nothing of the world of record deals, recording studios and pressing plants, and it would be another eight years before I would finally be on a proper album.

* * *

The first artist I ever saw perform live was Gary Numan. Not many pop or rock tours came to Plymouth, with most major artists only travelling as far west as Bristol. One day a school friend called Kevin Johnston managed to score tickets to see Gary Numan performing at Colston Hall in Bristol. Kevin was a budding musician too, and had recently written and recorded a song that was not dissimilar to Gary Numan; I remember being very impressed. So, on 6th October 1985, we drove to Colston Hall for my first ever experience of a pop concert.

We showed our tickets at the door and made our way excitedly into the huge, dark hall. First up was the support act, a little-known new wave band called Grey Parade, who had just released a promising single called *Asleep* on Gary Numan's own record label. They were a decent band and I later bought the single. Unfortunately, like countless bands that have come and gone over the years, they would discover that supporting a huge artist was no guarantee of superstardom, and sadly they never achieved mainstream success.

The lights dimmed and Gary Numan made his way onto the stage to the opening sounds of *No Shelter*. The crowd went wild. Gary looked iconic with black hair, white suit and red bow tie, in stark contrast to countless fans dressed in older Numan-inspired looks, many with blue hair and lipstick emulating his *Berserker* look from the year before. I wasn't too familiar with Gary's latest music, but his earlier hits *Cars* and *Are 'Friends' Electric?* (with his former band Tubeway Army) had made a huge impression on me, and when he performed these songs I was ecstatic. I remember watching Gary and knowing that the job of being a frontman didn't appeal to me at all. I would much rather be the one producing the evocative and powerful music behind him that had me captivated for the whole night.

* * *

With my time at school finally drawing to a close, I had to decide what to do next. Simon Rees had spotted a degree course called Electroacoustics in the Universities Central Council on Admissions handbook, a list of all the courses available at universities across the UK, and he thought I might be interested. Most students at Plymouth College were expected to attend university, but, with the possible exception of Computer Sciences, I had been struggling to find anything that I wanted to study. There were no courses related to popular music or studio engineering in those days, and I wasn't interested in a classical music degree. Besides, I was doing A Levels in Mathematics, Further Mathematics and Physics rather than Music, so I had already abandoned any thoughts of classical music studies.

The only university that offered the Electroacoustics course was at Salford, a town on the outskirts of Manchester in the north west of England. So I travelled up to Salford to attend an open day and was pleased to learn that most people who took the Electroacoustics course also tended to be aspiring musicians.

That sounded good enough to me; all I really wanted to do was form a band.

Chapter 3

You Hoped And You Prayed

AT THE END OF SUMMER 1986 I packed up all of my possessions and moved north to start my new life at Salford University. My home would be a small room on the ground floor of the Oaklands Halls of Residence in Salford, a student accommodation block a couple of miles north of the university campus. I soon discovered that one of the guys on my course lived just along the corridor from me. His name was Garvin Wills and it transpired that he was a bass player. We became good friends, and many evenings would end with us making toasted marmalade sandwiches (the only meal we knew how to cook) and listening to our favourite records.

Before long we started jamming together, playing our own versions of songs such as *Don't You Want Me* by The Human League and *Rio* by Duran Duran with its captivating bass line that Garvin could play perfectly. My set-up now consisted of a new Roland TR505 drum machine, the SIEL Mono and a Korg Poly 800 synthesizer, and with these I was able to produce a more professional sound than I had during my school days. Garvin knew of a guitarist called Ian Venner who lived on the other side of the halls, so it wasn't long before we formed a band. The only missing ingredient was a singer.

Salford was a tough place to be a student. It soon became clear that some of the locals intensely disliked their town being overrun by outsiders, and we started to hear regular reports of students getting beaten up by gangs of local youths while walking to and from the university campus. I was fortunate never to be attacked, but Garvin and I had a close call one afternoon when we were chased by an angry mob in a Ford Fiesta as we were skateboarding outside Oaklands Halls. Thankfully we just got through the narrow entrance gate before they caught up with us and managed to escape unharmed.

As a result of this constant threat to student safety, taxi sharing became the standard way of getting to lectures. Each morning there would be a long line of students queuing up on Oaklands Road to catch the next available taxi to the university campus. One morning after breakfast, Garvin and I were standing in the queue contemplating how we should go about finding a singer, when a girl behind us overheard our conversation. "I can sing," she said. At that moment the next taxi arrived. We both climbed into the vehicle followed by the girl and her friend. The girl was called Theresa Sawford, and by the time we arrived at the campus she had become our singer.

Our brand new four-piece band started rehearsing regularly and loudly in my small bedroom, with my Roland drum machine providing the rhythm section. After much deliberation we eventually settled on the rather dull band name of Up From Under, although for some reason we thought it sounded good at the time. We put together a set of original material that consisted mostly of songs I had written at school, along with a couple more recent compositions. It all came together very quickly, and before we knew it we had booked our first gig. Up From Under would be performing a 30-minute lunchtime set in the Union Bar at Salford University on Friday 5th December 1986.

Two things surprised me that day. The first was how many people showed up. It was a lunchtime gig, which is obviously not a normal time to put on a show. However, student bands were rare in those days, and as far as I could tell there were only two other bands active at Salford University at the time: a highly entertaining second-year Blues Brothers inspired group called Papa Demetrious & The Smurfs, and a more serious final-year band called File Under Q. So maybe the novelty factor drew people to our concert. It probably also helped that we had been very busy plastering the campus and halls of residence with photocopied A3 posters advertising the event. As we took to the stage that Friday lunchtime the Union Bar was packed out with about 300 fellow students.

The second thing that surprised me was that they actually appeared to like us. At my two previous concerts in Plymouth I hadn't noticed whether anyone had cheered or not; I was too busy focussing on the music. But today as we finished our opening number, an up-tempo track called *Your Dance* that would one day form the basis of the Threshold ballad *Avalon*, the crowd were ecstatic. I must confess that I was rather taken aback. It was just a song that I had written in my bedroom in Newton Ferrers the previous year, and now there were hundreds of people cheering it. I could get used to this.

More gigs followed and we made plans to record a demo tape. We booked a large room in Oaklands Halls and borrowed some recording equipment from the final-year band File Under Q. Unfortunately, as we were setting up, our guitarist Ian was subjected to a huge electric shock from one of the amplifiers, which wasn't earthed properly, and an ambulance had to be called. Thankfully he was fine, but our recording session was over before it had begun. The end of our first year at university was looming, so we all prepared to head home and the recording session never got rescheduled.

During the holidays I did some part-time work for my Dad, delivering furniture around the UK in a large van. Over the previous few years he had established a successful business designing and manufacturing furniture, and he now supplied a number of shops around the country, including the famous Harrods and Fortnum & Mason stores in London. He even had a couple of pieces in Buckingham Palace. He usually took care of the deliveries himself to stay in touch with his clients, but deputising the job to me during the holidays gave him a much-needed rest. As far as I was concerned, I was getting paid £2.50 an hour to listen to music. The van had a good sound system, and I absolutely loved the long road trips, getting to know the country to the soundtrack of my favourite albums.

I would happily drive for hours without a break, although sometimes I pushed myself too far. One evening I was approaching my destination after a particularly long day. I was getting very tired and it was a struggle to keep my eyes open. I had tried everything – turning up the music, opening the window, taking off one shoe, anything to keep me awake. Finally I saw the motorway sign that announced my exit and I breathed a sigh of relief. The next thing I remember was waking up in the next lane of the motorway. The shock of realising I had fallen asleep at the wheel coursed through my body and I was suddenly wide awake. It could have been fatal, and I was very lucky there were no other vehicles around me at the time. After that I was a lot more careful about my hours, and those long road trips would prove to be useful training for band journeys later on.

＊＊

As I returned to Salford for my second year at the end of summer 1987, it became apparent that Up From Under was over. Theresa was no longer interested in being in a band and Ian had joined a gothic rock group called

MPD (Missing Presumed Dead) with some other students. Garvin and I spent a few weeks searching for a new singer, but we couldn't find anybody suitable. Instead, I devoted my time to writing and recording songs in my room, with Garvin on bass and various other students performing vocals, guitars or the occasional saxophone solo as needed. As much as I missed being in a band, I was really enjoying producing music in my little bedroom studio.

The third year of my degree course involved being placed in a job for 12 months to gain some work experience. I requested a placement that would allow me to live alone in the remote countryside so I could focus on my music. I was duly handed a job at a telephone manufacturing company in the bustling city of Brighton and Hove sharing a house with four other students. It was the complete opposite of what I had sought, but I had an amazing time there, getting to know the local students and immersing myself in Brighton's thriving nightclub scene. I don't think I was much of an employee. I would often roll up at work looking exhausted and dishevelled after a late night out, do very little work apart from running the odd errand, and a couple of times I remember calling in sick so I could go to the beach. I was completely dumbfounded when the company called me a couple of years later to offer me a job.

At the end of my time in Brighton I made my final journey in the Fiat 126 back home to south Devon. The car was now very much the worse for wear. The accelerator pedal was rusty and occasionally got stuck in the down position, so I had looped a bungee strap around the steering column and hooked it to the pedal so that it would come up again. During the journey the gearbox broke and the poor little car limped home like an elephant heading for its graveyard. A few weeks later my Dad sold it to a man in north Devon. When he turned up to collect it, I was surprised to find he hadn't brought a trailer. "How are you going to get it home?" I asked. "I'm going to drive it of course," he answered. "If I stick to the back roads across the moors, I shouldn't get into any trouble." A few hours later his wife called to ask if he had collected the car yet. Evidently he hadn't made it home.

Back in Salford the following year, I spent most of my evenings at the university's nightclub and bar called The Pavilion, known by the students as The Pav. I slowly got to know the DJ, and after a while he started to let me operate the record decks during the first hour on Saturday nights while most people were still in the bar. I wasn't allowed to play the biggest songs of the time, as they were reserved for later on, so I would mostly choose older tracks, lesser-known hits or any new club music that was coming up from the underground scene.

When the nightclub was empty during the day, I would sometimes sneak in to practise, working out the tempos of the 7" and 12" singles with a stopwatch and learning how to seamlessly blend tracks together. It was an art form all of its own and I became obsessed with doing it well. As time went on, I was occasionally allowed to DJ for the whole night, and before long I was surprised to find that I had gained some sort of notoriety. Suddenly people seemed to know my name and they were queuing up to offer me drinks to play their favourite songs. It was an unexpected benefit; I was just there for the music.

By now I had written and recorded over a hundred songs of my own. Having spent so much of my youth making music, it had become like a second language, and I would happily compose full productions in my head, often oblivious to the conversation that was going on around me. However, the problem was how to download these productions out of my head and into the real world. My four-track bedroom studio was great fun, but I knew my results were a long way from sounding professional. I was longing to get into a proper recording studio.

In June 1990 I graduated from Salford University with an honours degree in Electroacoustics. It had been a wonderful four years during which I had formed a band, played some proper gigs, become a DJ and somehow avoided getting beaten up by the locals. As I headed back to Newton Ferrers for my final summer there, I had no idea what to do next. There was no particular music scene in Devon, so I saw no point staying there. I needed to be closer to London, the pulsing heart of the UK music industry. During my final few weeks at Salford, various companies had visited the university to scan for potential recruits, and I had been offered an interview for a job as an acoustics consultant in Sunbury-on-Thames, a small town located just outside London. So, I went for an interview and a few weeks later I was offered the job.

*　*　*

As the long, hot summer drew to a close, I said goodbye to my childhood home and moved into a small, rundown bedsit in Fulwell, a couple of train stops from Sunbury-on-Thames. I started work as an acoustics consultant, which involved a lot of reading, calculations and site visits to the BBC's new White City complex, which would open in London the following year. The first few weeks were tough; I wasn't used to working eight hours a day and by the evenings I was exhausted. I was also rather lonely as I didn't know anybody in the area. Then I remembered that Theresa, the former singer of Up From Under, lived only a few miles away, so I called her to see if she wanted to record some of our old songs together. She wasn't interested, but while we were talking she rather unexpectedly invited me to her local church.

During my time in Brighton I had gone to church a few times with a group of my nightclub friends. At the time I had just been through a difficult relationship break-up, which had affected me rather badly and left me with an underlying sense of depression, and I found that going to church made me feel a lot more peaceful. So, the following Sunday morning, I met up with Theresa at a small church in the nearby town of Staines. As the service was about to start it became clear that the piano player had not shown up. Theresa suddenly shocked me by volunteering my services, and after a few moments' hesitation I cautiously accepted. I was familiar with some of the songs and thought I would be able to play some of them by ear. I probably made a lot of mistakes, but I was invited back the following week and ended up as one of their piano players for many years.

It was there that I would also meet two people who would affect the course of my life forever. The second of these wouldn't arrive on the scene for a few more years, but the first was a fellow keyboard player called Richard Burge. He was a flamboyant character with shoulder-length, dark hair and a bohemian dress sense. He had somehow mastered the art of seeming both intense and laid back at the same time. He had an infectious enthusiasm and I liked him immediately.

Richard's former band Shout The Dream had recently split up and he was working with the guitar player on a new project. They had recorded a couple of promising demos with producers Mike Paxman and Paul Muggleton, the team behind a recent hit by pop heart-throb Nick Kamen, and they were looking to form a new band with the provisional name of Blue Cage. Richard had moved from keyboards to frontman, so he wanted me to take over as keyboard player. The guitarist was a quiet, relaxed guy with long, dark brown hair. He was a talented musician and appeared to be involved with several local bands. His name was Karl Groom.

Richard had built a small recording studio at the end of his garden, and I found myself spending many evenings and weekends there, learning how all of the equipment worked and producing demos for local artists. I essentially became Richard's apprentice, an invaluable experience for which I will always be grateful. I was finally in a proper recording studio. It was centred on an 18-channel Seck mixing desk, a 12-track Akai digital tape recorder and an Atari 1040 ST computer. There were some Yamaha NS10 loudspeakers, which we supplemented with a pair of larger second-hand PMC units that I had purchased from the editor of *Sound On Sound* magazine. Richard also had a nice collection of effect units and synthesizers, including a Yamaha DX7, Roland Juno 106 and Roland D50. It was a great place to learn, write and record, and for a long time it was like a second home to me.

One of our studio clients was a songwriter who wanted to record a track to pitch to a record company boss that he knew. I had recently met a singer called Marie at the Jazz Café in London, so I invited her down to record the vocals. The demo was duly submitted to the record company and we waited for the verdict. The name of the record company boss was Simon Cowell. Before he went on to achieve global superstardom on TV shows such as *Pop Idol*, *The X Factor* and *Britain's Got Talent*, Simon ran a small label called IQ Records as part of the huge BMG label. Our demo was being put forward for the American-born British singer Sinitta, who had first achieved UK chart success on Simon's former label Fanfare Records back in 1986.

Simon wasn't convinced by the demo. He kept asking for revisions, but the song never quite worked. In the end I asked Simon if I could pitch a song of my own and he agreed. I invited Marie back to the studio and we recorded *Free To Get Higher*, a dance-pop track with a harder edge than Sinitta's previous work and which I hoped would be perfect for her. Simon loved it and told me that it would be her next single. I was over the moon! The offer also promised a large advance, so I would be able to leave my acoustics job and become a full-time songwriter. I submitted a few more songs and got a couple of them shortlisted for other artists on Simon's roster, and waited eagerly to see what would happen next.

Unfortunately, what happened next was that the whole project got closed down. From what I recall, Simon was promoted within BMG and IQ Records folded. I was incredibly disappointed. Simon marched on with his career, eventually hitting gold with the duo Robson & Jerome in 1995, and Sinitta later teamed up with him again for the first series of *The X Factor* in 2004. Marie also went on to have some success with a couple of dance acts, but unfortunately the trail ran cold for me and my brief foray into pop writing was over before it had begun.

* * *

The early 1990s was a curious time for music. Having grown up in the 1980s, I had watched so many bands converge from their unique beginnings towards a sort of corporate rock/pop sound. Whether it was the elaborate art rock of Queen, the progressive rock of Genesis, the reggae-infused punk of The Police or the early synth pop of Tears For Fears and Spandau Ballet, by the mid-'80s they all seemed to be looking for that MTV sound. It was hard to believe that the creators of *The March Of The Black Queen* or *Roxanne* had gone on to make *Radio Ga Ga* or *Every Breath You Take*. And once this new corporate sound had reached its pinnacle at Live Aid in 1985, the only way was down. Adam Ant described Live Aid as "the end of rock and roll" and you could see what he meant. The bands who had enjoyed so much success in the early '80s struggled to stay relevant as the decade wore on. I had always assumed I would form or join that sort of band. But, although I hadn't realised it at the time, what I was looking for was already gone.

As it turned out, my acoustics job had gone too. The office had recently acquired its first computer to be shared among its eight employees. The manager had boldly predicted that one day there would be a computer for every person in the office. His prediction came true, but not quite in the way he had hoped, as one day we were told that the office was relocating 100 miles away to Suffolk. Nobody wanted to move to Suffolk, so most of us handed in our notice, leaving the manager sitting alone in the office with the computer. Meanwhile I was fortunate to secure another job a bit closer to home.

All prospects of a music career looked rather distant and one night I was feeling very low. I went outside and stood in the garden, stared up into the dark night sky and silently cried out: "Show me there's more to life than this!" I stood there for a while lost in my thoughts. Suddenly I noticed a strange flash of light across the sky. It looked like a small ball of pure white light, moving silently from west to east at an impossible speed somewhere between 50 and 200 metres above me. It was clearly not a man-made craft. While I was reeling from the shock, it suddenly returned, this time flying in the opposition direction along exactly the same path at the same impossible speed. I have no idea what it was, but somehow it felt like an answer to my silent cry. There obviously was something more out there, even though I had no idea what I had just encountered.

Following the disappointment of not becoming a full-time songwriter, I poured my time and creative energy into the new band with Richard Burge and Karl Groom. The group's name had now changed from Blue Cage to Mercy Train, and our line-up was completed by drummer Nick Harradence and bassist Peter Gee, who was also a member of the progressive rock group Pendragon. By the summer of 1992 we were ready to start performing live, and we did a handful of shows across the UK, starting with a local gig at the Brunel University campus on 24th June, followed by an exceptionally muddy outdoor festival in Castle Ashby called Greenbelt a couple of months later.

We recorded our only album *Presence* at Richard's studio, and this was when I really started to get to know Karl. Although the three of us had written and produced the record, Richard wasn't so interested in the mixing process, so that was left to me and Karl. Every evening after work I would meet him at the studio and we would mix late into the night. When we were too tired to continue, I would drive him home in my red Talbot Alpine to Maidenhead, where he lived with a bunch of other musicians in a large house that was home to another recording facility, known as Thin Ice Studios.

Karl shared my love of video games, and on arrival in Maidenhead we would often play into the early hours on a games console that belonged to another of the house's residents, a drummer by the name of Tony Grinham. We would happily spend endless hours driving around a rally circuit on a demo version of *Skid Marks* in the hope of shaving a few fractions of a second off our fastest lap times, or competing in World Cup tournaments on a rudimentary football game called *Sensible Soccer* where you could score with a throw-in from the halfway line, much to the annoyance of the opposing team. Eventually I would say goodbye and head back home to catch a few hours of sleep before getting up for my day job the following morning.

The Talbot Alpine was the first car I ever bought and I loved it. It cost me £150 from a friend of a friend and it gave me the independence I needed, having been reliant on local buses and trains to get me from place to place since parting company with the Fiat. However, the Talbot was barely roadworthy and went through three engines during the two or three years that I owned it. The heating system was broken, so when I drove to work during the winter months, I would have to put a hot water bottle on the dashboard to stop the windscreen from misting up. When the glass was finally clear I would enjoy a few precious moments with the hot water bottle on my lap to warm me up, before the windscreen became misty again and I had to return it to the dashboard. By the time I finally retired the Talbot, the front seat wouldn't stay upright and the bonnet wouldn't open. I was going to take it to the scrapyard when Karl said he would take it on, so for a while it became the official Thin Ice vehicle.

I wasn't entirely sure how many musicians lived at the Thin Ice house, but there seemed to be quite a few. Among them was another member of Pendragon called Clive Nolan. Clive had a couple of projects on the go with Karl, including a four-piece progressive rock group called Shadowland, whose line-up was completed by bassist Ian Salmon and our Mercy Train drummer Nick Harradence. That autumn Clive asked if I would go on tour with them. As he was both the singer and keyboard player for the band, he wanted me to play the keyboards so that he could focus on being the frontman. After a warm-up show in Rotherham in the north of England, we headed across the English Channel in a minibus for ten shows across Belgium, France, Germany and the Netherlands, co-headlining with another British progressive rock band called Jadis.

It was my first European tour and I absolutely loved it. It was far from glamorous – the journeys in the minibus were often very long and the accommodation sometimes left a lot to be desired, sleeping eight to a room on some nights – but I was on the road playing keyboards with a band and it felt fantastic. Karl and I would while away the long hours on the road playing *Double Dragon* on a Nintendo DS console, a game which kept us absorbed for hours in the absence of any other entertainment.

On stage I was in charge of five keyboards – three to the front of me and two to the side – so I was kept very busy, not only performing all the parts, but also remembering every time I had to select a different sound on each of the keyboards.

There are essentially three reasons for having so many keyboards on stage. The first reason is to have the widest palette of sounds available to you, as some keyboards are better at making certain sorts of sounds than others. The second reason is to hopefully reduce the number of times you have to change sounds on each one during the course of a song, so that when you turn to a particular instrument you know it will usually have the sound you want on there. And the third reason, of course, is because it looks good! For the Shadowland tour all of the keyboards belonged to Clive, and to the best of my recollection these were a Yamaha SY77 for wide, expansive sounds, a Roland D50 for some of the brighter sounds such as bells, a Roland Juno 60 for warm string sounds, a Kawai K4 for some other softer sounds and a Korg DW8000 for the all-important lead solos.

On 24th November 1992, three days before my 25th birthday, we were nearing the end of the tour and had a few days off in Lille in northern France before our next show in a small basement club in the city. During dinner, Karl asked if I would like to record some keyboards for his other band. I knew he was in a heavier sounding group but I had not heard their music. He told me he had already recorded most of the keyboard parts but he was hoping that I would come and add some solos and other moments. It was flattering to be asked. I was very much enjoying my new role as a session player, so I accepted the job on the spot.

The band was called Threshold.

Chapter 4
Get Your Mind-Set Altered Here

THRESHOLD HAD FORMED IN 1988 in the university town of Egham, located about 20 miles to the west of London. Guitarist Karl Groom had arranged some jam sessions with local drummer Tony Grinham, and they were soon joined by a second guitarist called Nick Midson, whom Karl had met at a Slayer gig in London. Jon Jeary joined shortly afterwards, initially as vocalist before switching to bass guitar. Karl and Nick shared a mutual appreciation of bands like Testament, Metallica and Deep Purple, while Jon was more influenced by progressive rock bands such as Rush, Pink Floyd and Genesis.

They had started out performing cover versions of heavy metal songs in local pubs and clubs, before venturing into writing their own material. In 1992 they had secured a record deal with a small British progressive rock label called Giant Electric Pea. Jon had decided to step down as vocalist to "get a proper singer in" as he put it, so Damian Wilson was brought in as the band's new frontman. The new line-up had so far released one song called *Intervention* and they were now in the process of recording their debut album *Wounded Land*.

Over the winter of 1992 I spent many hours at Thin Ice adding solos, textures and other parts to the Threshold recordings. The Shadowland set had contained quite a few lead solos, so I felt up to the challenge and was ready to stretch myself to the edge of my ability with some fast and complex performances. So, with that in mind, I laid down the solos in *Consume To Live* and *Sanity's End*, pushing myself as hard as I could, confident in my (subsequently incorrect) assumption that I would never have to play those parts again. It was a great experience, but I wasn't expecting anything to come of it. Threshold's heavy, progressive style was very different to what I was used to, and I was sure my future would revolve around rock and pop music, producing and writing for other artists or being part of a band with more commercial opportunities.

Meanwhile, Richard Burge had touted our Mercy Train album to various music industry contacts, but nobody was interested in managing or signing us. My cousin Bast kindly set up a meeting with one of his friends, the legendary record producer Glyn Johns, so I took a day off work to go and meet him. As I walked up to his front door, I unfortunately trod in something a dog had left behind. I tried desperately to get it off my shoe before Glyn opened the door, but I suspect his abiding memory of our meeting was the awful smell that I brought into his home!

Glyn had worked with the world's top artists from The Beatles to The Rolling Stones, Led Zeppelin and the Eagles, so I wasn't too sure what he would make of our fledgling efforts. He listened attentively to some of our songs and was very kind and encouraging, but ultimately he didn't feel it was something he could help us with. Fortunately, Karl had a bit more luck with his contacts, and we eventually signed to a small sub-label of the Dutch record company SI Music that had released the Shadowland album.

1993 kicked off with a couple more Mercy Train shows, one at the Windsor Arts Centre and the other at the Red Lion in Brentford. The crew at the Red Lion filmed the show and offered to sell us a VHS video tape of our performance for the princely sum of £50. It had been a good show, but we felt confident that there would be better ones, so we opted to save our money and wait for a bigger show. Ah, the foolish decisions of youth – how I would love to watch that Red Lion set now! Still, it looked like a busy year ahead, with more Mercy Train and Shadowland gigs on the horizon.

Furthermore, my status in Threshold had now gone from session player to band member. I don't recall a specific moment or conversation that marked the transition, but I was now being asked to attend photo sessions for the CD artwork, I was being listed in the booklet as a band member, and I was going to be performing live with them. It seemed new and exciting and slightly abstract at the same time. The world of heavy music was quite alien to me, so I felt like I was stepping into a mysterious universe that I knew nothing about. There was also the small matter of performing the songs live. I had pushed myself to the edge of my ability on the album, so if I was going to play those parts on stage every night, I had some serious practising to do.

And so, one day I found myself at Longcross village hall for my first ever Threshold rehearsal, running through most of *Wounded Land* along with the song *Intervention* which had been recorded before I joined. Of all the early material, this was my favourite track to play, with its ethereal keyboards and heavy guitars combining perfectly over the song's dark, powerful chord progressions in a very moving way.

My lead solos in *Consume To Live* and *Sanity's End* felt insanely fast and I had been practising like crazy for the last few months to speed up my fingers so I could play them as well as possible. The scales and arpeggios from my school piano lessons finally proved their worth, and coupled with some Hanon piano exercises designed to improve speed and precision, my playing had developed considerably. I would practise those Hanon patterns everywhere – not only on the piano, but also on my desk, my chest or the steering wheel of my car while I was driving. And thankfully, all of the hard worked paid off. The rehearsal went really well, although I was uncertain how clearly anybody could actually hear Damian or me over the huge wall of drums, bass and guitars.

On 7th April 1993 we performed our first Threshold show together at the Royal Standard in Walthamstow, north east London. After a brief sound check, Damian approached the microphone at 7:30pm wearing a white long-sleeved shirt and blue jeans, and with the words "Well, welcome to the Standard then", we launched into our opening song. The audience was small but appreciative, with a few of the band's friends there to cheer us on. The whole gig rushed by in a blur and we left the stage feeling like conquering heroes, very satisfied with our debut performance together.

After the show Damian told me he had been offered a job as vocalist in an up-and-coming band called LaSalle which had some major financial backing behind it. It sounded like an opportunity that was too good to pass up, so I wished him luck and before long he had left Threshold to pursue bigger dreams. Sometime later he gave me a copy of the finished LaSalle album and I thought it sounded pretty good, but unfortunately it was never released and the group came to nothing. That evening in Walthamstow was therefore the only time that Threshold would perform together as the original *Wounded Land* line-up, and when we found ourselves back at the same venue nine months later, it would be with a different singer.

MAYBE A WRITER

As well as marking my first Threshold show, 1993 would also mark my last shows with Mercy Train and Shadowland, both for different reasons. We played four more Mercy Train shows during the spring and summer, ending with an exhilarating, packed-out night at the prestigious Old Trout venue in Windsor. But, despite a few decent reviews, our album *Presence* had sadly failed to make an impact on the music scene. With no more gigs on the horizon, the band unfortunately lost its momentum and gradually faded away.

Live shows with Shadowland also continued during 1993, ending on 13th August at the Royal Standard in London, where I had played my first Threshold show a few months earlier. However, with a Threshold tour looming, I wouldn't be able to take enough annual leave from my day job to continue touring with both bands, so I reluctantly told Clive and Karl that the London show would have to be my last. They were very nice about it and paid tribute to me during the show, by which I was very touched. I had loved every moment of my time as a session player for Shadowland and I was hugely grateful for the opportunity, but now it was time to move on and focus on Threshold.

* * *

Our debut album *Wounded Land* was released by Giant Electric Pea on 1st September 1993 and earned a decent amount of critical acclaim in the underground music press across Europe. It also did well in Japan, and there were rumours that the song *Paradox* was used as a theme tune for a Japanese TV sports show. Karl once told me that *Paradox* had been his attempt at writing a song like *Cuddly Toy* by Roachford, although I must confess I struggled to spot the resemblance. As a keyboard player it felt more like the final movement of Widor's *Toccata*, a six-minute organ piece of high-speed arpeggios that I had recently performed with mixed success at a friend's wedding.

Everything seemed to be going fine when I had visited the church for one final practice on the day before the wedding. The church's electric organ was wired through a PA system and sounded particularly impressive when the reverb switch was engaged to simulate the sound of a huge cathedral. I quickly ran through the hymns and spent most of the time practising *Toccata*. I had memorised the lengthy arpeggios by heart so that I could concentrate on the piece's greatest challenge: the bass line had to be performed using both feet.

The organ had a pedal board on the floor comprising 30 notes laid out like a giant piano keyboard. I had never played with my feet before, so the only way to make sure I hit the right notes was to memorise the finger movements and spend the entire time looking down at my shoes.

The next day I sat nervously behind the organ waiting for the wedding to start. As we launched into the opening hymn, I played through the first line as is customary, before stopping for a second so that everyone would know it was time to start singing. However, as I started the first line again, nobody in the church sang a word. I was horrified. Should I keep going and hope they would eventually join in, or should I start again from the top? I opted to stop. The pastor made a quick joke and I suddenly realised what had happened. Although the reverb setting sounded great from where I was sitting, in the rest of the hall it was so echoic that nobody had noticed that I had stopped at all. I quickly switched off the reverb, started the hymn again and left an extra-long pause after the opening line for good measure. I was very relieved to hear everyone start singing.

At the end of the service, it was finally time to perform Widor's *Toccata* as the happy couple walked together down the aisle towards the exit. And it would have been fine. I got through the first two pages without any problems, and it wasn't until the couple had left the church and the congregation started to mingle that I ran into trouble. With my left hand playing chords, my right hand playing arpeggios, and my head facing down towards my feet as they crossed over each other in an unwieldy fashion to perform the walking bass line on the pedal board, someone thought it would be the perfect moment to come and have a chat with me. It really wasn't. I totally lost my place, missed out two pages of music entirely and fumbled my way towards an impromptu ending. Fortunately though, nobody seemed to notice.

With Damian no longer part of Threshold, we placed an advertisement for a new singer in the back pages of *Metal Hammer* magazine. Over the next few weeks tapes started to arrive in the post from a wide spectrum of hopefuls, ranging from blues rock pub singers to growling female death metallers. But, while there were one or two promising candidates, nobody sounded quite right. Our first European tour was looming and we were starting to get worried. What if we couldn't find anybody in time for the tour? Would our whole trip have to be cancelled?

MAYBE A WRITER

We anxiously held our nerve for one more week, and then a tape arrived from a guy called Glynn Morgan. He sounded amazing: melodic, powerful and enigmatic, just what we were looking for. We invited him down to Surrey for an audition and discovered that he looked great too, with long curly hair and a hint of a young Jon Bon Jovi about him. We gave him the job on the spot!

* * *

On 19th January 1994, a long nightliner tour bus pulled up outside our bassist Jon Jeary's house to transport us across the English Channel for our first European tour. Some of Jon's neighbours could be spotted peering out from behind their curtains to see what was going on. It was evident that a tour bus was not a normal sight in this quiet, residential street. The nightliner was a significant improvement on the minibus which had transported us during the Shadowland tour. Downstairs there was a living area, a kitchen and a small toilet, while upstairs there was a TV lounge and a suite of 18 built-in bunk beds. These were essentially rectangular wooden shelves, each fitted with a foam mattress and a curtain for privacy. If you were lucky, you would also have a small light, a power socket and some ventilation, but not every bunk seemed to offer every amenity.

Choosing the perfect bunk was very much a matter of personal choice. If you were too near the back of the bus, you would be kept awake by noise from the TV lounge. But if you were too near the front, then it was harder to get downstairs, as the corridor was invariably blocked by someone getting dressed or organising their bunk. Another factor to consider, especially for the lighter sleepers, was avoiding being too close to anyone who snored loudly. As a deep sleeper, this wasn't too much of a concern for me, but, as I was sometimes known to snore, it's possible I was one of the problems.

With our equipment and luggage loaded, the nightliner drove to the Port of Ramsgate on the east coast of England so we could board the Sally Line cross-channel ferry to Dunkirk in northern France. The Sally Line was an experience to be savoured, and over the coming years we would savour it many times. While Jon, Nick, Tony and Glynn would head off to the fast food café for a cheap burger and chips, Karl and I would head in the other direction to the smorgasbord. There you could load up a plate with a huge selection of food, from regular salads to more unusual delights such as rollmops, which consisted of pickled herring fillets rolled around an onion filling. In any other setting I wouldn't consider going anywhere near them, but in the Sally Line smorgasbord they were a luxurious feast.

It was here that we also discovered possibly the worst coffee known to man. Stewing for hours in large stainless steel urns, the dark, thick liquid looked toxic and had a taste that only faintly resembled coffee. But one of the delights of the smorgasbord was that the coffee was free, so by the time we arrived in Dunkirk we would have sometimes downed as many as ten small cups each, rendering our chances of falling asleep on the nightliner almost impossible.

Our debut European tour consisted of 13 shows spread across 16 days, mostly in Germany plus one in Belgium and one in the Netherlands. We had played a warm-up show at the familiar Royal Standard in London the week before and now we were ready to take on the world. Our co-headliners on the tour were a Norwegian progressive metal band called Conception, and they would be travelling with us and our crew on the nightliner. They had recently released their second album *Parallel Minds* on the German label Noise Records, and we proved to be a very good pairing. They were great guys, and both bands were well received by the fans. As well as having an excellent frontman in Roy Khan, their guitarist Tore Østby was an exceptional player and we would meet him again many years later in his next band Ark.

The tour kicked off with an exhilarating show in Hannover, Germany; our excitement was high and our adrenaline pumping. It was great to be back on the road again and I loved it. We alternated which band would headline each night and made our way across Europe, performing at a broad selection of professional rock venues, stuffy town halls and amateur youth clubs along the way. But none matched the heady euphoria of that opening night in Hannover.

We soon settled into a regular daily routine. At around midday we would emerge, bleary eyed, from the nightliner and make our way into the day's venue. Breakfast would normally be served in the bar, consisting of a selection of bread, cold meat, cheese, fruit and chocolate bars. Fresh filter coffee was served from thermos flasks with pump-action lids, which were considered by most of us to be the height of modern luxury, at a time when most cafés in England still served instant coffee.

The venues would generally smell of spilled beer and cigarette ash from the previous night. In 1994 smoking was still commonplace in bars and clubs. It was a smell that became synonymous with touring, and would cling to our clothes, instruments and flight cases. Even after the tour was finished, opening a flight case at home would flood the room with that familiar venue odour, a truly foul scent to all except those who had been there. It was the nostalgic smell of being on tour.

After breakfast, one by one everyone would shower. If a venue didn't have adequate facilities, a local hotel room or crew member's house would be sourced so that we could use the bathroom there. And then, the long afternoon would begin: unloading our drums, guitars, keyboards and amplifiers from the nightliner, setting everything up on stage, sound checking the instruments one by one, running through a few songs until the sound engineer was happy, adjusting our monitoring levels on stage so that we could hear each other properly, and practising any moments that had not worked so well the night before.

The afternoons would pass very slowly, with bursts of activity punctuated by long pauses while a microphone was checked, a cable was replaced or a monitor was set up. Many of the venues had table football games, especially the youth clubs, so the long pauses were an excellent opportunity to fit in a quick game. Karl and I became quite addicted to table football, and we would always make sure we had a ready supply of coins in the local currency for such occasions. However, we soon discovered that playing against the local crew was a mistake. Table football seemed to be a national sport in mainland Europe, and the speed and skill of the locals was astonishing. I had played a few times at university and thought I was quite proficient, but I was a hopeless beginner compared to these professionals.

When sound check was over, we would congregate for dinner, either provided in the venue by local caterers or in a nearby restaurant, before making our way backstage to prepare for the show. It was all about those 90 minutes: walking onto the darkened stage to the sound of our introduction music, looking out into the audience for the first time through the swirling smoke illuminated by red, green and blue stage lights, hearing Tony count us in with four hits on the hi-hat; and then we would start, producing our huge wall of heavy, powerful music as the audience cheered and adrenaline pumped through our veins.

After the show was over, we would mingle with the lingering crowd at the front of the stage, conversing enthusiastically about the gig and signing merchandise, flyers and occasionally body parts until it was time to pack everything down and load it into the nightliner. Back on the bus we would chat into the night, watch videos and down a few beers as we started the next leg of our journey. Eventually everyone would head to their bunks and by about 3am the bus was quiet again, apart from the steady purr of the engine and the occasional sound of snoring, rolling through the night towards our next destination where the whole routine would start all over again.

It was during this tour that I had my one and only encounter with drugs. After a great show in the Dutch city of Nijmegen, the whole touring party went into the city centre to enjoy the local nightlife. There was no show the following night, so everyone was happy to stay out late and have a few drinks. We found a bar with an outdoor table and our tour manager Ingo ordered us copious quantities of Dutch beer. Someone from our touring party was smoking a joint and handed it to me to share. I had never smoked a joint before, barely even touched a cigarette, but for some reason I accepted and we smoked it together.

After a while I didn't feel too well. I wasn't sure if it was because of the beer or the joint or a combination of both. A couple of the guys decided to get some burgers, so I went with them, hoping some food would help me feel better. However, as soon as we stepped into the fast food restaurant the smell of the fried meat and chips made me feel worse, so I went outside and waited for the others to order their meals. I was really feeling quite rough now, so I lay down on the pavement and curled up into a ball. When the others left the restaurant, they didn't notice me on the ground and headed off into the night.

A couple of hours later I woke up. The street was now mostly deserted. It was a cold January night and I was shivering. I had left my jacket on the tour bus and was only wearing jeans and a T-shirt. I had no wallet, no passport and no idea where the nightliner was. I tried to stand up but discovered, rather strangely, that my legs didn't work. I wrapped my arms around myself tightly to keep warm and fell asleep again. Sometime later I woke up to the sound of a loud Dutch voice talking to me and a torch being shone in my eyes. I looked up to see two policemen. They asked if I was OK and I tried to explain that I was cold, lost and that my legs didn't work. However, all I actually managed to utter was an incoherent mumble. The policemen shrugged and went on their way.

Things were now starting to feel serious. I was shuddering rather violently and I still couldn't walk. In a few hours the nightliner would leave Nijmegen and head off to our next destination. I had left the curtain of my bunk closed, so nobody would even know that I wasn't safely asleep on the bus. It was 1994, long before mobile phones became commonplace, and with no money or ID I had no idea what I would do if I missed the bus. I fell asleep again.

The next time I awoke, the sun was up. I staggered to my feet and was relieved to find that my legs were now working again. But I had no idea where the bus was. I chose a random direction and walked, not knowing if it might be 100 metres or a mile away. I said a prayer, walked a little further, turned a corner and kept on going. As I rounded the next corner, I miraculously saw the nightliner in front of me. I climbed on board and collapsed on my bunk. Half an hour later I felt the low purr of the engine and the bus drove off. Somehow, I had made it back just in time. I spent most of the following day throwing up, so I was grateful that it was a day off. Many years later, I met up with the person who had handed me the joint and I recounted the story to him. He put down his drink and looked into my eyes. "That wasn't cannabis," he said with a wicked smile.

The tour continued across Germany, eventually drawing to a close in the German city of Weimar on 4th February. The venue had a good atmosphere, but it was distinctly at the amateur end of the spectrum. There was no stage and some of the lighting had kitchen spoons for reflectors. There were no security guards or bouncers, and during our final song a member of the audience walked right up to our drummer Tony while he was in the middle of playing, and leant towards him hopefully, brandishing a CD and a pen. Quite how he thought Tony could sign his autograph at the same time as playing drums remains a mystery!

Sadly, the tour had finally come to an end, so we said goodbye to our Norwegian contingent and made our way back across Europe, enjoying another Sally Line smorgasbord before arriving back home in Surrey in the early hours of the morning.

Chapter 5
Control Is Hanging By A Thread

NOT LONG AFTER OUR EUROPEAN TOUR we started working on our second album. Our live performances were going down well and we seemed to be making new fans with every show. However, they were hearing a band fronted by Glynn only to go and buy a record sung by Damian, so we really needed to put out a new album that matched how we sounded on stage.

My first composition to make it onto a Threshold record was the short, piano-based song *Under The Sun*. There were two other songs that I thought about submitting, but they were both slightly longer progressive rock ballads that sounded too far removed from our sound at the time, so I focussed on *Under The Sun* as I thought it was slightly closer to the style of *Keep It With Mine* on *Wounded Land*. The other two songs, *Half Way Home* and an early version of *Sunrise On Mars*, would eventually find their way into our catalogue later on. Glynn presented four songs for consideration and two of these were chosen for the album, *Will To Give* and the power ballad *Innocent*. His other two songs *Fist Of Tongues* and *Open Your Eyes* would also crop up later on future projects.

Karl and Jon had written three new songs: *A Tension Of Souls*, *He Is I Am* and *Devoted*. They had also resurrected a couple of tracks from before I joined the band, one called *Aftermath* that had been rebadged as *Babylon Rising*, and another called *Endless Sea* that had been developed further to become the ten-minute epic *Into The Light*. Alongside these tracks, most of us had also been collaborating on the album's eventual opener *Sunseeker*. While *Wounded Land* had been solely written by Karl, Jon and Nick, our new album felt like a much more diverse melting pot of styles and sounds, so Jon suggested the title of *Psychedelicatessen* to convey the idea of a shop full of eclectic and colourful ideas. It felt suitable.

MAYBE A WRITER

During May and June 1994, we returned to the Netherlands and Germany for a few more shows. We started trying out some of the new material on stage, including *A Tension of Souls*, a slightly rough-and-ready version of *He Is I Am*, and Glynn's ballad *Innocent*, which would become our first official single. The following month we headed back to Belgium for our biggest show so far, an outdoor festival called Viarock. The headliners were the legendary British band Whitesnake and we were all excited to be on the same bill as them. Threshold used to perform their song *Here I Go Again* during their early days, and their 1980 hit single *Fool For Your Loving* had been one of my favourite rock songs during my chart-obsessed days, so I was very much hoping they would play it at Viarock.

We drove to Belgium in two vehicles, an old rented Ford Transit van for the equipment and Karl's Citroen BX for additional passenger seating. That night we parked outside our hotel in Belgium and headed inside for a beer or two, stoked with anticipation for our show the following day. When we awoke the next morning, we discovered to our horror that an outdoor market had been set up on the street outside the hotel. All along the road there were market stalls and traders selling their wares. Our Transit van was well and truly blocked by a large stall selling socks. It was quite impossible for us to manoeuvre the van onto the road and now we were panicking. We had no idea how we were going to get to the festival.

As luck would have it, staying in the same hotel as us were a film crew from the music television channel MTV who had come to record highlights of the festival. They had fortuitously parked on the other side of the town, having possibly gleaned some local knowledge about the market. Miraculously they had space in their vans for us and our equipment, and they offered us a lift to the festival. We unloaded our van and rolled everything across the cobbled streets towards the MTV vehicles. Unfortunately, the old cobbles were too uneven for Nick's speaker cabinet and one of the casters broke off, causing it to wobble forlornly as he tried to push it through the town. But eventually everything was transferred to the waiting vehicles and we climbed on board.

The MTV crew were a friendly bunch and we talked enthusiastically about the day ahead. When we told them we were recording a new album, they encouraged us to send them a video of our upcoming single. They sounded confident that they would be able to air it on their late night TV show *Headbangers Ball*. We were over the moon. MTV was about as big as you could get, and had played a major role in the stratospheric rise of fellow progressive metallers Dream Theater a couple of years before.

Fortunately, nothing else went wrong that day and we had an amazing show. The audience was huge and supportive, and there were even a few Threshold fans at the front to give us a loud welcome. Later that night the crowd went wild as headliners Whitesnake took to the stage. They were in the middle of their *Greatest Hits* tour, so we were rewarded with stadium anthems such as *Is This Love*, *Here I Go Again* and, to my great delight, *Fool For Your Loving*.

Viarock was our biggest show so far. But sadly, for our drummer Tony, it would also be his last. Tony was a good drummer and *Wounded Land* had suited his playing style well. But the songs we had written for our sophomore album were more technical than before, and it was becoming clear that he was struggling with them. We tried to encourage him to put in some extra practice because we really wanted our new album to sound perfect. However, as the time to record the drums got closer, it was evident that he would not be able to produce the performances that were required. And so, it was with the heaviest of hearts that Jon told Tony that we would have to find a new drummer. It breaks my heart to think about it today. Threshold meant everything to Tony. He had been there from the start and he loved everything about it. But, just as things were starting to get good, it had been suddenly taken away from him. I don't think he has ever forgiven us.

We drafted in Nick Harradence to record the drums. Nick had a proven track record as the drummer for Mercy Train and Shadowland and he was very happy to come on board. Thin Ice Studios wasn't equipped to record live drums, so these were recorded at Halfway Houses, the studio belonging to Pendragon frontman Nick Barrett. Karl had worked on their 1993 album *The Window Of Life* and would go on to become their go-to producer and mixer.

Back at Thin Ice we recorded the guitars, bass, keyboards and vocals. The record label had advanced me enough money to buy my first professional keyboard, a Korg O1/W. As much as I had loved the Roland and Yamaha keyboards from the Shadowland tour, the Roland's palette sounded too limited and the Yamaha seemed too complicated to program. I had borrowed a Korg M1, a predecessor to the O1/W, during my final year of university and had found it quite versatile. So, I decided to take a chance with Korg and see what their latest synthesizer had to offer. It proved to be the perfect choice, and I have been using Korg keyboards ever since. It was complex enough that I could design a diverse range of sounds, and intuitive enough to make programming relatively painless. I set about assembling a palette of new sounds for the album. I also had access to a dozen keyboards and sound modules at Thin Ice, so sonically it felt like the sky was the limit.

Having stretched myself to the edge of my abilities on *Wounded Land* and got away with it, I decided to do the same again for our new album *Psychedelicatessen*, pushing myself to play even faster and harder than before. As a result, the solos on the album's first two tracks *Sunseeker* and *A Tension Of Souls* are still a bit of a stretch to this day, and I would later find that I had to practise them regularly so that I could perform them consistently every night on our subsequent tours.

Karl had recorded Damian's vocals for *Wounded Land*, but for the new album I offered to take over the vocal production duties. Glynn was a joy to record and had a wonderful dynamic range, growing menacingly from a whisper to a scream on tracks like *Into The Light*. We worked our way through the songs, adding vocal harmonies to some of the choruses to make them sound bigger and wider, a process that would become one of our trademarks going forward.

When we reached *Under The Sun*, it started to become apparent that we had recorded the music in a rather high key and Glynn would have been more comfortable singing it lower. However, he soldiered on, running through the song a few times to see if he could get more comfortable with it. After four or five passes, he took off the headphones and said: "Sorry, Rich, I can't do it – it's just too high for me." I rewound the tape and played it back. What he hadn't known was that I had been furtively recording him while he was practising, making a note of which words needed replacing each time he ran through it, so that on the next pass I could quickly hit the record button and drop him in. By the time he took off his headphones, I had the whole vocal recorded and he sounded perfect.

Psychedelicatessen was released on 1st November 1994, 14 months after *Wounded Land*. It wouldn't sell enough copies to get us into the charts, but it achieved 'Album of the Month' in the Dutch magazine *Aardschok* and got some good reviews along the way.

* * *

We had one more show booked for 1994, a charity gig in Germany on 10th December. Nick Harradence joined us on drums for what would be his only show with Threshold before we started our search for a permanent drummer. We only had limited time to find a replacement because we had more European shows booked for the following spring. We eventually found Jay Micciche, an 18 year old drum prodigy who lived locally. Jay was a phenomenal drummer, and although his taste in music was much heavier than Threshold, he was delighted to join us and we were very happy too.

Our next job was to film a video for *Innocent*. Our budget was fairly low, so we decided to produce and direct it ourselves. A friend had recommended a good film crew who could look after the filming, lighting and final editing. But every good film needs a story, so Glynn came and stayed at my place for the weekend and we worked on a storyboard together.

We decided the video would need three locations: a large space to film the band, a café for the story shots and a bedroom for the death scene. The bedroom was the easiest location to source. Karl was the only person with a decent looking bedroom, so that was chosen by default. The café presented more of a challenge. After various reconnaissance missions to a number of local towns, I discovered a cool, shabby-chic café in Egham called Bar 163. It looked perfect and the coffee was rather good too. The owner was a friendly chap and was quite receptive to the idea, so we arranged a suitable time and date and crossed another task off the list.

The large space to film the band proved the most difficult location of all to secure. I had initially booked a suitable venue, but they had cancelled shortly afterwards. I looked everywhere, I phoned everyone, but nowhere suitable could be found. Our film crew was booked, the band was ready, but we had nowhere to go. With every passing day I grew a little more anxious. Suddenly it was the day before we were due to shoot. The film crew called to ask why I hadn't sent them the location yet. I nervously told them that I would let them know soon, and assured them that it was still going ahead. I mustered every ounce of faith I could find and kept searching. At around 7pm my phone rang. The voice on the other end of the line said: "I heard you were looking for somewhere to film tomorrow morning. Well, I've got the perfect film studio for you."

The following morning, we all made our way to London to our last-minute location. I removed the light bulb from my bedroom so it could be used for a slow-motion shot of the bulb swinging and smashing. On the way I had to pick up our drummer Jay, who had been tasked with making a large, black wooden box with an open front where Glynn would sit for some of the shots. He had done an excellent job, but when I arrived we discovered that it was too big to fit in the back of the car. Jay started panicking, worried that the whole day was ruined because we wouldn't be able to use the box. But after the stress I had just been through over the last 24 hours, there was absolutely no way we were going to fall at the last hurdle. "Can we unscrew it?" I asked. "Oh yeah, I hadn't thought of that," he replied, and he went to find a screwdriver.

The man on the phone had been right; it was the perfect film studio. The room was painted white and had curved 'infinity walls' so that the edges of the room couldn't be seen. It was exactly what we wanted. We set up the band equipment, while the film crew set up the camera, lights, floor track and smoke machine.

We were just running through the song when we saw a large gang of firemen emerging through the thick, swirling smoke and marching purposefully into the room. It looked just like a scene from a Hollywood movie, made all the more melodramatic by the powerful soundtrack of *Innocent* blasting over the PA. Evidently our smoke machine had set off the fire alarm and triggered an automatic response. Unfortunately, the firemen weren't too happy and we got a good telling off. Even more unfortunately, we hadn't captured their dramatic entrance on film, because it would have looked fantastic!

After that, the rest of the day passed without incident. The band was filmed performing the song from various camera angles, Glynn was filmed singing in Jay's reassembled wooden box, and my bedroom light bulb was filmed swinging and smashing just as we had planned it. After a long day we headed home. Somehow it had all worked out and I was terribly relieved. I walked into my rented room and turned on the light switch, amazed and grateful that nothing had gone wrong. The room remained dark. I had forgotten that we had smashed my light bulb for the video, and I didn't have a spare one.

* * *

It was sometime around now that I first caught a glimpse of the second person who would change the course of my life forever. It was a Sunday evening and

I was sitting at the church piano, playing softly in the background as people made their way in from the cold for the evening service. I knew most of the faces in the church by now, but, as I looked up, I spotted someone I hadn't seen before. She was sitting about four or five rows from the front, wearing a brown felt cap over long, sandy blonde hair that seemed to shine like gold as the light caught it. For a moment I was transfixed, as if there was nobody else in the room apart from her. But it would be a while before I saw her again.

Back at the rehearsal room we were preparing for what would be a busy year of touring. We had originally been slated to tour Europe supporting US progressive metallers Fates Warning, but for some reason this hadn't happened. So, as we waited for a replacement tour to be booked, we busied ourselves with a couple of UK festivals and some low-key headline shows in mainland Europe, once again driving ourselves there in a rented van and Karl's trusty Citroen.

Meanwhile another support tour was arranged for May 1995, this time with a different US band called Psychotic Waltz, who had just released their third album *Mosquito*. It's fair to say that the two bands didn't become friends. We were very different sorts of people: Threshold, the stereotypical, reserved Englishmen, more likely to ask "Please may I have a cup of tea?" than shout "Hell yeah!", and Psychotic Waltz, the stereotypical, crazy Californian band living a rock and roll lifestyle.

We didn't enjoy being on the shared nightliner very much. The air was constantly filled with the smell of drugs, courtesy of a device called a bong which appeared to be in constant use, and the TV screens were constantly filled with porn movies. It was a horrible place to be, and I developed a habit of taking long walks to get away from it all. Armed with a notebook and pen, I would head off towards the nearest river or area of countryside to enjoy the solitude until it was time to return to the venue to set up, sound check or perform. These long walks became a routine that has stayed with me over the years, and I've written many songs during these quiet moments.

On stage we were improving every night, honing our performances and getting tighter as a unit, an experience which would prove invaluable for our subsequent tour. Our set featured an assortment of songs from our first two albums, along with a new track called *Part Of The Chaos* that was under development and would slowly evolve as the shows continued. However, we were noticing that some of these shows were smaller than the headline gigs we had done earlier in the year. So, as well as not enjoying life on the bus, we were also starting to get disgruntled with the whole tour. To make things worse, Glynn was having problems with his throat and we had to cancel some of our appearances.

When we reached the town of Katwijk on the Dutch coast it all became too much. Jon looked out towards the sea and declared that he could smell Blighty (a slang name for England). A plan was hatched to abandon the tour and go home. There were still six shows left, but, with the added rumour that no tickets had been sold for the upcoming Paris concert, it was decided that enough was enough. Looking back, it seems astonishing that anyone would even consider not finishing a tour. But we were young, foolish and extremely fed up. We made our way to the Hook of Holland and took the long, seven-hour ferry ride back to Harwich in England, followed by a staggeringly expensive taxi ride back home.

When I returned to work the following week, I was told that I had taken too much annual leave and I wouldn't be allowed to take any more time off. While this was disappointing news, it didn't matter too much because there were no more shows planned anyway. But the very next day I got a phone call. We had just been booked to support Dream Theater.

Dream Theater was the most successful progressive metal band in the world. With the help of heavy rotation on MTV, their debut single *Pull Me Under* had launched them into the big time two years earlier. Our MTV moment hadn't quite worked out. Before we could send them the final version of our *Innocent* video, they had announced the sudden cancellation of the *Headbangers Ball* show and our video was never shown. But now we were touring with Dream Theater and we were over the moon. They were coming to Europe to play at a few festivals as part of their *Waking Up The World* tour. In between the festivals they had arranged a few club shows, and we had been booked to support them for six of these dates in Germany. These would be the most important shows of our career so far.

We hastily released a live album called *Livedelica* featuring two songs from *Psychedelicatessen* and three from *Wounded Land* to capitalise on our upcoming shows, and headed back to our rehearsal room to prepare for the tour. My boss was very kind and agreed that I could take a few more days off. I had him wrapped around my finger to some extent. He knew that I would be back soon and there was no way he could hire and train up someone to replace me in such a short space of time. And so, on 19th June 1995, Threshold headed back to Europe once more in a Transit van and an MPV.

I was very much a loner and quite shy, so I didn't talk to Dream Theater much, something I regret looking back, but they seemed like nice guys. However, some of their crew members were less than hospitable. On the first day, I took a shower backstage at the Musiktheater in Kassel and dried myself with the towel that was hanging next to the shower. A couple of minutes later I was being shouted at furiously by one of the crew because I had used Mike Portnoy's towel. Later that day, the band invited us to help ourselves to food and snacks that had been provided backstage, only for us to be shouted at five minutes later by another crew member because we had eaten the band's strawberries.

My only encounter with their then keyboard player Derek Sherinian was when I was invited to sound check his rig. Derek had recently replaced original member Kevin Moore in the band. Being offered to sound check his keyboards was quite an honour and it would be a rare opportunity to see his set-up at close quarters. I climbed nervously onto the stage and started playing. One of the keyboards was set up to play a powerful lead solo sound, so I raced through the fastest moves and tricks I could think of, clearly desperate to impress anyone who was listening. After I had finished, I walked off the stage and through the hall. At that same moment Derek was heading towards the stage, and, as he walked past me, he said "Slick fingers!". I beamed, but I was too nervous to look him in the eye.

Our shows with Dream Theater were a great success. We made a lot of new fans across Germany and we were playing and sounding better than ever. Behind the scenes, however, tensions were rising. Writing had begun for our third album, and we were going through a classic case of 'musical differences', so often cited as the reason for band altercations and break-ups. On one side, the band's original members Karl, Nick and Jon (whom Jon now referred to as the 'triumvirate') wanted to go in a more progressive direction. On the other side, the new boys Glynn and Jay wanted us to sound heavier and less progressive. I found myself caught in the middle. I wasn't too heavily involved in the songwriting at this stage, so I was happy with either option as long as the material sounded good.

Among the songs that had been put forward for our third album so far, *Part Of The Chaos* had been mostly composed by the triumvirate and was probably our most progressive track yet, while Glynn had submitted a heavier, more direct song called *Always Never*. When we played our last show of the year, a rather spectacular stylistic mismatch that saw us supporting The Enid at London's Astoria on 6th December 1995, both songs were on the set list, representing two opposing sides of an ever-widening divide. Eventually things came to a head, unkind words were spoken, and we had another line-up change on our hands. Glynn had been fired and Jay had decided to go with him. Threshold would continue in their more progressive vein, while Glynn and Jay would go on to form a heavier sounding band called Mindfeed. The song *Always Never* would end up on their first album instead.

I was sorry to see them go. Despite the obvious 'tension of souls' that had built up within the band, we had sounded great together and I thought our future had looked promising. I offered to help out on the upcoming Mindfeed album, but Glynn politely declined as he had no plans to use keyboards. However, it felt as though there was some unfinished business between us, so we left the door open for possible future collaborations.

In the meantime, my old band Mercy Train briefly reappeared on the radar. Richard Burge had continued writing songs since our *Presence* album and he was hoping to get the band back together. I put forward a couple of songs too and we shortlisted a handful of them for a new demo tape. We got together for a jam session to run through the tracks before taking them to the studio, and it felt nice being back together. The new material had a good energy and we were sounding great. But the spark that had driven us forward in 1992 and 1993 had gone out. Having done all that work and got nowhere last time, it was hard to imagine doing it all again with no prospect of a better outcome. Still, we recorded demos of the songs in the hope that something would come of them.

But nothing happened and no doors opened, so unfortunately Mercy Train ground to a halt once more.

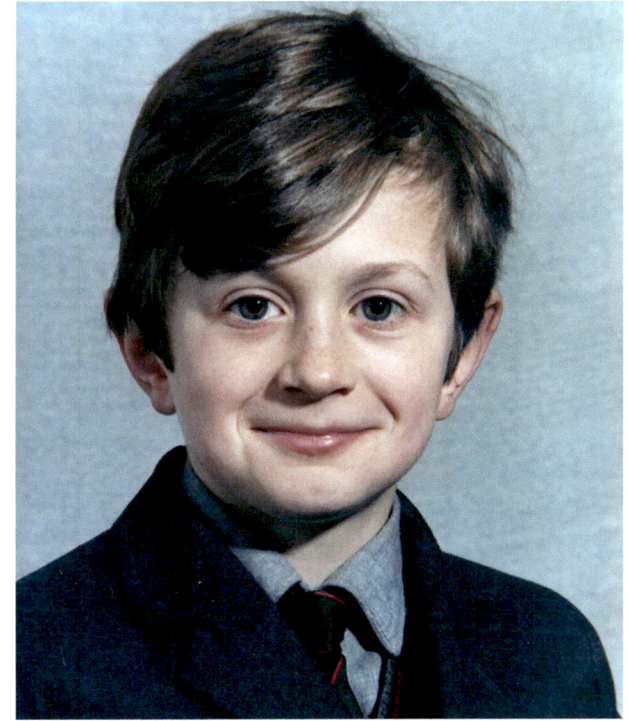

All dressed up for Plymouth College Preparatory School. The side parting was never going to last (1977).

Playing an unconventional piano duet with Dad in Newton Ferrers (1978).

Practising the ukelele on holiday at Widemouth Bay in north Cornwall (1980).

Emergency Exit, comprising Geoff Warren and me, trying to look too cool for school (1984).

Songwriting on the shore of Lake Plansee, Austria, during a family camping holiday (1985).

Mercy Train photo shoot on the streets of London. From left to right – Nick Harradence, Karl Groom, me, Richard Burge (1992).

Looking young and moody with Mercy Train (1992).

*Early Threshold photo session in a church in Maidenhead.
Clockwise from left – Tony Grinham, Karl Groom, Nick Midson, Damian Wilson,
me, Jon Jeary (1993).*

*Another early Threshold photo session at The Long Walk near Windsor Castle.
From left to right – me, Nick Midson, Tony Grinham, Damian Wilson, Jon Jeary,
Karl Groom (1993).*

Recording keyboards for Threshold's debut album
Wounded Land *at the original Thin Ice Studios in Maidenhead (1993).*

Hanging out backstage at our first European festival, Viarock in Belgium, headlined by Whitesnake.
From left to right – me, Karl Groom, roadie Mark Shergold, Nick Midson (1994).

*Long-haired lads on tour across Europe.
Clockwise from top left – Glynn Morgan; Karl Groom; me; Jon Jeary and Nick Midson (1994-1995).*

Photo shoot for Threshold's third album Extinct Instinct.
Clockwise from top left – me, Nick Midson, Karl Groom, Mark Heaney, Damian Wilson, Jon Jeary (1997).

On 13th June 1998 I married the love of my life, Kelly Farrah West. Our first dance was a song I wrote for her called You Alone, *a romantic piano ballad that we have no plans to release!*

We started recording music under the name Farrah West long before we thought of the name League Of Lights. Our first official photo session was shot at our flat in Walton-on-Thames (1998).

Photo shoot for Threshold's fourth album Clone *at Wisley Airfield, where we would return 19 years later for* Legends Of The Shires.
From left to right – Karl Groom, Nick Midson, Mac, me, Jon Jeary (1998).

*Impromptu photo shoot in a field on the way back from Wisley Airfield.
From left to right – me, Jon Jeary, Mac, Karl Groom, Nick Midson (1998).*

Performing at London Astoria 2 (LA2) on the second night of our Clone *tour. From left to right – Nick Midson, Jon Jeary, Johanne James, Mac, me, Karl Groom (1998).*

Another shot from our LA2 show. The venue has since been demolished to make way for Crossrail, a high-speed railway running underneath central London (1998).

At Thin Ice Studios in Virginia Water during the recording of Hypothetical. *From left to right – me, Jon Jeary, Nick Midson, Mac, Johanne James, Karl Groom (2001).*

Official photo shoot for Threshold's Critical Mass *album. From left to right – Karl Groom, Jon Jeary, Mac, me, Nick Midson, Johanne James (2002).*

Recording sessions for Threshold's Subsurface at Thin Ice Studios. Clockwise from top left – Mac; Johanne James; Nick Midson; me; Karl Groom, Steve Anderson (2004).

Mac absorbing the atmosphere from the crowd during the filming of our Critical Energy *DVD in Zoetermeer (2003).*

On stage in Weert during our Subsurface *tour, with my Korg Triton brandishing an extra 'I' in honour of the Corgi breed of dogs following a joke about my alleged royal ancestry (2004).*

Hard rocking on the Rock Hard stage in Gelsenkirchen, Germany (2005).

Relaxing behind the stage of the Rock Hard Festival on the bank of the Rhein-Herne-Kanal.
From left to right – Johanne James, me, Steve Anderson, Nick Midson, Karl Groom, Mac (2005).

RIAA gold disc for production work on the DragonForce album Inhuman Rampage *(2005).*

Karl Groom getting dragged along the floor during the filming of our video for Pilot In The Sky Of Dreams in Germany (2007).

On location in the industrial unit where we filmed the video for Pilot In The Sky Of Dreams (2007).

Outdoor photo shoot on a cold winter day in Germany (2007).

First official photo shoot of our new temporary line-up following Mac's departure. From left to right – Pete Morten, Steve Anderson, Damian Wilson, me, Johanne James, Karl Groom (2009).

Drinks at the Wheatsheaf Hotel, the closest pub to Thin Ice Studios in Virginia Water. From left to right – Karl Groom, Johanne James, me, Pete Morten, Damian Wilson, Steve Anderson (2009).

Relaxing in the Netherlands with Damian Wilson during one of our long weekenders (2011).

*The tour bus casino!
From left to right – Karl Groom, me, Damian Wilson (winning as always) and roadie Justin Hulford (2011).*

Chapter 6

No Straight Lines, No Simple Answers

WHEN IT CAME TO CHOOSING a singer to replace Glynn in Threshold, there was really only one choice.

Damian was available again after the collapse of LaSalle, the band he had dropped us for in 1993. With Threshold having already gone through one vocalist change and two drummer changes in the last couple of years, bringing back a former member to maintain some sort of continuity felt like the most sensible option.

Much of our third album was already written. *Part Of The Chaos* had slowly evolved but it was essentially complete, and we had even released a demo version of it as a bonus track on the Japanese edition of *Livedelica*. Another song called *Life Flow* was almost ready. We had performed an early version of it under the working title of *The River* at our recent London show, and after some final adjustments it was ready to record. There was also an early version of *Somatography* kicking around. Karl and Jon had played us a demo tape of the song at one of our rehearsals the previous year, although the vocal parts were rather different at that point.

Before Glynn's departure, our new album had sported the working title of *Always Never*, named after his song that we had performed in London while we were trying to forge ahead with our previous line-up. However, with Glynn now gone, Jon had chosen the slightly more abstract title *Extinct Instinct* instead. At this stage of Threshold's journey, Karl and Jon were still the band's main songwriting team, with Nick occasionally contributing guitar riffs to some of the songs. Karl would typically put together full instrumental demos at Thin Ice, and Jon would then write vocals over the top of them. It was a process that worked very well, and most of our third album was written in that way.

MAYBE A WRITER

Having contributed a fairly simple piano song for *Psychedelicatessen*, I was looking forward to flexing my writing muscles and composing something more elaborate for our new album. The first result of my efforts was *The Whispering*, which I put together at Richard Burge's studio. Originally based around a distorted Hammond organ riff, the song kept growing until it was eight minutes long, complete with numerous different sections and time changes. I later became worried that my original organ riff was a little off-genre, so I asked Karl to play the part on guitar instead. It was my most complex composition so far and I was proud of my efforts.

My other contribution was the ballad *Forever*. Its original title had been *Just Another Dream*, but I later changed it because I had already written a song called *Just Another Dream* for my school band Emergency Exit. I thought there was a faint possibility that I might want to re-record it one day, so I called the Threshold ballad *Forever* to avoid confusion. As it turned out, many years later, and outside Threshold, I would release another song called *Forever*, so I probably should have just stuck with the original name.

With seven songs from Karl, Jon and Nick, and two from me, the album was almost written. The final track came one day at the studio, as Karl and I accompanied Damian on acoustic guitar and piano to complete a song called *Clear*. Jon had also written a short acoustic piece which became known as *Segue*. This was initially positioned at the end of the CD as a hidden track when such practices were in vogue. And so once more we entered Thin Ice Studios to record our new album.

Thin Ice had now moved from Maidenhead to Virginia Water, a secluded Surrey town on the border of Windsor Great Park. The new property had a triple garage and workshop on the ground floor which had been converted into a recording studio. With my acoustics background I was asked to help out with the studio design, so I drew up plans for a two-room layout with an acoustically isolated live area. This meant that we could now record live drums at Thin Ice, something that hadn't been possible at the studio's old location due to the layout of the property.

But, before we could record any drums, Threshold needed a new drummer. For this we turned to a London-based session player called Mark Heaney, who would end up as our studio drummer for the next two albums. Mark had been recommended to us by Damian after they had worked together on a project called Jeronimo Road. He was the perfect fit. He was just as technically proficient as his predecessor Jay, but he had a lighter, more subtle touch that seemed to suit our new material perfectly.

Our recording sessions followed a similar pattern to *Psychedelicatessen*, with Karl taking charge of drums, bass and guitar while I looked after keyboards and vocals. I continued to rely heavily on my Korg O1/W alongside a selection of keyboards and modules at the studio. And once again I pushed myself to the limit for some of my keyboard solos, most notably on the album's two epics *Eat The Unicorn* and *Part Of The Chaos*. However, I had learned my lesson on our previous album and established the fine line between playable and unplayable parts. When you're on stage and the band is pumped with excitement, nerves and adrenaline, sometimes the songs can run a little faster than usual, so the last thing you want at that moment is a keyboard solo that you can only just cope with at normal speed.

The vocal sessions took a lot longer than our previous album. Every evening I would collect Damian and take him to the studio, and we would record late into the night until he was ready to stop. With most singers I would usually expect to record the main vocal three or four times and then compile a final version from the best moments. But, on *Extinct Instinct*, Damian would often insist on recording a song as many as 20 times before he was happy, constantly striving for perfection, even though most of the takes sounded virtually identical. By the time he finished a song I would have completely lost track of where all the best moments were, so it took a long time to compile the final versions. The process worked though, and we got a great result, but I do have vague memories of wanting to bang my head against the wall a few times during those sessions.

* * *

Towards the end of 1996 I decided to cut my hair short. I had been slowly growing it since joining the band and I now had long, flowing locks that looked a lot more on-genre. I loved having long hair on tour; it made it so much easier to look good during the shows. With just a few head movements you could look and feel like a rock god. Performing with short hair was a lot trickier, as the same movements could easily make you look weird and uncoordinated.

But, as wonderful as long hair was on tour, it was becoming a lot less wonderful for everyday life. Over the previous few years, British trends and fashions had become uncharacteristically conservative, and all of the men now seemed to have short hair. The flamboyance of glam rock in the 1970s and new romanticism in the 1980s were long forgotten, and nobody seemed to want to look different anymore.

Having long hair made me stand out, and it seemed as if people were starting to look at me suspiciously and treat me differently. One morning I went shopping to buy a new shower hose for the bathroom. With my long hair and black leather biker jacket I looked very different to everyone else in the town, who mostly wore shell suits. I found a suitable shop and asked the proprietor if he sold shower hoses as mine had broken. He eyed me up and down with the utmost contempt, looking like he wanted to spit on me. "You're not supposed to swing around the bathroom on it," he hissed condescendingly.

So eventually I succumbed to the spirit of the age and cut my hair short. The first cut looked truly awful because I foolishly asked for a bob, so I had to avoid seeing anybody until I could get another appointment the following day to cut it shorter.

Having short hair also looked a lot more suitable for my day job. Although working in acoustics wasn't how I wanted to spend my life, it could be quite interesting and sometimes involved solving some curious noise problems. Perhaps helping to make the world quieter by day was penance for making the world noisier by night.

One job earned me a certain amount of notoriety when I exorcised 'The Ghost of Rye Water Tower'. The company had received reports that a large, elevated water tower in the town of Rye near the south coast of England was haunted. On dark, stormy nights the locals would complain of hearing the ghostly sounds of *Amazing Grace* whistling eerily across the town. The music appeared to be emanating from somewhere near the old water tower. I was hired to visit Rye on a windy day to see if I could solve the mystery.

I climbed carefully to the top of the tower, which thankfully had a circular handrail around the edge to stop me from being swept away by the strong winds. I stood and waited for the wind to blow. And sure enough, before long I heard the opening notes of *Amazing Grace* floating all around me. It was the most mysterious sound, and it was rather disconcerting. It seemed impossible to locate the source of the noise because it was coming from everywhere.

Whenever the wind picked up, the tune would start again, sounding like a deathly orchestra of flutes practising their arpeggios.

It occurred to me that flutes only made a sound when air blew over their holes, which could potentially produce overtones similar to the opening notes of *Amazing Grace* if the air speed rose and fell in the right way. Then I noticed that the handrail which surrounded the top of the tower was made of long metal tubes with drainage holes at each end. Could those be the ghostly flutes?

I had some gum in the car, so I retrieved it and started chewing. One by one I plugged up the holes with the gum, and slowly the eerie whistling sound vanished. I had exorcised the tower's ghost. I vaguely remember a crowd of people gathered below cheering as I told them the news, and as I went home that night I was pleased with a job well done. But I also felt slightly wistful; I had destroyed a local legend.

Another job involved a report that some local primary school children had complained about a high-pitched whistling noise in their classroom. None of the teachers could hear it, so they had initially assumed that the children were just being naughty and making up stories. But, as the complaints continued, I was called in to investigate.

The head teacher escorted me to the classroom and I asked everyone to be quiet. I could just about make out a faint whistling sound. It was incredibly high-pitched, so it was likely that the older teachers at the school could not hear it because they had lost that part of their hearing range with age. I told the head teacher that I could hear the noise, but he just stared at me dubiously. He looked like he wanted to send me to the corner for being badly behaved. He clearly hadn't believed the children's stories.

The sound seemed to be coming from above me, so I asked for a ladder and climbed up into the dusty crawl space above the suspended ceiling. Eventually I spotted an old PA system mounted at the top of the wall. It had obviously not been used for a long time, but for some reason it had not been switched off. I found the source of the power and disconnected it. Below me I could hear the children shouting excitedly that the sound had finally stopped. I climbed back down, handed the ladder to the head teacher and explained what I had done. He eyed me very suspiciously. I had solved the problem, but I don't think he believed a word of it.

* * *

Far outside of the world of acoustics and progressive metal, I had been slowly getting to know the girl with the brown felt cap and long, sandy blonde hair who I had seen at church. She had now joined the church's music group as a singer, so we saw each other fairly regularly at music rehearsals and services. But, although we felt a strong connection to each other, most of our conversations had been limited to a few words between songs or in the company of other friends. Her name was Kelly, although most people in the music world would later come to know her by her middle name of Farrah.

Every month the church would send a few musicians to the local Young Offender Institution to hold a Sunday service for any inmates who wanted to attend. Occasionally Farrah and I would be on the team together, and it didn't go unnoticed that some of the young men were more interested in Farrah than they were in the service. After each meeting I would act as her bodyguard, shielding her from the more enthusiastic inmates who wanted to get close to her. In the years that followed, when people asked us how we first met, we always enjoyed seeing their shocked faces when we told them we had got to know each other in prison.

Farrah had heard that the Celtic rock band Iona would be performing in London on 31st January 1997, so she decided to arrange for a large group of friends to attend the concert together. Among those she invited was me. I hadn't heard of Iona, but the thought of going to a gig with lots of friends sounded good, so I signed up. It would also give me a chance to get to know Farrah a little better.

Over the course of January a few people changed their minds and cancelled, and then a few more, until eventually only Farrah and I were left on the list. It was starting to look a lot like a date, and we were both secretly pleased at this sudden change of circumstances. However, she later confessed that our date was almost lost at the last minute, as somebody phoned her the morning before the gig to ask if they could join us. But, instead of inviting him to travel to London with us, Farrah nonchalantly told him that we would probably see him there and hung up the phone. She had no intention of having a third wheel joining us for the night.

The whole concert went past in a haze. I was totally intoxicated by the girl standing next to me. During our journey into London, we had been so lost in conversation that at one point we found ourselves driving in the opposite direction to where we had been heading 20 minutes earlier, a navigational achievement that I cannot explain to this day. We both loved every moment of our unplanned date and neither of us wanted the night to end. I was head over heels in love, and from that moment on we would see each other every day until the next Threshold tour took me out of the country in April.

＊＊

For the last seven years I had been renting rooms in other people's houses, and I was starting to feel the need to buy a property of my own. Work was going well and I had a decent salary, so, with the help of a small loan from my parents, I was able to put down a deposit on a modest, two-bedroom flat above a bakery in Walton-on-Thames in Surrey. I converted the second bedroom into a small recording studio, borrowed some old furniture from my parents and settled contentedly into my first home.

It was from this two-bedroom flat that the Threshold fan club was run, based around printed fanzines that we would post out to subscribers. Our fan club was called *Devoted*, named after the song on our second album, and the magazines contained a selection of articles such as tour and studio diaries, interviews, band member profiles and the latest news about Threshold and other side projects. With the advent of the internet and online printing services it's hard to imagine doing it now, but I would print out the magazines at the office after work, fold and staple them and trim the edges with a guillotine for a tidy finish. It was a long-winded process and many of the copies would end up in the rubbish bin if the staple didn't go through properly or the trim wasn't good enough, but Threshold now had its very own fan club magazine.

Over the following 18 months we would end up producing three issues of *Devoted*. I don't recall how many fans subscribed or how much we charged, but we got quite a good response. We also sold a range of merchandise through the magazine such as CDs, cassettes, T-shirts and tour posters. Fans could pay using the antiquated method of Eurocheque or Travellers Cheque, and we promised to deliver their items within a wonderfully speedy 28 days. By the time we published our third and final edition of *Devoted* the following winter we had launched our first official website, so the need for a printed fanzine disappeared and no more issues were produced.

In 1997 I also auditioned to be the keyboard player for an up-and-coming singer-songwriter called Imogen Heap. Richard Burge knew her manager and had kindly recommended me for the role. Threshold was going well but it wasn't paying any bills. I really wanted to work full time in music and to do that I needed more opportunities, so I decided to give it a try. Imogen was in the process of making her debut album *I Megaphone* and was putting together a live band. Her songs were quirky and beautiful and reminded me a little of Tori Amos. I spent a couple of days learning the songs and programming up the sounds on my keyboards, and then headed up to London for the audition. All the hard work paid off and the audition went really well.

The following week I was called back for a second audition, and I was starting to feel quite confident of getting the job. However, a few days later I received a phone call to say they had given the role to someone else. I asked why I had lost out and they told me it was because I was too old. I was only 29, but apparently I was already over the hill! Imogen went on to do really well, and a few years later I saw her perform at the Roundhouse in London. I couldn't help noticing how young her band looked.

Around that time Threshold started to get some regular radio play in the UK. Alan 'Fluff' Freeman was a legendary DJ who had started his career at Radio Luxembourg before making his name at the BBC. By 1997 he was hosting *The Friday Rock Show* on Virgin Radio and had started to play our music. Jon was particularly chuffed with one episode when Fluff opened the show with *Paradox* and proceeded to quote several lines of the lyrics live on air, describing them as chilling.

Threshold's third album *Extinct Instinct* was released on 19th March. To promote the album, a 14-date European tour had been put together for us by a new German record label called InsideOut. The company had been formed by Thomas Waber, one of the directors of Giant Electric Pea, and had started out by reissuing progressive metal albums by US bands such as Symphony X and Shadow Gallery before going on to sign some acts of their own. Thomas had arranged for the tour to be promoted by the German magazine *Rock Hard*, so it was comprised mainly of German shows along with dates in the Netherlands, Switzerland, Spain, France and England.

Our new drummer Mark was unavailable for the tour because he had been offered a year-long contract performing in the musical *Joseph And The Amazing Technicolour Dreamcoat*, so a temporary replacement had to be found. Our new blood came in the form of Johanne James, who had been recommended to Damian as being the best drummer in Europe. And he did turn out to be rather good. He had a broad range of experience, not just with his other band at that time, London-based rockers Scrap Iron Scientists, but also from playing live sessions for some of the country's top popular music acts including Imagination and The Shadows. For a while, it seemed that every time we spoke to Johanne we would discover a new famous name that he had worked with.

Our crew for the tour rather unusually included three record company executives and a bass player. Thomas Waber was our tour manager, and his partner at InsideOut Michael Schmitz came along to sell merchandise. On lighting we had another of Giant Electric Pea's directors Laurence Dyer, and our stage technician was our long-time friend Ian Salmon, who, as well as being the bassist in Shadowland, had played acoustic guitar on Threshold's debut album *Wounded Land*. Our final crew member was Pendragon's sound engineer Andy Brookes, an exceptionally tall, ginger-haired Englishman with a dry sense of humour, who lived and worked in Germany.

Four weeks after the release of the album we performed our first show with our new touring formation. The band worked together really well, with Johanne slotting in perfectly and Damian returning as if he had never been gone. For the first two German shows we were supported by a local band called Hydrotoxin before our main support act arrived, a progressive rock group from the US west coast called Enchant, who were signed to InsideOut. They had missed our first two shows because they were out supporting Dream Theater, the privilege we had enjoyed a couple of years earlier. They arrived in the early hours of the morning after our second show, and our crowded nightliner headed off into the night with 17 people on board.

Our set list for the tour consisted mostly of songs from our new album, starting with the trio of *Exposed*, *Virtual Isolation* and *Eat The Unicorn* before weaving in a few songs from *Wounded Land* alongside *A Tension of Souls* from our second album *Psychedelicatessen*. Our closing song was always *Paradox*. It was the perfect way to end a show and was easy to extend if there was a good crowd and we wanted to carry on for a bit longer.

Overall, the tour ran fairly smoothly, as we made our way across Europe performing in a variety of venues, some pleasantly large and others so small that we could hardly fit everybody on the stage. However, things didn't run quite so smoothly when we got to Barcelona. After a lengthy 12-hour drive from Switzerland, we had spent a relaxing day looking around the Spanish city, sampling the local food and walking along the city's beach promenade. But we were all exhausted from the long journey, and as we walked onto the stage that night tempers were fraying.

The venue's sound system wasn't particularly powerful, and although Damian's on-stage monitor speakers were turned up as loud as they could go, he was still struggling to hear himself properly. Part way through our set, his frustration boiled over. He picked up one of the monitors, hurled it off the stage and stormed out. The remaining band members were rather unsure what to do, so we just stood there like rabbits staring into the headlights. The audience stared back, wondering what was going to happen next. Eventually we realised that nothing was going to happen next. Damian evidently wasn't coming back. We apologised politely to the audience and shuffled off the stage, feeling rather embarrassed and deflated.

The reaction from Thomas was priceless: "If you're going to do something like that again, make sure you've got more music journalists in the audience!" He understood that all publicity was good publicity, but for us it was just an uncomfortable incident that we would prefer to forget. As the crowd started to exit the venue, rather earlier than they had expected, Thomas handed out free promotional CDs to anyone who wanted one in consolation for the curtailed gig, and we headed back to the nightliner for our next long journey. As we left, the local promoter informed us rather curtly that we would never perform in Barcelona again, and for the following 22 years that would prove to be true.

Our final show in mainland Europe was at the Noorderlicht in the Netherlands. Karl and I had previously experienced an amazing crowd there on the Shadowland tour back in 1992, and we weren't disappointed on the Threshold tour either. The venue was packed out and it was our largest headline show so far. After a dozen concerts together our performances were really tight. It was the best night of the tour and we loved every minute of it. We were rock stars, and this was our moment. We returned to England feeling like conquering heroes, ending the tour in the northern town of Rotherham before making our way back home to Surrey.

Farrah travelled up to Rotherham to see our final show. I'm not too sure what she made of our performance, as progressive metal wasn't really her sort of music, but it didn't seem to put her off. We continued to see each other every day. Farrah worked about half an hour from me, so I would often stretch the limits of my lunch break to race over and join her for a few precious minutes together, before meeting up again after work to enjoy the long summer evenings getting to know each other. I knew she was the one for me. It's possible that I had known from the moment I first saw her.

In October I arranged for us both to go on a hot air balloon ride over Devon and Cornwall. As our balloon rose into the air, I remember thinking how unsafe it felt to be so far up in what appeared to be little more than a wicker basket. But after a few minutes it felt perfectly normal and we enjoyed the beautiful views and the peace and quiet, punctuated only by the sound of the hot air balloon's burners and the occasional police siren on the roads below. And this was the moment that I asked Farrah to marry me. Rather scarily, the hot air balloon ride ended with us crashing through some trees in the twilight as the pilot struggled to find a place to land, with the basket eventually hitting the ground and toppling over on a steep hill. Even more scarily, Farrah said yes.

Chapter 7
Goodbye Mother Earth

TOWARDS THE END OF 1997 I started developing health problems. At the time I thought it was just the result of doing too much and burning the candle at both ends, so for a while I ignored it. But I was starting to feel exhausted all the time. I couldn't stop yawning and I was increasingly getting brain fog. Quite often I would get half way through a sentence only to forget what I was talking about, and if somebody spoke to me, it was hard to follow what they were saying. At the time, Farrah and I were trying to refurbish the new flat, but after a few seconds of rubbing down a door frame or sawing a piece of wood, I would be totally out of breath and have to sit down. It was disconcerting and frustrating, and the strange thing was that Farrah was showing the same symptoms too.

We were both diagnosed with Chronic Fatigue Syndrome and had to stop work. It felt like our bodies were overloaded with something that they couldn't cope with. The doctors had no idea what to do, and we spent the next few months feeling exhausted, lethargic and cloudy headed. Our problem was only solved much later when we started seeing a nutritionist, who put us on a heavily restricted diet, and we slowly started to see some progress.

Meanwhile, Karl and Jon had started work on a new Threshold album. *Extinct Instinct* had focussed on our progressive side, resulting in our most unconventional sounding record so far, but for our fourth album it was decided to lean more towards our metal side and do something heavier and more direct. The irony was probably lost on us that this had been close to what Glynn and Jay wanted before they left the band. However, there would still be plenty of progressive moments, just with a darker and heavier sound than our previous effort.

Glynn and Jay's new band Mindfeed had signed to InsideOut, where they would release two albums produced by Andy Sneap. The first one included the song *Always Never*, which had been originally destined for Threshold, along with *Open Your Eyes*, which Glynn had previously put forward in 1994. Their second album also included a new recording of the song *Innocent*. They were both great records, showcasing Glynn's songwriting and powerful vocals really well, so I was sorry to learn that, after a couple of tours supporting Skyclad and Symphony X, they had eventually broken up before they could complete their third album.

Jon thought our new Threshold record should be a concept album. He had thought up a storyline that involved a genetically cloned child with special abilities who felt out of place on Earth and moved to Mars. It was a slight departure for Threshold, but the idea of making a concept album sounded appealing so we started writing songs to fit the story. I completed my old composition *Sunrise On Mars* and wrote a couple more songs, *Goodbye Mother Earth* and *Change*, as well as taking some of Karl and Nick's unused riffs to write *Angels*. Meanwhile, the rest of the album was composed as usual by Karl and Jon, with the occasional contribution from Nick. The album was given the working title of *Replica*, although we would later change this to *Clone*. With everything going according to plan, Karl and I convened at Thin Ice and prepared to start recording.

Mark Heaney travelled over from Germany where he had been hosting a series of drum clinics. He had some good sponsorship deals and consequently turned up with an excellent new kit. He was surprisingly fast to record, and once again proved that he was more than a match for whatever we could throw at him. However, as we approached the end of the week, Mark dropped a bombshell. He had been asked to join another band and would not be able to continue with Threshold. They were called The Seahorses, an alternative rock band formed by John Squire, guitarist of The Stone Roses. Obviously, it was too good an opportunity for him to turn down, so all we could do was accept the news and wish him well. Finding a permanent drummer was clearly proving to be a problem.

Jon came to the studio next to record his bass parts. The sessions went well, so apart from our unexpectedly empty drum stool, most things appeared to be going to plan. However, as if to prove that lightning can strike the same place twice, with only five days to go before Damian was due to start recording the vocals, he phoned us to say that he wouldn't be coming. He had been offered a role in the musical *Les Misérables* and would not be available to record our album for a while, possibly for up to 18 months. It's fair to say that the band was not too happy about this. In the space of two weeks we had lost both our drummer and our vocalist. And for the second time we had been upstaged by a musical.

We discussed our latest dilemma with Giant Electric Pea, and Thomas sent over some CDs of vocalists who he thought might be suitable to replace Damian. I don't recall who all the options were, but one album stood out from the crowd. It was by a German band that had recently broken up called Sargant Fury. The vocals sounded amazing: rich and melodic with some of that grit that we had loved so much about Glynn's voice. It turned out that the singer was British and had moved to Germany to join Sargant Fury after hearing their demo tape. His name was Andrew McDermott, also known as Mac. We decided to look no further, we were sold. We sent a copy of our demos to Germany and he accepted the job on the spot. No auditions, no meetings, just a lot of trust and a very good voice.

We modified our studio schedule and continued with the rest of the production until Mac could come over. Alongside our final guitar and keyboard parts we also recorded some guest appearances by other people. The first of these was Darren 'The Badger' Redick, a radio DJ who lived locally and sometimes played Threshold on his show. He had a rather useful American accent that sounded great for voice-over work, so he recorded a countdown for the start of *Goodbye Mother Earth* along with various other phrases that didn't actually make the final cut. Another part that didn't get used was an overdriven harmonica solo by Simon Forster on *The Latent Gene*, although this was later reinstated for an extended version of the song. Farrah also made her CD debut as part of the choir on the majestic *Voyager II*.

With the album almost complete apart from the vocals, it was finally time to visit London Heathrow Airport to meet our new singer for the first time. The only photo I had to go on was from the artwork of Sargant Fury's last album, featuring Mac pouting moodily through long, flowing hair with his shirt half unbuttoned. So, I figured he should be quite easy to spot. I stood in the arrivals hall and watched the flood of people pouring in from their flights. However, there were no men with long hair and everyone's shirts appeared to be properly buttoned. I waited and waited. After what felt like an age, a short-haired man wearing a brown leather flying jacket approached me and asked in a thick, Geordie accent: "Are you Richard? It's taken bloody ages to find you, I thought you had long hair!"

I drove Mac to the studio, and we were profoundly relieved to discover that we all got on well. He was very laid back with an easy-going, infectious sense of humour. The following days recording his vocals were highly enjoyable. His voice sounded every bit as good as we had hoped. We changed a few melodies to suit his vocal range, but mostly he just performed the songs as they were written, and he made them sound as if they had been written for him. We had fallen on our feet and found a truly special vocalist. After a few more weeks of production, editing and mixing, we had somehow got through another turbulent chapter of Threshold history, and our fourth album *Clone* was complete.

* * *

Outside the studio, life was even busier. Farrah and I had been putting together the final preparations for our wedding, and on 13th June 1998 we were married in a little church in Staines surrounded by our family and friends. I was as nervous as the day I had first dropped her home after the Iona gig. It rained for most of the day, but it didn't matter because I was marrying my soulmate, the love of my life. The ceremony was followed by an afternoon wedding breakfast, an evening reception and multiple attempts to capture some outdoor wedding photos in between the rainstorms. Karl was my best man, and the rest of the band came to celebrate with us too. It was one of those very long days that go by far too fast, and one of the best days of my life.

A few months later *Clone* was released on 20th November. However, despite a smattering of solid reviews across Europe and the US, the record didn't sell too well. Whether this was due to our constant line-up changes, the shift in style from our previous album, or just because people didn't think it was as good as the last album I don't know, but it only sold about half as many copies as *Extinct Instinct*. It was a frustrating outcome. We had worked so hard to produce our fourth album against all the odds, but our seemingly upward trajectory had now taken a serious dip. We rested our hopes on our upcoming European tour, trusting that it would help to boost our profile and reinvigorate our disappointing album sales.

We also decided to release a compilation album of remixes and rarities. Karl had been revisiting some of our older mixes and thought the results sounded better than the original versions. We also had various radio edits of tracks that were not yet available on CD, as well as some alternative mixes of songs from *Clone* and a couple of unexpected dance remixes. Our record label wasn't interested in putting out a compilation at this stage of our career, but we felt sure that our fans would want to hear it, so we decided to press the CDs ourselves and sell them through our website and live shows. And so, with the blessing of our record label, our 'Direct-to-Fan' CD concept was born.

We called the compilation *Decadent*, partly to mark the first decade of the band, and partly to acknowledge that the compilation was possibly a little self-indulgent. We found a fantastic cover image in a stock photography catalogue of two men sitting in the control room of a large power plant. The men didn't look too dissimilar to me and Karl, so we rather liked the idea that some people would think it was a picture of us working at Thin Ice Studios. We released the album on the first day of our *Clone* tour in February 1999 and it proved to be very popular.

* * *

Our *Clone* tour started with two shows in the UK. The first of these was in Rotherham where we had ended our previous tour the year before. The venue was a rather reverberant sports hall in a leisure centre where a number of progressive concerts were arranged by the Classic Rock Society, an organisation set up in 1991 to support and promote progressive rock music. Supported by Welsh band Ezra and the Society's customary raffle, we took to the stage for the first time with our new singer Mac, who appeared to have fully embraced the word 'leisure' at the bar before we got to the stage. We put on a highly energetic show, much to the delight of our fans, who didn't appear to mind too much that our new frontman was rather drunk and couldn't remember all of the words.

The following night we were back at London's Astoria where we had previously supported The Enid, although this time we found ourselves downstairs on the smaller LA2 stage. The show was well attended, including many friends and family members who had been waiting for us to do a London show for a long time. We had arranged to record the concert to release as another Direct-to-Fan album. We brought in a sound engineer and some recording equipment to capture the show and hired a photographer to make sure we had some good pictures for the album artwork. Unfortunately, some of the audio channels overloaded during the recording process. We didn't have the technology to restore the sound quality at the time, so the album never got made. However, the photos looked good, so we used them in the booklet for our subsequent studio album instead.

After our two UK shows we had a week to wait until we were due to travel over to mainland Europe for the rest of our tour. I had felt a little uneasy during the last two shows because of how I looked. I had never really got used to having short hair and thought I looked much too ordinary to be in a rock band. So I decided to take radical action. I would bleach my hair white for the rest of the tour. I knew this wouldn't go down too well at work and probably not at church either, so I decided to do it in secret. I would bleach it just before we headed off to Europe and dye it brown as soon as we got back, so nobody outside of the tour would ever know.

Farrah thought I was crazy. She was perplexed that I felt the need to dye my hair to feel like I belonged. However, my mind was made up, so on the Friday before we were due to depart, I left work early and went to the local hair salon. They sat me down and started the treatment. It seemed to take quite a long time, and after a while the stylist was looking worried. "The colour's not lifting," she said nervously. After almost four hours I still didn't have white hair. It had gone a strange yellowish colour, not what I wanted at all. But she told me it wasn't going to go any lighter in one session, so I left the salon looking and feeling slightly off-colour. It wasn't really what I had hoped for, but at least I could rest assured that none of my friends outside of the band would ever see it.

When I arrived home that night, I received a phone call from Karl. He told me that our nightliner was going to collect us slightly later than expected, so it would now be leaving on Sunday night instead of Saturday. This was no problem; I would have a bit more time to prepare for the tour. I would just have to lay low until Sunday night so that nobody saw me. Then the phone rang again. It was the church's music director. "We have an emergency; no one's available to play the piano on Sunday morning. Please could you help us out?" I was mortified, but I didn't feel I could really say no. I got a lot of strange looks during that service. I suspect quite a few people prayed for me.

On Sunday night we finally sailed across the English Channel for the European leg of our tour, where we would be joined by two support bands from the InsideOut label: Italian power-metallers Eldritch and Swedish prog-metallers Pain Of Salvation. Although we weren't totally convinced that having two support bands for the tour was a good idea, we were pleased to learn this that meant we would have a little more space on the nightliner, as the support bands would travel on a second bus. Our nightliner's entourage therefore consisted of Mac on his first outing with us, Johanne on his second, the rest of the band and four crew members.

Our next gig was at the Markthalle in Hamburg, Germany, a venue with an amazing atmosphere and a wide, spacious main stage looking out over a long, tiered hall. Over the years it has become one of my favourite places to play. The venue also has a much smaller second stage called the MarX located in a side room. On arrival at the venue we were rather horrified to discover that we would be performing on the smaller of the two stages due to low ticket sales. It had barely enough space for one band, let alone three, and changing gear between acts would be almost impossible. Somehow, we got through the evening and the crowd were a lot more enthusiastic than we were. As we packed up our gear at the end of the night, we could at least look forward to a better day tomorrow.

Unfortunately, due to an argument between the show's organisers, the following day turned out to be considerably worse, and our gig in Minden was cancelled. The frustration among our touring party upon discovering that the show had been axed for such an unnecessary reason was palpable. We spent the rest of the day in a small lorry park on the outskirts of nowhere in particular, with nothing to do, nowhere to go, no money and no enthusiasm.

Thankfully, the next four shows in Germany and Switzerland went according to plan. Fans showed up wearing an assortment of Threshold and Sargant Fury shirts, and while we didn't feel quite as polished as the line-up that had performed with Dream Theater four years earlier, we were at least starting to feel like a band again. The audience at our Swiss show included a large contingent of Italian fans, so we were suitably encouraged that our first ever gig in Italy the following night would be a memorable one.

Our first ever gig in Italy the following night was indeed a memorable one, but not quite in the way we had hoped for. We didn't know whether it was because we were in a small hall in the middle of nowhere, or because there was an important football match on that night (a well-worn excuse used by many promoters over the years), or because the whole progressive metal fan base of Italy had been at our Swiss show the night before, but for whatever reason this was one of the worst attended gigs we ever played.

The day had started well enough. We woke up a few miles from Biella to the most beautiful weather and scenery of the tour. After a relaxing walk through the countryside to pass the time, the staff arrived to open the venue and we enjoyed a delicious continental breakfast as we watched the Formula 1 Grand Prix on a TV behind the bar. However, as we started to set up on stage, we discovered that there was a problem with the venue's power supply. This promptly caused Nick's amp to blow up, followed by mine and several other pieces of our equipment. It was all downhill from there, so when only thirty people turned up to the show, much to the embarrassment of our Italian support band, we just took it with a resigned shrug as Mac invited the entire crowd onto the stage for a memorable rendition of our encore *Paradox*.

The next day was a driving day, with a lot of miles through treacherous weather conditions separating us from our next venue, the Blue Sport Café in Clermont Ferrand, France. While our road crew negotiated with the local venue staff over the problems of parking two rather large buses outside a rather small café, I spent the afternoon looking for a new amp and having coffee with my sister Caroline. She lived in nearby Le Puy and had travelled up to see the show, her journey hampered slightly by a protest in the town centre by local farmers, who had covered one of the roundabouts with several tons of manure. The gig itself was a good one, despite the diminutive size of the stage forcing Johanne to play his drums from a small dining area in the corner of the café. An arena tour it was not, but at least things were going smoothly again.

Unfortunately, all the smoothness vanished when we were informed that the following night's show in Paris had been cancelled due to poor ticket sales. This was the second show we had lost. We consoled ourselves with an afternoon at Disneyland instead, but it felt as though our tour was close to falling apart. The next night in Lingen, Germany, was only slightly better. The gig had been advertised for the wrong month, so we spent a rather unenjoyable evening playing to a very small crowd of people who had heard about the gig by chance. To make matters worse, Nick's amp blew up again during the show. We briefly wondered if we were expected to return a month later to play on the advertised date, but we thought better of it.

Thankfully, the next three shows were much better and helped to lift our spirits. A fantastic crowd in Vosselaar, Belgium, coaxed three encores out of us and reminded us how good it felt when things were going well. The following night in the Dutch town of Uden was even better and provided the loudest crowd of the tour, before we headed to what was now to be our final show in Verviers, Belgium. This was because we had received yet more bad news: poor ticket sales in Pain of Salvation's homeland meant that our final shows in Halmstad and Stockholm had also been cancelled.

Our concert in Verviers therefore became our end of tour party. We swapped band shirts and said our goodbyes, and as we performed our final encore everyone from all three bands appeared on stage together. Everyone, that is, apart from Nick, whose amp had blown up one final time before the encore, so instead of joining us he spent the last few moments of the tour sitting gloomily on his own backstage.

**

With the tour now over, we headed home across the English Channel with mixed emotions. We tried to put a brave face on it, but it had been our least successful tour so far and we had endured some thoroughly miserable moments. Combined with the commercial failure of *Clone*, it was starting to feel as if Threshold had gone as far as it could go. And so, in the summer of 1999, I decided it was time to leave the band. I felt that I had strayed for too long from my original dream of producing music that would get into the charts, so now was the time to devote myself to that pursuit again.

I resolved to tell the band of my impending departure after our upcoming show at Germany's Wacken Open Air. Wacken was one of the biggest heavy metal festivals in the world, so it would be a memorable place for my final show. We took to the stage in the early afternoon of 7th August and put on one of our best ever performances, powering through a selection of songs from *Clone* and some of our older tracks in the afternoon sun. Mac was having a lot of fun and at one moment I turned to see him singing while doing a headstand. He was later voted the best frontman of the festival in the German music press. Funnily enough, Glynn Morgan was also there, and I watched him perform with his band Mindfeed, which no longer featured our former drummer Jay, for what would turn out to be their final show.

Back in England after the festival, Karl was gracious when I told him I was leaving. He accepted the news reflectively, thanked me for all that I had done and confessed that he never thought I would stay as long as I had. As it turned out, I wouldn't be gone for too long. But as I drove home that day, I felt a buzz of excitement about the possibilities that the future held.

I busied myself writing rock and pop songs in the hope of placing them with other artists. Once I had a few songs ready I visited my publisher in London, hopeful that he would snap up my compositions and start shopping them to potential artists and labels. It was a good meeting, but I was disappointed that he didn't spend longer listening to the songs; he seemed more interested in telling me about his own success than helping me with mine. In hindsight, it is very difficult to break through into the mainstream pop market, and although I had got close a few years earlier, it was obvious that lightning wasn't about to strike twice. I left his office feeling totally deflated. I had pinned a lot of hope on that meeting, and I wasn't sure what to do next.

Meanwhile, Threshold had booked two more concerts, starting with a return to Rotherham followed by the inaugural ProgPower festival in the Netherlands. I had assumed that the guys would have found a replacement for me by now, so I was rather surprised when Jon called to ask if I was available to do the shows. As it turned out, they hadn't taken my resignation too seriously and had made no attempt to look for someone else. Having made no headway with my songwriting career I hesitantly agreed to help out. And so, a few days later I found myself in a rehearsal room with the band again, not sure if my return was temporary or permanent. And I must confess that it felt good to be back. They had a great set list planned for ProgPower. It would be our first time headlining a European festival and it had the potential to raise the band's profile considerably.

The ProgPower concept was a perfect fit for a band like Threshold and would go on to spawn sister festivals in other countries. It was masterminded by Dutch music enthusiast René Janssen and some fellow music fans who had noticed there were no festivals dedicated to the progressive metal scene. Over the years Threshold had often struggled to secure festival appearances, deemed too heavy for progressive rock events and too progressive for heavy ones. ProgPower solved that problem perfectly, and the first edition of the festival at the 013 in the city of Tilburg boasted an impressive line-up including Evergrey, Superior and Poverty's No Crime, with Threshold booked as the event's headliner.

However, quite how we survived those 90 minutes on stage remains a mystery. We had travelled to Tilburg the night before the show so we could arrive fresh-faced at the venue the following morning to set up, sound check and fully immerse ourselves in the event. However, Mac decided to spend the day fully immersed in the local refreshments, so by the time we hit the stage that night he was in a pretty bad state. During our set a helpful member of the audience handed Mac something to smoke, and that was the beginning of the end. My lasting impression is of Mac lying semi-conscious on the stage as we laboured our way through *Exposed* and *Somatography*. He couldn't remember the songs at all and could barely stand up, so he just lay there holding the microphone in the air hoping that the audience would cover for him.

Mac was very apologetic afterwards, but the damage had been done. It felt like he had shot us in the foot instead of helping us shoot for the moon and wasn't exactly the return to the band that I had hoped for.

Chapter 8
The Storm That Won't Be Calmed

BACK HOME I BUSIED MYSELF with my day job. By now I had taken a step back from acoustic consultancy to focus on promoting some specialist software that the company had developed. I immersed myself in the world of graphic design, website coding and marketing, skills that would prove very useful in music for the years to come. My work caught the attention of the company's IT department and I ended up changing roles to work on their internal and external websites. This resulted in a good pay rise, and before long I was earning more than ever and driving a beautiful black Alfa Romeo GTV, a car I had dreamed of owning for years. Threshold may have been faltering both professionally and financially, but my career was going more successfully than ever.

The GTV was a small, two-door sports car with black leather racing seats and virtually no luggage space, making it thoroughly impractical for transporting music equipment. For band rehearsals I usually had to carry two keyboards and a large rack case, and the only way to fit them in the car was to put the rack case on the narrow back seat and recline the two keyboards on the passenger seat next to me. The leather was quickly ruined. At one point I even managed to fit a large Soundcraft mixing desk in the car, jammed precariously across the passenger seat and onto my left shoulder, making it rather hard to steer or change gears. But it was such a beautiful car to drive that it was worth putting up with such minor inconveniences.

My pay rise also meant that Farrah and I were able to move out of our flat in Walton-on-Thames to a tiny cottage a few miles away in Lower Feltham. In fact, it was so small that our sofa wouldn't fit in the living room and we had to buy a smaller one, and I often got my flight cases stuck half way down the narrow staircase when I took them to rehearsals. However, it was good to be moving up the property ladder.

Threshold was about to move home as well. Our record contract with Giant Electric Pea had expired, and, following the poor sales of *Clone*, we were politely dropped from the label. However, as one door closed, another one opened, and we were offered a deal with InsideOut. Despite our performance at ProgPower I had decided to stay with the band. My songwriting career had not progressed as I had hoped, and it now seemed rather foolish to say goodbye to the band that had been such a huge part of my life for so long. Although there were problems that needed resolving, there was also a lot of potential, and I was hopeful things would improve over time. And so, one day I found myself travelling to London with Karl, boarding a small plane at London City Airport and flying to Germany to sign a record contract with InsideOut Music.

Karl had started writing two new long songs which would become *The Ravages of Time* and *Narcissus*. But before I launched into composing any new material, I decided to review what I had written over the last two years to see if there was anything suitable that I could use. Two songs stood out as possibilities, so those became my starting point. The first of these was *Long Way Home*, although it was a very different song when I first wrote it. It wasn't meant for Threshold, but I thought it just might work, so I sent a copy to Mac and he recorded a rough version of the vocals in Germany. But even with his powerful voice it didn't really sound like a Threshold song, so I turned to Nick for inspiration.

Nick wrote guitar riffs that had a dark, brooding quality that suited the band perfectly. He used to record his ideas onto C90 cassette tapes, so I borrowed a copy of his latest recordings and started listening through for something I could use. I struck instant gold, with the song's main riff and pre-chorus both coming from his cassette. I rewrote the chorus to sound a bit more progressive and before long I had a whole new version of the song. Several years later we would record the original version for our *Paradox* box set, using the rough vocal that Mac had recorded in Germany. However, it didn't come close to the version of the song based on Nick's guitar parts.

The other composition to emerge from my review process at the time was *Keep My Head*, a rather unlikely Threshold song that Jon thought was closer to the style of the folk-rock group Crosby, Stills & Nash than it was to Threshold. Mac did a great job of the vocals, and it ended up sitting fairly comfortably on the final album between the heaviness of *Long Way Home* and the closing epic *Narcissus*. However, we all knew that it was probably a little off-genre, and although fans have been kind about the song over the years, it unsurprisingly remains one of the few tracks that we have never performed live.

Writing *Light And Space* was a curious experience. Other songwriters have previously described moments when it felt like they were receiving music from another world or picking up songs from the floor of heaven. This was one of those moments. It was August 2000 and I was in Radčice, a small village in the south Bohemian region of the Czech Republic. Farrah and I were on holiday with her family, and we had fallen in love with the area's beautiful countryside and picturesque towns. The only musical instrument in the cottage was an old acoustic guitar hanging on a wall with one solitary string on it. One morning I woke up with a simple riff in my head, four repeated notes that would have worked even on that old guitar. Then I heard an answering phrase, a fat synthesizer line that sounded huge. I wrote the two ideas down in a small notebook that I kept in my pocket.

During the course of the day I found myself reaching for that notebook every few minutes. Next I heard another riff, an opening lyric and melody, a strange time change, a chord sequence, a few more words. The whole song came one line at a time, I had no idea where it was going or what it was about. But by the end of the next day I had the whole song, even down to the keyboard solo. I read the finished lyrics and I was blown away; they had a profound message but I felt as though I couldn't take credit for them. It was more like a gift than a composition, as if somebody had already written it and my job was just to write it down.

Once we arrived back in the UK, I got into the flow of writing and the songs *Oceanbound* and *Sheltering Sky* came quite easily. I had wanted to compose an atmospheric ballad with a darker sound than my previous efforts *Forever* and *Change*, and as soon as I had come up with the opening piano hook of *Sheltering Sky* with its backdrop of floating harmonics, desert winds and reverse acoustic strums, I knew I was on to something and the song was a joy to write.

There was just one more track waiting to be finished. Karl had given a six-minute instrumental to Jon but he had been struggling to come up with lyrics for it. After a while I became concerned that the song wouldn't be ready for when Mac arrived to sing it, so I wrote some lyrics and melody as a backup in case we needed them. My version of the song was called *Undertow*, but I kept it quiet because I didn't want to cause any arguments or upset Karl and Jon's writing partnership. As it happened, Jon finished working on the song a few days later, so I never needed to present my version. He had called it *Turn On Tune In*, in homage to the American writer and drug advocate Timothy Leary. And it was fantastic, one of the catchiest songs he had ever written.

One night I went over to Jon's house to discuss how the album was coming along and try to decide on an album title. While we were chatting, I explained that some of my song lyrics were essentially conversations with God. Jon and I had very different views on faith and religion, so he suggested the title *Hypothetical* to emphasise the point. I felt slightly affronted at first and I drove off that night with a sense of disappointment. But the more I thought about it, the more I warmed to the idea. I turned the car around, drove back to Jon's house and agreed to the title. I shouldn't expect anyone to endorse my opinion any more than I would expect to endorse theirs. So, for an album that was a melting pot of conflicting lyrical themes and ideologies *Hypothetical* was the perfect title.

The cover artwork for the album was designed by German artist Thomas Ewerhard. He had previously worked on our *Clone* album, as well as Glynn Morgan's second Mindfeed album, but this was something else. Comprising a city on a rock floating over a rugged, rocky beach, it evoked the classic progressive rock covers of the 1970s by legendary artist Roger Dean. But it also possessed a darker quality that instantly let you know that, as well as sounding progressive, this album was going to sound heavy and atmospheric. It's a rare thing for an album cover to perfectly match the music, but with *Hypothetical* Thomas had done just that, creating not just one of our best Threshold covers, but in my opinion one of the best album covers of all time.

We recorded *Hypothetical* at Thin Ice Studios during November and December 2000. Johanne James had now become our permanent drummer following Mark Heaney's departure in 1998. Having already been our drummer for the *Extinct Instinct* and *Clone* tours, Johanne was part of the Threshold family and was the only and obvious choice. The album was released on 20th March 2001 and was named 'Album of the Month' by Germany's *Rock Hard* magazine. There was even a brief glimmer of hope that we might finally make it into the album chart in Germany. But although this goal ultimately eluded us, we were very proud of what we had achieved with

Hypothetical. It was such a marked contrast to the release of *Clone* just over two years earlier, with its low sales resulting in the termination of our first record deal. *Hypothetical* marked the start of a new chapter for Threshold and we looked forward to taking it on tour.

* * *

Meanwhile, Farrah and I had been recording some music of our own. Over the last few years, we had written and recorded various songs in our home studio, drafting in Ian Salmon and local musician Tim Walker to play guitar on them. One of these was called *Horses* and would go on to form the basis of the Threshold song *Smile At The Moon*. Another was called *Summer* and would later end up on a US charity compilation album, marking our first official release together under the name Farrah West. We had converted our tiny spare bedroom in Lower Feltham into a recording studio, and although it was quite hard to move around once we had squeezed in the mixing desk and keyboards, we managed to make a few good recordings there.

However, Lower Feltham never felt like home and we were soon looking for somewhere new. Although we were just a stone's throw from Freddie Mercury's childhood home, it didn't feel like a very inspiring place to be. While the local newspapers delivered to our previous flat in Walton-on-Thames used to feature gentle headlines like 'Cat in tree rescued by firemen', the Feltham headlines read 'Man stabbed to death on street with Samurai sword' or 'Girl attacked in pub car park'. It turned out that the pub in question was right next to our house. It was definitely time to move.

But before we could start house hunting, it was time for me to head back to mainland Europe once more. Threshold had been booked to perform at a Dutch festival called Bospop in July 2001 alongside bands including Megadeth, Savatage and Pendragon. We hadn't played live together since our catastrophic ProgPower show in the same country almost two years earlier, so we thought it would be wise to do a couple of warm-up gigs before unveiling our new material to a festival crowd.

One of the warm-up shows was at the Radhaus in Kleve, a small German town near the Dutch border where we had played our second ever European concert in 1994. The venue was just as we remembered it, an unlikely shed in the middle of nowhere with a car inexplicably sticking out of the roof. However, it was filled with heady memories of those early experiences of touring life: signing our first autographs, endless games of table football, free beer and meeting fans that seemed to be seven feet tall and looked far more rock and roll than I did. The place was mostly unchanged since our first visit, although it was a relief to discover that the stage was no longer powered from a single socket.

As we neared the end of the show, we launched into the song *Light And Space* and the crowd started clapping along. This is an endeavour that rarely ends well because the song has a complex time signature, so every fourth bar the music skips a beat and most of the clapping goes out of time. Unfortunately, Mac also lost the rhythm and when we reached the first verse he didn't start singing. However, instead of just letting the music repeat for a couple of bars and joining us later, he threw his hands in the air and told the band to stop playing. After a few bars of uncertainty, we reluctantly stopped, and he asked us to start the song again. This we duly did, rather frustrated with him for making us look so unprofessional. But when we got to the verse he missed his cue again.

This happened four times, each time ending with Mac stopping the band. We were rather furious with him at this point. Johanne was staring him down so hard that I thought death rays would shoot out of his eyes. Thankfully, on the fifth attempt he finally got it right and we made it through to the end of the show. It's fair to say that a few strong words were spoken after the gig, but Mac was so drunk that it was hard to know if he had really noticed.

The following day we made our way to the Bospop festival site. Although we were initially disappointed to discover that we would be performing in the Rock Tent rather than on the main open-air stage, in some ways this turned out to be a blessing, as the weather took a noticeable turn for the worse. So, as Pendragon played on the main stage to an ever-decreasing crowd of drenched fans with raincoats and umbrellas, the Rock Tent started to fill up with a combination of Threshold fans and others seeking shelter from the storm. By the time we started our set we had a full house. We performed an hour-long show, bravely including *Light And Space* despite the difficulties of the night before.

Unfortunately, Mac had been drinking heavily and spent a fair amount of the show lying on the stage forgetting the words. However, during our final song he was back on his feet and staring up at the huge lighting gantry above the stage. For some reason he decided it would be a good idea to climb it. So, with his microphone stuffed into his back pocket, he started to scale the vertical frame at the corner of the stage. Once he reached the top, he manoeuvred himself onto the horizontal beam and crawled upside-down towards the centre of the stage, suspended precariously several metres above the ground. The band and audience stared up at him in disbelief and horror. Although it made for a memorable climax to the show, one slip could have been fatal. Thankfully he got down safely, but afterwards he confided that when he was half way across he suddenly had a moment of lucidity and thought he was going to die.

* * *

2001 saw the rise of a new technology that allowed multimedia content to be added to music CDs. This meant that when you put a music CD in your computer you would be able to access extra content such as photos, screensavers and other bonus material. InsideOut were keen to release special edition versions of our early albums, so we decided to add multimedia content to them. I bought some software for designing and compiling the content and before long we had a good selection of bonus material for the albums. The record label was pleased with my work, so they asked me to produce content for a couple of upcoming releases by other artists: *The Rainmaker* by The Flower Kings and *Bridge Across Forever* by Transatlantic. I found the combination of artistic and technical input quite satisfying and I really enjoyed the work.

I decided that my new side-line business should be called something. I had thought of eight areas that the business might cover, from writing, performing and producing music to designing artwork and multimedia. Eight is also a fundamental number in music, so I decided on the name Eightspace. Over the years that followed I would end up venturing into most of those areas, operating under the moniker of Eightspace instead of using my own name.

The special edition versions of Threshold's early albums also gave us the opportunity to fix a problem that had been troubling us for years. Our original 1994 mix of *Psychedelicatessen* just didn't sound very good. I don't know if it was because we had been uncomfortable with our studio equipment or because we had been burned out when we mixed it, but despite doing our best the original version sounded thin and lacked power. We had remastered it at Abbey Road Studios in London for the second pressing but that had not solved the problem. The whole album needed to be properly remixed. So, Karl and I reconvened at Thin Ice Studios and started again from scratch, replacing various guitar and keyboard parts and making the whole production sound more like we had originally intended. It was a great success, so whenever I come across someone who owns the original 1994 edition, I implore them to buy one of the later versions. The difference is palpable and I would love to destroy all of the original copies.

Farrah and I continued with our thoughts of moving out of Lower Feltham. I was beginning to feel what my Dad had felt back in 1970 when he had been travelling up to London every day, tired of the long days commuting and working in an office. I longed for more hours in the week and more space for a studio and a garden; but living in the south east of England was expensive, and those things cost more money than we could afford. We wanted to record more music together, but we had very little time or space to do it.

One day we went strawberry picking at a local pick-your-own farm, and it was there that we had our idea. Why not move to the Czech Republic? We had both fallen in love with the country. Farrah was half Czech on her mother's side, so if we could go anywhere in the world, why not go there? It was an absurd idea. We discussed it some more. At the time, property prices were incredibly low in the Czech Republic, so you could buy a large house with some land for the fraction of the price in the UK. Living costs were low too, so if we could make a little money from Eightspace, we could work shorter hours and have more time for music. The plan was starting to sound a little less absurd. Clearly, visiting pick-your-own farms was a dangerous pursuit; it could turn your life upside down. I've been slightly wary of strawberry picking ever since.

*　*　*

But before we could progress any further with our plans to turn our lives upside down, there was another Threshold tour to do. Our itinerary even included a show in the Czech Republic, so I was especially looking forward to that one. Our support band for the tour was another InsideOut act, the insanely talented Ark. Comprised mostly of session musicians who had toured with Swedish guitar virtuoso Yngwie Malmsteen, along with guitarist

Tore Østby, whom we already knew from our tour with Conception, it seemed astonishing that they would be supporting us and not the other way around.

It was around this time that we started to enforce a 'black clothes only' rule. Thomas had often despaired at our choice of stage clothing but up until now we had not taken much notice. Our show at Wacken had been a good example. We were performing at Europe's largest heavy metal festival and Nick wore beige cargo trousers, Johanne and Karl opted for lime green T-shirts and Jon strode out in striped shorts and a shirt with a big yellow lemon on the front. Heavy metal we were not. I wasn't immune to the problem either, having spent much of our *Wounded Land* tour in white jeans and a neon-yellow shirt with the words 'Vacation Valley' scrawled on the front. Thankfully, by the time we toured *Hypothetical* we wore mostly black, a rule that we've tried to follow ever since. It's not that black is the only colour that works, it's just that it works so much better than what we used to wear.

Our bus driver for the tour was rather worrying. He was a very old chap who we had nicknamed Django. On his dashboard there was a wicker basket filled with miniature bottles of gin, vodka and other strong alcohol. At first, we thought they were quaint souvenirs or possibly gifts for his passengers, but after a while we realised that he wasn't offering them to anyone. He appeared to be drinking them as he drove through the night.

The next morning, we woke up to discover that our Sega Dreamcast games console had gone missing. After much searching around, we found that Django had hidden it in a cupboard because we had been too noisy when we used it. He told us he didn't like rock bands and would rather be driving old age pensioners across Spain. The following evening, he pretended that the nightliner's power was faulty to try and stop us plugging in the Dreamcast again.

One night, before our show I went out into the audience to watch our support band Ark. I had really enjoyed their *Burn The Sun* album and I was interested to see how it came across live. I watched a few songs and it was obvious how talented they were; the playing and singing were fantastic. But for some reason it wasn't coming together. It was like watching five individual soloists rather than one united band. Later that night their bass player, Randy Coven, asked me what I had thought of the show. He was worried that the band wasn't really working together, but he couldn't work out what was going wrong. "Are you all playing the same parts that you recorded in the studio?"

I asked. He looked at me with wide eyes. "Hell no!" he exclaimed. It was possible that we had located the problem.

After one of our shows I stayed up late drinking with Ark's drummer John Macaluso. We had become good friends and we were happily shooting the breeze as usual. For some reason he asked what my middle name was. I told him it was Lansdowne and expounded the story behind the name. It was alleged that the Lansdowne line of our family had a distant claim to the royal throne of England. I have never researched this to corroborate the story, but the name had eventually ended with four sisters, one of whom was my Great Grandmother. I have seen an old photograph of the four women, and my enduring impression was how sturdy and formidable they looked. I have no doubt they would have made fearsome leaders.

"So, you're in line to the throne of England?" gasped John. "In that case you've got to knight me!" There were no swords on the nightliner, so I knighted him Sir John of Ark using a plastic spoon. We may have been rather drunk at this point. The following day he recounted the story at breakfast, and when I walked onto the stage later that afternoon I found that Karl had added an 'i' to the logo on my keyboard. It was now a Korgi, in honour of the Corgi breed of dogs kept by Queen Elizabeth II.

Threshold's set list for the tour typically featured tracks from all five of our studio albums, opening with *Sunseeker* and closing with *The Ravages Of Time*. My favourite song to play at the time was *Light And Space*. With its fat synth hook, distorted organ parts and flowing solo, it fell under the fingers beautifully and was always a feel-good moment.

After three shows we arrived in the Czech capital of Prague, where we had a day off before our performance at the Rock Café in the city centre the following night. I went for a long walk, happily absorbing the sights and sounds of the beautiful city. Suddenly I felt compelled to write down some words. I took out my notebook and starting writing "There's a storm coming in, I can feel it in my bones, there's a cloud across the ocean and the darkness grows". I don't know what prompted me to write it, but the next day was 11th September 2001.

As we entered the Rock Café the following day, everyone in the building was watching a TV mounted on the wall. It was showing live news coverage from the USA where an aircraft had just crashed into the World Trade Center in New York. We watched in total horror as a second aircraft flew into the building. There are no more words to say about that tragic day. Two members of Ark were from New York and our hearts were with them. Everyone was numb. Nobody wanted to play the show, but it was decided not to let the terrorists win, so the show went on. However, not many fans wanted to leave their homes that night.

After the show, Django did his best to take our minds off the terrible events of the day by managing to drain the nightliner's battery so that it wouldn't start. Mac jokingly suggested that we should push the bus to jump-start it. It was a crazy idea that would never work, but it was the only idea we had. So, as several perplexed fans watched from the pavement, eight musicians in black leather jackets attempted to start a large tour bus by pushing it along the road. And, rather unexpectedly, it worked. The engine roared to life, we jumped on board and drove off into the night.

The following day our tour manager sacked Django and we looked forward to having a more professional driver at the wheel instead. But sadly, this was not to be, as a couple of nights later we were awoken from our slumbers to discover that our new driver had beached the bus on the edge of a motorway. Somehow, he had driven down a steep slip-road and got the bus stuck on the curve of the slope, with both the front and back of the vehicle wedged into the ground. What was worse, the front of bus was protruding dangerously into the first lane of the motorway. Maybe Django hadn't been so bad after all. Eventually the bus was rescued and the tour continued across the Netherlands, Germany and France.

The tour ended with a fantastic night at the prestigious Élysée Montmartre in Paris, a stunning venue dating back to 1807 that was originally used as a ballroom. Joining Threshold and Ark that night was Swedish rock band Freak Kitchen, so we shortened our set to allow enough time for all three acts. Fortuitously, Freak Kitchen's frontman Mattias Eklundh had brought some recording equipment to capture their performance, and he kindly recorded our show too. The result was the album *Concert In Paris*, an hour-long set featuring four songs from *Hypothetical* and four older numbers. The atmosphere on the night was amazing and it made for a really good live album. InsideOut were happy for us to continue with our Direct-to-Fan concept, so a few months later *Concert In Paris* became our second self-released album.

Overall, our performances during the *Hypothetical* tour had been much stronger than our *Clone* shows. Mac had been on excellent form and as a band we had recaptured some of the consistency that we had built up at the height of our powers supporting Dream Theater in 1995. It was good to be taking positive steps forward again, and that momentum would see us back in the studio only seven months later to record our next album.

Three weeks after the tour ended, Farrah and I travelled to the south Bohemian region of the Czech Republic to explore the possibility of moving there. Our hope was to find a property that was a little out of the ordinary; not a regular house on a regular street, but preferably a secluded property in the countryside with enough space for a recording studio. We visited an estate agent in the picturesque town of Třeboň and told him what we were looking for. There were very few properties for sale that fitted our criteria. In fact, there were very few properties for sale at all, and most of them tended to be in the town centres. However, eventually the estate agent pulled out two folders that captured our imagination.

The first property was a very old house on the edge of a forest where deer were known to come into the garden during the long, snowy winters in search of food. It was an idyllic spot and we were very taken with it. However, we noticed that there was a row of electricity pylons running through the forest very close to the house. Living next to huge power cables didn't sound like an especially healthy way to start our new life in the countryside, so we reluctantly crossed the property off our list and drove off to see the other one.

The second property was a large, 300 year old house set into the hillside on the outskirts of a small village, with long views across the fields and forests below. It had a large, vaulted cellar containing a natural spring that provided water for the house and fed a small pond in the garden. Unusually, there was also a long, covered bowling alley in the garden. It turned out that the property had been used as a public house between the two World Wars, but had eventually fallen into disrepair and needed a lot of work. But it was stunning. We just stood in the large living room, utterly speechless. Could we really move here? Should we really move here? But there was no way back now. Our hearts had already moved in.

Chapter 9

There's Purpose In The Sky

IN APRIL 2002 THRESHOLD RETURNED to the studio to record *Critical Mass*. Building on the momentum we had achieved with *Hypothetical*, we had been busy writing new material and by the time we reached the studio, we had 11 new songs ready.

Most of the guys were involved in the writing process for the album. Karl had co-written four new songs with Jon in the form of *Choices*, *Fragmentation*, *Round And Round* and *Critical Mass*. Jon had also composed a short acoustic piece called *Lucky*, which he and Karl had decided to add to the end of *Critical Mass*, making it the longest song in our catalogue at 13:34. Mac had put forward an acoustic song of his own called *Do Unto Them*, which I converted into a full band arrangement for him. Even Nick, who up until now had mostly just written isolated riffs, had composed a full-length track with Jon called *New Beginning*.

I had written four new songs for the album namely *Echoes Of Life*, *Falling Away*, *Avalon* and *Phenomenon*. I had originally proposed *Echoes Of Life* as a possible album title, with the idea of making an album that consisted of five long tracks called *Echoes Of Life (Parts 1-5)*. However, Jon had already started writing lyrics with a different theme, so the idea was soon forgotten. The song itself was a cry from the heart, with the words 'the clouds are rolling by, there's purpose in the sky, I'm rooted to the ground procrastinating' echoing how I was feeling. Even the clouds seemed to know where they were going, but I was going nowhere, stuck in a day job I had never wanted. I longed to make a full-time living from music instead; that was my heart's desire. The same sentiment flowed through the album opener *Phenomenon* with the words 'I don't want many things, just a chance to spread my wings, don't know what the future brings but I want to be there'.

The song *Falling Away* had come quite quickly in a wave of feeling and emotion. I was driving Farrah's sister Debs home one day and the song had started growing and repeating in my head during our journey, getting slowly louder and louder until I couldn't think about anything else. I suspect I was very poor company; I don't think I said a single word for the whole drive. I was just desperate to stop the car and write everything down. So, as soon as I dropped her off, I pulled over in the first available layby and started scribbling furiously in my notebook. Before long, most of the song was finished.

For the ballad *Avalon*, I repurposed the chorus of the song *Your Dance* that I had written when I was 18 and had performed several times during my university days with Up From Under. However, although I had recorded various demo versions of the track over the years, it had never made it onto a commercial release. I had always loved the chorus and was pleasantly surprised to discover that it worked just as well as a slow song. So, after a few adjustments, I found that I had the makings of a new Threshold ballad.

After all the personnel changes we had gone through over the years, it felt good to be back in the studio with the same line-up as our previous album. Rather incredibly, it was the first time that we had managed this throughout our entire history together. We tracked up Johanne's drums first, followed by Karl and Nick's trademark dual guitars and Jon's bass as usual. For keyboards, I had a new toy to add to my arsenal of sounds, a Korg Trinity workstation on which I was able to create some powerful new lead sounds.

Mac travelled over from Germany and spent the week staying with Farrah and me in Lower Feltham. It had only been seven months since I had last seen him, but he had changed a lot. Apart from growing his hair long again, he had stopped drinking alcohol for health reasons and had lost quite a lot of weight. Now, instead of the obligatory cans of cider in the vocal booth, he was drinking nothing but herbal tea. In fact, he was drinking it rather obsessively and asking for a fresh cup as soon as the previous one was empty. He enthusiastically told us that he felt better than he had in years, as if a weight had been lifted off his shoulders. He had a great sense of humour and he would often have us in stitches as we relaxed and chatted into the evening after a long day at the studio. We had a wonderful week together, the best in all the time that I had known him.

Karl and I spent the last two weeks in the studio crafting the mixes. We cut down the running order to eight songs to improve the flow of the record, consigning two of the slower songs to a bonus disc alongside a radio edit of *Phenomenon*. *Critical Mass* was ready to release and we were sounding stronger than ever.

***

Meanwhile, Farrah and I had also been busy as we made the final preparations for our new life in south Bohemia. We had bought the 300 year old house with the vaulted cellar, sold our tiny cottage in Lower Feltham, left our jobs, secured some freelance multimedia work to keep us going and packed up all of our possessions for the long journey to the Czech Republic.

And so, on the day of our fourth wedding anniversary, Farrah and I left the UK to move overseas. One of our friends had a van and had volunteered to help us move, so the day before our journey we started loading it up with our possessions. However, as the van got fuller and fuller, we realised to our horror that there wasn't going to be enough space for everything. It was a stunning miscalculation on our part. After a mild panic, we made some phone calls and somehow managed to commandeer Farrah's Dad and another friend to drive a second van in convoy with us. We were extremely grateful; I don't know what we would have done without them. With everything finally packed and loaded, early the following morning we started our 800-mile journey to our new home in the small village of Nové Hrady.

The journey was slow going. One of the vans was so heavily laden that every time we came to a hill we lost all of our speed and took forever to regain it. It was the middle of the night when we finally arrived, exhausted and cramped, at the Czech border. In 2002 the country was not yet part of the European Union, so although all of our paperwork was in order, we were slightly apprehensive about crossing the border. We stopped at the imposing barrier and handed over our passports at the control booth. The guard studied them for a very long time. He eventually got up and walked out of the booth with a second guard. They approached our vans with torches and asked us to open them. Our hearts sank. Would we have to empty out all of our possessions onto the road? Would we be refused entry into the country? Or worse, would we be arrested for a problem with our paperwork?

We opened up the first van and it was a complete mess. The load had moved a lot during the journey and all of the loose items on top such as small boxes, lampshades and rolled up rugs were strewn everywhere. The guards stared in disbelief. It looked like a very long night's work for them. After a long pause, they sighed, handed back our passports and told us to go on our way. We drove off into the night, extremely relieved. And so, as the sun started to rise on a new morning, our weary convoy finally arrived at our new home.

Over the previous few months we had hired a builder to make the house habitable before we moved in. When we had bought the property the heating system needed replacing, the roof needed repairing and there was no kitchen or bathroom. The builder was a friend of the family and he had told us horror stories of foreigners getting ripped off by local builders, so we felt safer knowing that the work was being done by a friend. However, what greeted us on our arrival filled us with horror.

First of all, there was no central heating. We had asked for a new gas system to be installed, but when we arrived all we found was the broken coal-fired boiler that had been there when we bought the house. Secondly, there was no new roof, just some temporary repairs that wouldn't last the winter. And thirdly, where there was supposed to be a kitchen, there was just an empty room with a water pipe sticking out of the wall in the corner. This was not the dream start to our Bohemian adventure that we had hoped for.

The following week we visited the nearby town of České Budějovice and found a shop that sold kitchens. There was a display kitchen mounted on the wall, fully assembled, on offer at a reduced price. The wall looked roughly the same size as our kitchen wall, so we bought everything on the spot without even bothering to measure it. A few days later it was all delivered to our house and we fitted it ourselves, relieved to find that everything was just the right size for the room. Over the next few weeks I also spent several afternoons with my head sticking through the roof, replacing various old and broken tiles.

But sorting out the central heating proved to be more difficult. We asked a local plumber if he would install a gas system for us but he refused, saying they were so expensive that we would be better off jumping out of the window. It wasn't quite the response we had expected. We asked a different plumbing company and got much the same answer. Evidently the locals were used to burning coal and wood for heat. So, in the end, we settled for a replacement coal burner, a decision that we would come to regret a few months later.

There's Purpose In The Sky

Later that summer I got a phone call from Clive Nolan, asking if I would be interested in doing a remix of a song by Arena, a band he had formed a few years earlier with former Marillion drummer Mick Pointer. They had just finished recording their new album *Contagion* and wanted to produce an EP of extra material to accompany the release. I was delighted at the opportunity, and spent the next few days producing an industrial rock version of their song *Witch Hunt*. I thoroughly enjoyed the whole process, and the remix was released the following year on their *Contagious* EP.

* * *

Threshold's sixth studio album *Critical Mass* was released the following month. For the first time ever we appeared on a chart listing, reaching a modest number 78 in the German national album chart. Although this was still some way off my childhood goal of getting in the Top 40, it was a milestone achievement, and we were delighted to see that our popularity was growing and our record label was doing a good job of promoting us to a larger audience.

Following performances at Metal Dayz Festival in Switzerland and Bloodstock Festival in the UK, a European tour was booked for October. We were a little perplexed to discover that, despite the launch of our new album, the booking agency had only managed to secure nine shows for us. After two runs of 15 shows to promote our last two albums, this was rather shorter than expected. However, it would soon end up feeling like a very long tour indeed, courtesy of a nightliner and driver that would make us long for the days of Django and his antics.

The problems started before we even arrived at our first show. A Dutch company had been booked to provide a bus and driver for the tour. It was scheduled to collect us at 2pm from Thin Ice Studios and transport us to our opening show at The Underworld in London. It was a tight schedule because it would take us a while to load the bus before the hour-long journey to the venue. Normally we preferred to start setting up on stage by 2pm, especially if there was a support band that needed time to set up as well, so we were going to have to move quickly once we arrived at the venue.

By 3pm the nightliner had still not arrived. After some difficulty we finally managed to contact the driver via his company's office, who rather unexpectedly informed that us that he was still in the Netherlands. How were we supposed to get to our first show? After a heated debate we sprang into action. It was clear that, if we were going to get to London, we would have to arrange some transport ourselves, so by 4pm we were loading all of our equipment and luggage into a rented van. By 5pm we had arrived at the venue, drawing heavily on Johanne's past skills as a motorbike courier in London to navigate our way through the backstreets and avoid the worst of the traffic. The show itself went smoothly despite the stress of the afternoon, and later that night, as our fans headed home, we packed down our equipment and waited for the nightliner to arrive.

However, outside the venue there was still no sign of the bus and no longer any way of contacting the driver. We loaded everything back into our hired van and waited. We had some coffee and pizza in a late night café and Mac went to sleep in the back of the van. We waited. We chatted to a few lingering fans and got hassled by some local lowlife. Still we waited. At 3am the phone rang. Our driver was finally in London and was looking for the venue. Our sense of relief was profound. We were exhausted, stressed, and until this moment we hadn't even been sure if the driver would turn up at all. But by 3.30am we were finally heading to the cross-channel ferry to Europe, via a detour through Surrey to return our rented van.

Unfortunately, our driver's chauffeuring skills were no better than his time-keeping. I was once told that a chauffeur should drive as if his passengers were all holding glasses of champagne and the ride should be so smooth that not a drop was spilled. However, our driver appeared to have learned his chauffeuring skills on a go-kart track, resulting in Jon sustaining a nasty, deep red bruise on his arm during the first night as the driver slammed on his brakes at a road junction.

Thankfully our second show was two days later, so we had an opportunity to rest and recover from the night before. We spent our day off in Belgium in anticipation of our show the following night, where we would be headlining ProgPower again. After our performance at their debut festival three years earlier, which had been memorable for all the wrong reasons, it was rather surprising that we had been invited back at all, let alone as headliners again. So, we knew that we owed it to the organisers and fans to put on the best possible show to make up for last time.

As we were wondering what to do on our night off in Belgium, we learned that our original vocalist Damian was performing not too far away with the

Star One project. Star One was a star-studded group of artists assembled by Dutch musician Arjen Anthony Lucassen. The vocalists alongside Damian included Russell Allen from US progressive metal band Symphony X, Swedish musician Dan Swanö, who would later guest on a Threshold album, and Dutch singer Floor Jansen, who would go on to join symphonic metal legends Nightwish. It was an impressive cast. They had recently released their first album *Space Metal* and were performing a short run of live shows across the Netherlands, Germany and Belgium.

I hadn't seen Damian since he left Threshold in 1998, so I thought it would be nice to meet up again and see the show. That evening I headed off in a taxi, joined by Mac and our roadie Steve, to watch Star One in concert. Our taxi driver seemed to know the city streets very well, and proceeded to show us most of them. Then he kindly gave us a tour of the motorway, in both directions, before finally dropping us off at the venue and charging us a lot of money.

The Star One show was excellent, with a great stage set and a top-quality cast of performers. Damian was in fine form, with unexpectedly short hair and dressed in a space-age silver outfit, a far cry from his long-haired rock look of our 1997 tour. We had hoped to go backstage after the show to see him, but by the end of the concert our previous late night had caught up with us, so we headed back to our nightliner, this time on a cheap local bus which took us there in no time at all.

That night Jon sustained another nasty, deep red bruise, this time on his leg. In an attempt to coax our driver into improving his chauffeuring skills, Jon showed him the injuries, but the driver only responded by saying he would probably have another bruise tomorrow. The nightliner itself was also in quite a poor condition, so we were heartened to learn that a new replacement bus was due to arrive later in the day. But, unfortunately, the new bus rather ominously broke down before it could reach us.

The following night at ProgPower went well and we were relieved that we had been able to make up for our previous performance there. Back on the bus after the show there was no power, as the driver could not work out how to connect the power line to provide electricity without draining the battery. To make matters worse, he also had no idea how to empty the chemical toilet, so before long the environment on the bus became rather unpleasant.

Our tour continued across Europe and the shows went well, although some of the audiences were a lot smaller than usual. Our set list would typically start with *Phenomenon* and close with *Light And Space*. *Paradox* was still used for an encore, but by now we were starting to feel that we had overplayed it, and a couple of years later we would finally drop it from our set.

After the first five shows we enjoyed a welcome day off at a golf course in Düsseldorf. We were all completely hopeless at golf, but fortunately we were all as hopeless as each other, so we had a great time. In between our constant searches among trees and shrubs for our wayward golf balls, we occasionally managed a good shot or two, although during one swing I was rather surprised to see the head of my club soar off into the distance along with my golf ball. As the sun finally set over the darkening golf course we headed back to the bus smiling, and hoping the club house wouldn't notice that one of the rented golf clubs no longer had a head on it.

By now, our driver had finally worked out how to operate everything on the nightliner, which was a profound relief to everyone. However, when we got back from the golf course, we discovered that the vehicle had now developed battery problems and had to be replaced. The new bus turned out to be equally squalid and slightly smaller, and the driver didn't appear to know how to operate that one either. After a night with no heating or ventilation, we all woke up with colds and sore throats. As a result, we had to drop a couple of songs from the set the following day, as Mac's voice was struggling to last for the whole show. Our driver responded to our complaints by spending much of the next night driving over the reflective studs that lined the edge of the motorway, causing the bus to judder heavily and making it hard for us to sleep.

The tour finally ended with two excellent nights in Switzerland and Slovakia. But our driver still had one more ace up his sleeve. Nick couldn't handle one more night on the bus, so on the way home from Slovakia we stopped at Vienna Airport so that he could fly back to England. As Vienna was only a couple of hours from my house in the Czech Republic, I left the bus too and rented a car to drive home. However, the others were not so lucky. As the bus stopped in Germany to drop off Mac, the driver informed Karl, Jon and Johanne that he would not be taking them home. Instead, he dropped them on a street corner with all of their belongings and told them to wait for a van to come. Eventually, after several hours worrying that they had been forgotten and abandoned, a van finally arrived and drove them back to the UK.

* * *

Winter came early that year in the Czech Republic. The snow started in October and didn't disappear until March, with temperatures regularly below freezing and sometimes as low as minus 20° C. Farrah and I ordered a delivery of coal to power our replacement coal burner and hoped it would provide enough heat for the winter. However, the system didn't work very well, so our radiators very rarely got hot. Consequently, we could often see our breath when we talked and resorted to wearing coats, hats and gloves indoors.

One morning we heard a strange hissing noise. It started softly and grew slowly louder until it sounded like an express train was going through our house. Farrah was absolutely petrified. It got more and more intense until it sounded like something was going to explode. And then something did explode. All of the hot water in the heating system suddenly flooded out of the boiler and flowed through the house towards the front door, which was fortunately downhill from the boiler. The house filled with steam and our only option was to open the door and let the water flow out, as the icy winter air filled the house and made it even colder than before. We drove to České Budějovice with heavy hearts, bought an electric heater and spent most of the winter huddled around it trying to keep warm. The local plumber visited a number of times to try and fix the boiler, but for some reason he was never able to fully repair it.

We also had another problem. Over the summer, heavy rains had caused serious flooding across the Czech Republic and much of Europe. It was the worst flooding in Prague's 800-year history, and the nearby historic town of Český Krumlov had been completely submerged. Our house in Nové Hrady was half way up a steep hill, so flood water constantly flowed down towards it and we had to continually manage the drains and gullies around the house to make sure the water got safely past. However, the heavy flow of water had gradually weakened a large retaining wall on the hill behind our property, until one day the wall and part of the hill collapsed onto our house. When we saw the damage our hearts sank. Things seemed to be going from bad to worse.

However, despite our problems south Bohemia was a beautiful place to live. Covered in a blanket of crisp white snow, the landscape of spruce forests and frozen lakes looked like a scene from a Christmas card. We visited the nearby towns, dined in the local hospodas and enjoyed regular walks through Theresa Valley with its pretty woodland paths, historical buildings and frozen waterfall. We slowly got to know a few people in the village and welcomed a steady flow of friends and family who travelled over from the UK to visit us.

We put together a makeshift recording studio in the main bedroom and started working on a few songs together. Our most promising track was *Bring It On*, the song that I had written in Prague the day before the World Trade Center attacks in 2001, so we decided to record that one first. I was comfortable playing the keyboards, bass and main guitar parts, but the song needed a good guitar solo and I felt that was beyond my abilities. We therefore enlisted the services of Tore Østby, who sent us a CD in the mail containing a stunning solo that fitted the track perfectly. It was just what the song needed, and provided a welcome boost to warm our spirits, if not our bodies.

Meanwhile, our plans for making money had got off to a slower start than we had hoped. Before leaving the UK, I had secured agreements with a number of record companies to produce multimedia content for their new releases. However, during our first few months I was only offered one album. This was the debut release by OSI, an American band formed by Fates Warning guitarist Jim Matheos and ex-Dream Theater keyboard player Kevin Moore. It was a phenomenal record and I was proud to be involved with it. However, one job wasn't enough to cover our bills. As a stop-gap we started to sell our CD and DVD collection online to bring in some extra money, but it was obvious that something would have to change soon.

It was therefore somewhat of a relief to have the distraction of travelling to Atlanta in November 2002 to perform at ProgPower USA with Threshold. The US edition of the festival had formed as an unofficial partner to the European event, and we would be performing alongside an impressive array of acts including the Devin Townsend Band, Blind Guardian and Edguy. Farrah and I drove to Prague Airport to fly to London and left our car in a secure on-site car park. Before moving to the Czech Republic, we had sold my black GTV and replaced it with a second-hand Audi 80. The Audi was far more practical for the long trips to the UK and back, and as it was quite old it was far less likely to get stolen. After we landed in the UK, Farrah stayed to spend a few days with her family, while I flew on to Atlanta with the rest of the band.

The festival was a phenomenal success. Mac was on fine form and his British banter went down very well with the American audience. ProgPower USA was our first show in America, and it felt like a real milestone. Sadly, it also marked quite a different milestone, as Jon decided it would be his final show with the band. Jon had been with Threshold since the beginning, originally starting as the band's vocalist before moving to bass guitar. He remained fairly quiet about his reasons for leaving, but I got the impression that the band had just run its course for him, and it was time to move on to other things. He had been a cornerstone of Threshold and his presence would be missed by all of us.

After the festival we flew back to the UK and I met up with Farrah to catch a further flight to Prague Airport. After going through passport control with our luggage and my keyboards, we made our way to the secure on-site car park to find our Audi. We had made a note of the parking space number so that we could locate it easily. But when we found the correct space our car was not there. We realised that we must have written down the wrong number, so we searched the whole parking level, but there was no sign of our car. We tried the other levels, but there was no Audi 80 to be found. After an hour of frantic searching, double-checking and panicking, we finally had to accept that our car had been stolen.

There was a police station not far from the car park, so we made our way there to report the theft. The police appeared to be more interested in what we were doing in the country than trying to help us locate our car. After an hour of interviews and form filling, we were told there was nothing they could do, so we made our way forlornly back to the airport. It was too late in the evening to catch a train to our house, so we found a taxi driver who was willing to make the 100-mile journey to Nové Hrady and eventually arrived home in the middle of the night. When we woke up the next morning in our freezing cold house, with no money, no car and no hope, we seriously considered giving up on our Czech adventure and returning to the UK for good.

Chapter 10

Can We Go On?

IN DECEMBER I PHONED KARL about the possibility of making another Direct-to-Fan album. Having just released *Hypothetical* and *Critical Mass* in quick succession, we thought it would be fun to do something a little different before we started work on another studio album. We had previously recorded an acoustic version of *Life Flow* as a bonus track for *Hypothetical*, and we had often discussed the idea of taking the concept further to make a whole acoustic album. So, we began looking through our back catalogue for suitable songs to record, and before long we had come up with arrangements for ten songs, included two previously unreleased tracks from the band's early years. So, after Christmas, we all convened at Thin Ice to record what would become *Wireless (Acoustic Sessions)*, complete with a video for the opening track *Fragmentation* that was filmed on the shore of nearby Virginia Water Lake.

While Farrah and I were home for Christmas we had been grateful to discover that my Dad had an old Vauxhall Astra in storage that had belonged to my late Grandfather. He kindly handed us the keys and a few weeks later we found ourselves driving the 800-mile journey back to the Czech Republic. Over the weeks that followed we completed our recording of *Bring It On* and released it online, our second official release following *Summer* two years earlier. As the spring finally arrived, the snow started to melt and our house finally warmed up again. It was a huge relief to see the countryside restored to its lush green beauty once more. We finished two more songs and pressed up some promotional CDs to distribute to prospective music managers and record labels. And so, at the end of May 2003, almost a year after we had started our Czech adventure, we drove back to the UK to look for a record deal.

There were also some more Threshold shows to prepare for. Germany's *Rock Hard* magazine had invited us to perform at their 20th anniversary festival in Gelsenkirchen. We had always been well reviewed by the magazine and many of our albums had been awarded 'Album of the Month' status over the years, but this was the first time we had been offered the opportunity to play at their festival. One booking had quickly led to more, and our record company decided that the short tour would provide the perfect opportunity to film a show to release on DVD. The Boerderij in Zoetermeer was duly booked for this purpose, and we looked forward excitedly to producing our first ever concert movie.

With Jon no longer in the band, Karl turned to one of his old school friends called Steve Anderson to join us on bass guitar for the shows. Steve was a relaxed, affable sort of guy and a highly accomplished bass player, and he slotted into the band very easily. We drove to Germany in the first week of June for a couple of warm-up shows on Tuesday and Wednesday night before heading to Zoetermeer where our concert would be recorded by a professional film crew on the Friday. We had also been offered a support slot with Whitesnake in nearby Zwolle the night before, but our record company had declined the offer to allow us an extra 24 hours to set up for our DVD recording. Unfortunately, this turned out to be a huge mistake.

On the day of the Zoetermeer show, fans started arriving from all over the world to be in the crowd for our concert movie. We had previously released two live albums, *Livedelica* and *Concert In Paris*, but it was a special moment to have a show professionally captured on film. We had planned a two-hour set full of our most popular songs, including an acoustic segment in the middle of the show where we would perform *Clear*, the acoustic version of *Life Flow* and a new arrangement of *Narcissus* that had been carefully crafted to avoid the possibility of Mac forgetting the vocals during the long middle section. However, as it turned out, *Narcissus* would prove to be the least of our worries.

Our additional 24 hours for setting up meant that Mac had long periods of time with nothing to do. Unfortunately, instead of using the time to run through the lyrics and make sure he was ready for the show, he spent the day drinking. Sadly, his abstinence from alcohol the year before had not lasted. That evening, as we walked onto the stage to start our opening number *Phenomenon*, he was in quite a bad way. It soon became clear that he was struggling to remember the songs, and the mood of the band quickly turned from euphoria to disappointment. We had worked so hard to get to this point, and now that we finally had the chance to film a concert for posterity, it looked like it would be a night to forget.

When we reached the acoustic segment of the set, Mac started *Life Flow* on the wrong note and proceeded to sing the whole song in the wrong key. By this point I couldn't concentrate on our performance anymore, I was just trying to think of how we could possibly salvage what was looking to be a total disaster. The film crew and mobile production truck outside had cost a small fortune that is still being recouped from our royalties today, so there was no way we could afford to cancel the project. Our only option would be to fly Mac back to England to re-record the vocals, something that we had hoped very much to avoid.

We laboured through the rest of the set, longing for the night to finish. We briefly considered repeating a couple of songs at the end of the show in the hope of capturing some better performances, but after our experience with *Light And Space* at our warm-up show for Bospop two years earlier, we knew there was no guarantee of getting a better result. So, we left the stage, thoroughly deflated and knowing there would be a lot of work to do in the studio.

We still had two shows to go, and these would also prove to be quite memorable. The following night in Switzerland, Mac had a sore throat and after the first song he announced to the crowd that he would have to stop. The crowd protested loudly, so, after a short pause, we continued with Mac holding the microphone out to the audience to sing the choruses, before he took things a step further and invited a fan onto the stage to sing a whole song. The fan did such a good job of *Falling Away* that Mac responded as if to a challenge and proceeded to complete the rest of the concert.

The final show of our short run of dates was the Rock Hard Festival, which took place in an outdoor amphitheatre. Storm clouds were gathering overhead as we took to the stage. We started our opening song *Phenomenon*, and as Mac sang the words 'so if the sky's about to fall', the heavens opened and the sky fell. As the wind and rain blew wildly across the stage and through our hair, it looked like we were performing in an epic heavy metal video. By the time we had reached our third song, the rain was falling horizontally and soaking everything on the stage. Just about the last words Mac sung were 'I see the sunrise but only taste the rain' from *Long Way Home* before the stage got so wet that the power was turned off for safety reasons and we had to stop the show.

A hard-core group of fans crowded around the front of the stage, finding whatever shelter they could below the edge of the stage roof, but as the minutes ticked by it was clear that we wouldn't be able to continue. Eventually we dried off our gear with towels and packed it away, hoping that it would all still work when we got home.

Later that month I dropped in at Thin Ice to see Karl. Over the years he had built up a good roster of clients at the studio, from progressive rock artists such as John Wetton, Pendragon and Arena to power metallers like DragonForce, Intense and Power Quest. Karl's calm, relaxed demeanour coupled with his ability to get on well with everyone made him a popular choice of producer, while his attention to detail and skill as a recording engineer kept them coming back for more. We poured some coffee and started to discuss what to do about our live DVD. To my surprise, while I was there two bands offered me multimedia jobs before I had even finished my cup. After a year of struggling to survive in the Czech Republic by working remotely and relying on the internet for communication, it turned out that the best way to get work was just to see people face to face the old fashioned way.

With more potential work from Thin Ice later in the year, Farrah and I decided to stay in the UK for a while, earn some money and assess our best way forward later. We drove back to the Czech Republic to collect everything we thought we would need for a few months in England and rented a spare room at Nick Barrett's house a few miles from the studio. It felt good to be back in the UK and reassuring to have some work lined up. Nick was a gracious host, and we enjoyed many long chats solving the world's problems from beside the pool. However, we still weren't making enough money to cover our costs, so a few months later we said our goodbyes and moved in with Farrah's parents.

There was something very humbling about moving in with parents-in-law as a grown adult. It represented failure, a total inability to look after ourselves, an admission that we had got it all wrong. But it was also a time of love and acceptance. Farrah's parents are such wonderful people, and I will always cherish the time we spent with them and their unconditional support and kindness as we went through that difficult moment.

Meanwhile, Karl and I turned our attention to the live DVD. Mac understood that his vocals would need some work and was happy to come over from Germany to record some overdubs at the studio. We mixed the concert in both stereo and 5.1 surround sound. It sounded glorious; so, although we were disappointed that it was no longer completely live, we were delighted to have ended up with such a good result. With the addition of some bonus features, including a short documentary called *Critical Moments* and some footage from our appearance at ProgPower USA, we now had everything we needed for our concert DVD package. *Critical Energy* was finally complete and was released by the record label the following year.

* * *

Following Jon's departure from Threshold, Karl turned to me to be his new songwriting partner. Jon had set a high bar lyrically over the years and had left some big shoes to fill. I had been reading a lot of books and articles on philosophy, politics and faith, as well as revisiting novels such as George Orwell's prophetic *Nineteen Eighty-Four*, so all of these topics were swirling around in my thoughts as we started work on our new studio album. I didn't harbour any ambitions to devise a full-on concept album, but I liked the idea of combining all of these elements to form a common theme, a loose concept that would help the songs flow together and feel like a coherent body of work.

I had already started work on *Stop Dead* over the summer, and during the autumn I completed *Ground Control*, *Static* and *Flags And Footprints*, partly in the UK and partly in the Czech Republic. Karl had also started sending me instrumentals for what would become *Mission Profile*, *Opium*, *The Art Of Reason* and *The Destruction Of Words*. The music for *Mission Profile* sounded the most like an album opener, so I decided to tackle that one first. I must confess I was slightly anxious, hoping I would meet Karl's expectations as a replacement for Jon. I wrote a lot more lyrics than I needed, originally under the working title of *The First Protocol*, and then set about honing the words and melodies until everything sat perfectly. I recorded the vocal parts over his demo, sent it back and waited apprehensively for his response.

His first reaction wasn't quite what I had expected. "Didn't you want to use the melodies I had suggested?" he asked. This was news to me. I felt terrible. Had I missed something? Had I totally failed on my first attempt? On further investigation it turned out that he had meant to send me a MIDI file (essentially a file of musical notes) which contained some suggested melodies, but either I had never received it or I had simply not noticed it. Whatever the reason, thankfully Karl seemed happy with my work, and I don't think he's ever suggested melodies again (unless I didn't notice them!).

Some lyrics that I was particularly fond of were for *The Destruction Of Words*. The song title was inspired by a quote from *Nineteen Eighty-Four*, namely 'It's a beautiful thing, the destruction of words'. In the book, the concept involved removing superfluous words from the dictionary to narrow people's thinking and stop 'thought crime'. In the verses of the song I worked my way through the alphabet to symbolically destroy words one letter at a time, starting with 'I don't need allusion [A], I don't need blame [B]' and so on. However, the verses weren't long enough for me to go through all 26 letters, so I found a creative shortcut to get from K to Y: 'I am just [J] the knowledge [K] that's found its way to you [Y]'. The song therefore found its way to the end of the alphabet and closed with 'now I've reached my zenith [Z]'.

One of the things I love about writing progressive music is that, in amongst trying to come up with interesting concepts and often having to fit them into someone else's music, there's still room to make the whole process even harder by coming up with ideas like this. But it's something I love doing, so while it's probably the sort of detail that goes totally unnoticed by most listeners, I find it very fulfilling.

With eight songs complete we felt that the album needed one more up-tempo track. So far there was nothing from Nick on the album. He had given Karl a cassette tape of riffs as usual but none of them had been used so far. I started listening through to see if I could find something suitable. As always, he had come up with some great ideas, but as most of them were slow or mid-tempo I kept on going. Finally I found what I was looking for. It was the very last idea on the tape, and it was perfect: a single note melody that would become the song's opening section. I modified the part for the verses, added a chorus and I had the makings of the song *Pressure*. Karl had an unused remnant from his writing sessions, a great keyboard motif over a syncopated guitar part, so I added that too and the song was complete. It was the first time we had put together a song that way since *Angels*, and I was really glad that one of Nick's ideas had made it onto the album at the eleventh hour.

Johanne had also put forward a song called *What About Me*, which he had been performing live with his other band Kyrbgrinder, a hard rock trio in which he was both drummer and lead vocalist. Although it wasn't exclusively a Threshold song, we agreed to record it as a bonus track. Johanne would later go on to release his own version of the song on the Kyrbgrinder album *Defiance*.

We decided to call our new Threshold album *Subsurface*. This had originally been the working title of the song *Opium*, so I renamed the song to reinforce the theory that television and the media had replaced religion as the new opium of the masses. The album artwork was another masterpiece by Thomas Ewerhard, who had now designed our last four covers. It was progressive and sophisticated, featuring three unrelated elements brought together beautifully, with an old-fashioned television set placed on an ancient tree stump standing in a lake. On the television screen was the word 'Reflect', while on the screen's reflection in the lake was the word 'Conceal'. Thomas had originally proposed the words 'War' and 'Peace', but he obligingly changed them to fit the concept of the *Opium* lyrics. Alongside *Hypothetical* I consider it to be one of his finest pieces of work.

In between the writing sessions I also took on some vocal production jobs at Thin Ice Studios, including an enjoyable reunion with our former vocalist Damian Wilson, who was recording his third solo album *Let's Start A Commune*. To the best of my knowledge the album features Damian's highest ever recorded note. Back in 1997 he had belted out a stunning top F# in the chorus of *Somatography*, and on *Let's Start A Commune* he managed to go a semitone higher on the infectiously funky *Fine Weather*. I also produced the vocals for an up-and-coming power metal band called DragonForce, who were making their second album *Sonic Firestorm*. It was great to be working with other artists and I was hopeful of more work like this in the future.

We recorded *Subsurface* at Thin Ice Studios between February and April 2004. Steve Anderson had now become our new, full-time bass player in much the same way that Johanne had joined after our *Clone* tour, easing seamlessly from live session player to full-time member as if he had always been there. While everyone was at the studio, we decided it would be a good opportunity to record another Direct-to-Fan album in parallel with *Subsurface*. We opted for a format broadly similar to *Decadent*, comprising a selection of remixes and acoustic versions alongside some previously unreleased tracks. We gave the album the name *Replica*, the original working title of our *Clone* album, and got to work compiling a list of possible songs.

We put together some new acoustic arrangements of *Ground Control* and *Forever*, approached in much the same way as we had done on *Wireless*. We also mixed a longer version of *The Latent Gene*, with the previously omitted harmonica solo added back in along with one of The Badger's unused voice-overs. Among the other highlights were new recordings of *Surface To Air* and a song from the band's formative years called *Endless Sea*. The collection closed with a synthesizer-based remix of *Opium*, which I had really enjoyed putting together. I secretly harboured plans to release a whole album of remixes by different bands, but along with countless other projects I've dreamed of over the years, time and opportunity haven't come together for that one yet.

Subsurface was released on 2nd August 2004. The album's reception was phenomenal, with 'Album of the Month' awards in 15 publications and glowing reviews across the world. We were still struggling to conquer the album charts, but we reached number 66 in Germany, 12 places higher than *Critical Mass* had managed two years earlier, so we were over the moon with the result.

The song *Mission Profile* was used to promote the album, featuring on music magazine cover discs across Europe and occasionally garnering some radio play. However, our record label thought that producing a music video would not be a good investment, so we decided to take matters into our own hands and make one ourselves. We remixed an edited version of *Pressure* at the studio, hired some camera and lighting equipment from a local rental company, booked a hall and enlisted a friend to operate the camera. The overall look and feel of our finished production were more 'underground' than professional. I don't think it was ever shown on TV, but we had a lot of fun making it.

* * *

Shortly after the release of *Subsurface* we were back on tour, and the difference from our 2002 shows was plain to see. The success of our latest album meant that our audiences were two or three times bigger than before, and we were playing to packed-out venues almost every night.

The tour started with three UK shows, including a performance at Bloodstock Festival in Derby and two nights in London and Rotherham supported by Power Quest. Across the channel in Europe we performed a dozen more shows, including a return to the Markthalle in Hamburg. But this time there was no possibility of us playing on the smaller MarX stage that we had been relegated to in 1999. This time we were on the main stage and the auditorium was packed. Our support band for the shows in mainland Europe was Dead Soul Tribe, led by the frontman of Psychotic Waltz who we had toured with nine years earlier. Somehow, he hadn't changed a bit, in stark contrast to Karl, Nick and me who were now almost unrecognisable from how we had looked as long-haired lads on that memorable tour bus of 1995.

With seven studio albums to choose from, our set list was mainly focussed on our most recent releases, opening with *Mission Profile* and closing with *Fragmentation*. We still played a few of our earlier songs though, with *Freaks* regularly featured alongside the occasional older long track such as *Into The Light* or *Surface To Air*.

After our show at the Markthalle, our booking agent offered us a three-month tour supporting Saxon. Mac was good friends with their guitarist Paul Quinn and said yes in a heartbeat. Three months on the road would have been tough on our family lives, but this was what we were here for, and I was desperate for us to reach the top, so I also said yes. Johanne's answer to any potential touring opportunity was always "My bags are packed!", so three of us were on board. However, unfortunately the rest of the band was less enthusiastic. There were understandably a lot of practical issues to weigh up, family commitments, prior engagements and financial considerations. So, we sadly had to decline the offer. Looking back, it's hard to know if the tour would have made us or broken us, but I was hugely disappointed not to have the opportunity to find out.

The tour ended in the Belgian town of Vosselaar on 19th September where we had performed regularly since our first tour ten years earlier. Not everything had gone smoothly, and Mac had caused some frustration because of his continued heavy drinking and inconsistent performances. On any given night we never knew if he was going to be exceptional or embarrassing, whether the alcohol would fire him up or knock him down. For this reason we would end up doing just two more shows in the two years that followed.

Back in the UK, I turned my attention to the Farrah West project again. We presented our demos to various management and record companies, but unfortunately we put our hope in the wrong people and found ourselves going down a cul-de-sac. It was very disappointing, and it would be a while before we felt ready to record together again.

I continued working at Thin Ice with Karl, mostly producing albums for power metal bands. In May 2005 I was recording DragonForce vocalist ZP Theart for their third album *Inhuman Rampage*. DragonForce had gained a lot of attention from *Sonic Firestorm*, leading to tours supporting W.A.S.P. and Iron Maiden. As a result, they had secured a deal with Roadrunner Records for their third album which would come out the following year. ZP was a pleasure to work with and we became good friends. One morning he was sounding a little tight in the throat, so I asked him what his warm-up routine usually involved. "A cup of tea and a joint," he laughed. I asked if he would like some more specific warm-up exercises and he sounded interested, so I called Farrah and she came over to the studio.

Farrah had been coached a few times by Tona de Brett, a London-based vocal teacher who had worked with everyone from Paul Young to Ozzy Osbourne. She had also once coached the singer of a notorious punk band. She told me that she had got a few good notes out of him, after which he had politely thanked her and told her that nobody was ever going to hear him doing that again. Farrah ran ZP through a few of Tona's vocal exercises, encompassing everything from scales and arpeggios to mouth exercises such as 'va-va-va-vi-vi-vi' and 'red lorry, yellow lorry'. He was a little embarrassed but he obediently followed her instructions. He then returned to the vocal booth to start the day's session. When the rest of the band arrived at the studio that evening to hear the results, they were blown away. "What happened?" asked guitarist Herman Li. "You've never sounded that good before!" The next morning I arrived at the studio to find ZP warming up with a cup of tea and a joint. "Don't get me wrong," he said, "the vocal exercises were great. But nobody's ever going to hear me doing that again!"

 Farrah and I continued to travel over to the Czech Republic, but it was mostly just for routine property maintenance and emergencies. We had finally managed to install a gas boiler at the house, which had made living conditions there a lot more pleasant. However, over the winter Farrah's family went to stay for a holiday only to discover that the new heating system had broken and leaked water all over the floor. The water had subsequently frozen and turned the living room into an ice rink. We dropped everything and travelled over. The temperature inside the house was below 5 °C and it was impossible to sleep there, so we checked in at a local guest house and stayed until everything was repaired. As much as we loved our Czech house, it had become more like a millstone around our necks. And as most of our work was now coming from the UK, we weren't sure if we would ever be able to return to the Czech Republic permanently.

Back in England, Karl and I put the finishing touches on another Direct-to-Fan release, a live album called *Surface To Stage* that we had recorded at the Z7 in Switzerland during our 2004 tour. I continued to work on more albums with Karl for bands such as Arena, Landmarq and Shadowkeep, but, of all the records we worked on together during that period, it was the DragonForce album *Inhuman Rampage* that would enjoy the greatest success. Its opening song *Through The Fire And The Flames* was featured on the popular video game *Guitar Hero*, propelling the album to number 1 on the US *Billboard Heatseekers* chart and getting certified Gold for selling 500,000 copies. As a result of their success, I am very proud to have a gold disc on my studio wall.

In March 2006, Threshold returned to the rehearsal room to prepare for the first ever ProgPower UK Festival which was being held in Cheltenham. Following the success of the Europe and US editions of the festival, a UK event had been launched and we were on the bill alongside bands such as Freedom Call, Firewind and Swedish headliners Therion. It was really positive to see a festival like that happening in England, where our sort of music had so far failed to garner the same level of attention that it had received in other countries. Mac put on a masterful show, confidently prowling the stage in his black and white kilt as he posed for photographs and joked with the audience between songs.

However, none of us knew at the time that it would turn out to be Mac's last ever live performance with us.

Chapter 11

There's A Storm Outside

FOLLOWING THE SUCCESS of our *Subsurface* tour in 2004, we were surprised to learn that it had made a huge loss and we were facing a hefty bill. We knew that progressive metal wasn't the most commercial genre of music, and we had no illusions of suddenly becoming global superstars or millionaires. However, we did at least hope to make a profit, so the news of our tour's financial failure hit us hard. There was a certain amount of confusion about how this could have possibly happened, so we decided that if we were going to continue, then it was time to make some wholesale changes.

One of those changes was to move record labels. We had reached the end of our three-album deal with InsideOut Music. They had done an excellent job of taking our career to the next level, but there had also been some frustrations along the way, such as the lack of video support, so we found ourselves considering our options. By chance, another German record company called Nuclear Blast got in touch and asked if we would like to sign with them. Nuclear Blast was one of the biggest independent labels on the planet, with huge selling artists on their roster including Nightwish, Meshuggah and Sepultura. Although most of their bands sounded a lot heavier than Threshold, the label were confident that they could do a good job for us and we were thrilled at the opportunity. We declined the option to extend our contract with InsideOut and signed a three-album deal with Nuclear Blast. InsideOut were understandably frustrated at our decision and tried their best to convince us to stay, but our minds were made up. It was the start of an exciting new chapter for the band.

Meanwhile, Farrah had secured some part-time work at Bray Studios in Berkshire, initially providing catering for the studio's clients before later working for the studio manager. Bray Studios had four sound stages and had been used for making movies since the 1950s, including cult classics such as

Dracula, *The Hound Of the Baskervilles* and *The Rocky Horror Picture Show*. However, it was now mostly used as a rehearsal space for bands and tours, and Farrah found herself providing food for an eclectic range of rock royalty from Status Quo to The Who. One day, Pink Floyd guitarist David Gilmour was rehearsing on one stage while his former colleague Roger Waters was on another one. The two were not on good terms and seemed to be initially unaware that they were both there at the same time, so there was a fair amount of drama when the two camps ran into each other at lunch.

With a new Threshold album to write and nowhere suitable to write it, I visited Bray Studios one day to see if there was anywhere I could rent as a writing space. I was hoping for something like a small disused office, but to my surprise I was told there was an abandoned recording studio in the complex. Among its previous clients were Marillion, who had written much of their *Misplaced Childhood* album there in 1985, but it was currently sitting empty. The control room was very damp after a long period of disuse, so I installed a dehumidifier and was surprised to find it collected five litres of water every day for the next few months. This greatly improved the atmosphere in the control room, transforming it into a warm, welcoming place to work. The studio was mostly empty apart from a couple of green leather sofas, so I moved in all of my recording equipment and started work on the new album.

I installed a coffee maker in the lobby, and this attracted the attention of various visitors to the site who were in search of a good brew, including Jimmy Page's roadie who was there working for another artist. One day he invited me into the adjoining building, handed me an electric guitar and asked me to play a few chords through a new amplifier that he had got for Jimmy to try out. I'm not the world's best guitarist but I must confess it didn't sound too good – muddy, indistinct, nothing noteworthy at all. I thought little of it and headed back to my studio. The following morning I was walking through the complex when I heard someone jamming on a guitar. It sounded absolutely amazing, a mind-blowing performance with a wonderful, powerful tone. I later learned that it was Jimmy Page, using the same guitar and amplifier that I had made sound so awful the day before.

My keyboard set-up at the time consisted of two synthesizers, a Korg Triton and a Roland JP-8000, which I had been using since our *Hypothetical* album, and was responsible for sounds such as the fat keyboard riff at the beginning of *Light And Space*. Our new album would need a new palette, so

I sold both instruments to fund the purchase of two new Korg keyboards, a Triton Extreme and an MS2000. I was excited to have been offered an artist deal with Korg, which gave me money off their products and the added bonus of an article in their magazine. As it turned out, the MS2000 didn't quite offer the range of sounds I was looking for, but the Triton Extreme was perfect and became my main keyboard for many years to come.

I had recently started writing a piano-based piece of music on Farrah's piano. I had tried to come up with the most beautiful chord sequence that I could imagine, and I ended up with a seven-chord progression that I thought sounded totally captivating. I kept writing, and before I knew it I had a new song on the way. Over the following days the song became longer and more complex, with my original seven-chord sequence supporting the main guitar solo. It was the longest song I had ever written and I loved every moment of it, but there was a problem. To coincide with our move to Nuclear Blast, we had decided that our new album would be our darkest and heaviest one yet. My new song was the polar opposite, so I wasn't sure if I should put it forward. I discussed it with Karl and we decided to record the song anyway and assess it later. I finished the lyrics and the final line I wrote became its title, *Pilot In The Sky Of Dreams*.

Karl had sent over four excellent pieces of music for me to write the vocal parts for. One song stood out as an opener for the album, an up-tempo track with a half-time anthemic chorus which would become *Slipstream*. The original demo had a longer instrumental section at the beginning, but we opted to edit it down to provide more impact to the start of the album. The lyrics for the verses needed a call and response style vocal, so I pondered a while on the best way to do this. The response phrase was 'Oh do you really think so?', and on any other record we would have probably chosen to do this using backing vocals or a synthetic vocoder effect. However, as we had decided on a heavier sound for this album, I wondered whether a death metal growl would work.

I recorded a demo vocal for the song, doing my best impression of a growl, which gave me a sore throat for the rest of the day. Mac was happy with the idea and joked that "we do progressive rock, so if you don't progress, you don't rock"! However, he couldn't perform that sort of vocal himself, so Karl contacted Swedish record producer Dan Swanö to ask if he could recommend a suitable guest vocalist. To Karl's surprise, Dan performed the parts himself and sent them over the following day. They were perfect and just what we were looking for. As we were so happy with the results, I wrote some more growl parts for the song *Elusive* and Dan once again obliged.

By September we had eight songs written. We were pleased to find that the heavier songs like *Slipstream* and *Elusive* balanced out nicely against the softer approach of *Pilot In The Sky Of Dreams*, so there was no need to exclude it from the album. It felt like the only thing missing was a slow track. Karl had an unfinished piece of music that he was working on which he thought might offer the solution. It sounded dark and atmospheric and was just what we were looking for. I added a chorus section and the song became *Safe To Fly*. We finally had all the songs for our new album. However, Nuclear Blast also wanted a bonus track, so there was still more work to be done.

Bonus tracks were nothing new to us and we had provided many over the years, either for limited edition releases or Japanese versions of albums to offer something extra to our fans. For a long time we had been contemplating recording some cover versions of songs reworked in a Threshold style, and for a while we had our minds set on the 1982 song *Hymn* by British new wave band Ultravox. However, when we heard Muse's recent top 10 single *Supermassive Black Hole* we changed our minds. It was a great track and we thought it had the potential to work really well with a heavier arrangement and Mac's classic rock vocal sound, so we abandoned all thoughts of the Ultravox song and put together our own version of *Supermassive Black Hole* instead.

With our album now fully mapped out and ready to record, it was time to commit to an album title. The only song name that had felt like a good option was *Pilot In The Sky Of Dreams*, so this had become our working title for a while. We had even commissioned Thomas Ewerhard to design an album cover for it, asking him to visualise what a pilot would see approaching the floating city on our *Hypothetical* cover. But the artwork didn't feel right and the title started to feel wrong too. With the exception of *Critical Mass*, we had tended to shy away from using song titles for album names, as we didn't want our albums to be defined by a single piece of music. I had pondered changing the title of the song to *Landing Lights*, but that seemed to take away from the beauty of the track, so I focussed my efforts on looking for another possible album title instead.

The album's lyrics were generally about navigating through the storms of life. I had intentionally moved away from the more political leanings of

With Farrah for our first official photo shoot as League Of Lights (2011).

Ruud Jolie recording guitars for the first League Of Lights album at his studio in the Netherlands (2011).

March Of Progress *photo shoot*.
From left to right – Steve Anderson, Pete Morten, Johanne James, Damian Wilson, Karl Groom, me (2011).

March Of Progress *photo shoot*.
From left to right – Karl Groom, me, Damian Wilson, Johanne James, Pete Morten, Steve Anderson (2011).

I don't remember what the joke was but clearly some were better at hiding it than others!
From left to right – me, Pete Morten, Damian Wilson, Steve Anderson, Johanne James, Karl Groom (2014).

Reviewing the mixes of For The Journey *with Karl Groom at Thin Ice Studios (2014).*

Outside Thin Ice Studios with Damian Wilson and Steve Anderson waiting for the tour bus to arrive (2014).

*Lining up for our traditional end-of-show bow.
From left to right – Pete Morten, Johanne James, Steve Anderson,
Karl Groom, me, Damian Wilson (2014).*

Sharing a joke on stage with Damian Wilson during our For The Journey *tour (2014).*

Pouting through the smoke at Bang Your Head Festival, Germany (2016).

A stage-eye view of the Masters Of Rock Festival in the Czech Republic.
From left to right – me, Karl Groom, Damian Wilson, Johanne James (2016).

Opposite page: Pulling shapes (2014).
From left to right – Pete Morten, Steve Anderson, Karl Groom.

*Back at Wisley Airfield to photograph our latest line-up.
From left to right – Glynn Morgan, Johanne James, Steve Anderson,
Karl Groom, me (2017).*

*An impromptu sit down on the drum riser before our encore in Aschaffenburg
during our* Legends Of The Shires *tour.
From left to right – Steve Anderson, me, Karl Groom, Johanne James, Glynn
Morgan (2017).*

Filming the audience in Aschaffenburg during our Legends Of The Shires *whole album tour (2018).*

Trying to look cool at the Night Of The Prog outdoor festival in Loreley, Germany. I'm sure it was sunnier than it looked (2018)!

The guys rocking out at the Markthalle in Hamburg, Germany. Clockwise from top left – Glynn Morgan; Johanne James; Steve Anderson; Karl Groom (2018).

With our crew and support bands The Silent Wedding and Maxxwell in Essen, Germany. Too many names to mention but a great touring family (2018).

The last night of our Legends Of The Shires whole album tour in London. From left to right – Karl Groom, me, Glynn Morgan, Johanne James, Steve Anderson, and of course our wonderful fans (2018).

A master class in the art of mixing with the legendary Manny Marroquin in the south of France (2019).

On set with Farrah filming our League Of Lights video for Kings And Queens *in the magnificent grounds of Pałac Marianny Orańskiej in Poland (2019).*

Photo shoot with Farrah for our second League Of Lights album In The In Between *(2019).*

Farrah on stage with Power Quest in London for the anniversary of their album Neverworld *and to commemorate the life of their late bassist Paul Finnie (2019).*

Our third visit to ProgPower USA in Atlanta, each time with a different singer! From left to right – Karl Groom, Glynn Morgan, Johanne James, me, Steve Anderson (2019).

Outside Oslo Airport after our first shows in Finland and Norway.
From left to right – Karl Groom, Steve Anderson, Johanne James, Glynn Morgan, me (2019).

*League Of Lights at Artrock Festival in Germany.
From left to right – Ruud Jolie, David Sievers, Farrah West,
Toby Schwietering, me (2020).*

Another shot of Artrock Festival, one of the few European festivals to take place in 2020.

When Damian met Glynn. Astonishingly this chance encounter at Thin Ice Studios during the recording of Threshold's Dividing Lines *was the first time the two vocalists had ever met (2021).*

Threshold photo shoot for Dividing Lines. *For some reason we always seem to choose cold days!*
From left to right – me, Karl Groom (bravely opting not to wear a coat), Glynn Morgan, Johanne James, Steve Anderson (2021).

Back on stage for Threshold's only shows of 2021, two consecutive nights for the HRH Festival weekend at the O2 Sheffield Academy followed by the Shepherd's Bush Empire in London.
Clockwise from top left – me; Glynn Morgan; Karl Groom, Steve Anderson; Johanne James (2021).

Subsurface, and if our new album had a subtitle, it would have been *How To Fly Well And Land Safely*. So, I started searching for ideas connected to navigation. I discovered that there were literally hundreds of navigation-related phrases that were totally unsuitable as progressive metal album titles: *In the Doldrums*, *Lateral Marks* and *Bum Steer* to name just a few. I finally came across the phrase *Dead Reckoning*, a method of calculating your position based on direction and distance travelled. It was just what I was looking for; it sounded dark and mysterious and fitted the album perfectly.

* * *

Bray Studios was a fascinating place to work. Every day there would be nightliners and tour trucks driving on and off the site as bands set up their full tour productions in the sound stages, complete with huge PA systems, lighting rigs and staging. Some bands would just book in for a couple of days after completing their initial rehearsals elsewhere, while others such as Cliff Richard would be on site for weeks, initially using one of the smaller rooms for band practices before setting up the complete production in one of the larger sound stages later for full dress rehearsals.

Farrah and I were invited to one of Cliff's final rehearsals just before he headed out on his *Here And Now* tour, and it was a truly impressive production. The previously empty sound stage had been transformed into a multi-level performance area with full backing band, a troupe of dancers and an amazing light show. A few weeks later we were kindly offered VIP tickets to his concert at Wembley Arena, and it was great to see the whole show performed in front of a live audience. I had seen bands at Wembley before where the sound quality had been quite poor because of the arena's reverberant acoustics, but that night the sound was pristine, a testament to the excellent crew and meticulous rehearsal routine.

In October, Mac travelled over from Germany to record the vocals for *Dead Reckoning*. He stayed at Karl's house, so each morning I would go and collect Mac and bring him to Bray Studios to record the vocals. Meanwhile, Karl tracked the drums, bass and guitars ten miles away at Thin Ice Studios. Everyone seemed to be excited about the new album, and our fresh start with Nuclear Blast provided an added impetus to make sure it was our best one yet. However, a few days into the guitar sessions Nick Midson announced that he wanted to take a break. We all knew that he hadn't enjoyed touring very much and it turned out that he wasn't enjoying the studio work either, so he had decided to step away from the band for a while and reassess his position further down the line. We all hoped that he would come back soon; he was one of the band's founder members and very much a part of its DNA. However, as it turned out, he would never return.

With Nick no longer involved in the recordings, Karl performed all of the guitar parts, doubling up the rhythm guitar sections to retain our trademark sound. By December the recordings were complete, so I joined Karl back at Thin Ice to mix the album. We also edited some of the songs to use as potential singles. We were both convinced that *Slipstream* would be the main single from the album, with its heavier feel and death metal growls seeming perfect for our new, heavier record label. However, Nuclear Blast had thrown us slightly by suggesting an edit of the longest song, *Pilot In The Sky Of Dreams*, believing that it had a better chance of appealing to a mainstream audience. As it turned out, the edit worked surprisingly well and this became the main single instead.

Having decided against using Thomas Ewerhard's *Pilot In The Sky Of Dreams* artwork for the album cover, we thought it wouldn't hurt to look around and see what other options were out there. We discovered an Italian artist called David Nadalin. Some of his work for his fellow compatriots Extrema had stood out and looked very promising, so we got in touch. He found the perfect concept with a stunning monochrome image of Zeppelin airships approaching by night over the sea, complete with rugged rocks redolent of our *Hypothetical* album. Once again we had a classic cover that I thought would work equally well as a piece of art hanging on the wall. Our record label took the look one step further by issuing a limited edition version of the CD as a digipack printed on silver card, an effect that really made it stand out from the crowd.

In January I flew to Germany to meet up with Mac and representatives from Nuclear Blast to attend our official listening party for *Dead Reckoning*. The record label had decided to hold the event at a Zeppelin Museum in the city of Friedrichshafen, birthplace of the Zeppelin airship. Music journalists from across Europe had gathered at the museum to hear our new album for the first time, with Mac and me there to answer questions and pose for photographs. We were given a full tour of the museum and I was disappointed to discover there were no actual airships there. Instead, there was only a 33 metre long partial replica of a Hindenburg Zeppelin. However, when the curator explained that the original airship had been a staggering 245 metres long it became obvious why there was only space for the partial replica.

After the tour of the museum, we all convened in a large meeting room while our new album *Dead Reckoning* was played to the assembled party. Reactions were positive and it was a great way to make us better known to the music press. It was the first time we had ever done a listening session and it added to the sense of optimism that we were already feeling. Here we were with a new album, a new record label and a new sense of purpose. Nuclear Blast was now talking about music videos, longer tours and the hope of proper chart success. It felt like we had finally arrived and the sky was the limit.

Later that month, Threshold travelled to Altenburg in Germany to film a video for *Pilot In The Sky Of Dreams*. Mac travelled up by train from Hannover, while Karl, Johanne and Steve flew over from the UK. At the time, Farrah and I were in the Czech Republic to fix our roof which had been hit hard by the winter storms. There had also been some damage to a wall that joined our garage to our neighbour's property, so one morning I went to see him to discuss the problem. He invited me in, and using a combination of Czech, German, English and a few illustrations, we quickly agreed how to repair the wall. He poured us both a glass of lethal looking home-made slivovice. With the words "Na Zdravi!" ("Cheers!") we downed our drinks. He refilled our glasses before I could stop him, repeated the words and we drank again. After a third glass I had to insist on no more. What I didn't know was that it was customary to refill someone's glass when they finished it. When I got home Farrah thought I looked a little green and unsteady on my feet. "Goodness, what happened?" she asked as I promptly threw up in the bathroom. "You've only been gone 20 minutes!"

The following day we caught the train from České Budějovice to Altenburg via Prague, enjoying the rather beautiful journey that took us through huge forests and meandering river valleys. In Altenburg we met our flying contingent to discover that their journey had been rather less idyllic. Apparently, their rather large plane had landed at a rather small airport and subsequently overshot the runway, leaving them all rather shaken, especially Johanne who wasn't at all keen on flying.

The young team at Film M Productions were aspiring movie makers who had some great ideas for our video, which was to be shot in an abandoned warehouse and beside a nearby lake. The final result looked absolutely beautiful, although I must confess to having no idea what it's all about. One particular sequence involved Karl being dragged backwards along the floor by a rope, which would later be made invisible during post-production. It's a blink-and-you've-missed-it sort of moment but it looks great, although we all thought that Karl had drawn the short straw because it wasn't a particularly comfortable sequence to film. Steve had been given the rather easier task of walking along and looking up at the camera, while Johanne was chosen for a moody, menacing moment in the warehouse's lift.

Then it was time for my acting cameo, a short sequence where I had to walk to the edge of a cliff, look out over the water and throw a bag into the ocean. In reality the cliff was a small mound and the ocean was the local lake, but the wonders of CGI brought the scene to life. One scene that didn't make the final cut was of me and Karl walking up a hill. I presume it was relevant to the story, but it was ultimately left on the cutting room floor because, we were told, we both "walked funny"!

Mac was nervous and only wanted to be filmed after everyone had left, so once we had finished our scenes we said our goodbyes, headed back to our accommodation and left him working into the night.

It was the last time we would ever see him.

***

Dead Reckoning was released on 23rd March 2007 and reached number 64 in the German national album chart, two places higher than its predecessor *Subsurface*. To be honest this was slightly disappointing as we had such high hopes for our new release, but it was still a small step in the right direction. We also reached number 95 in the Netherlands, a low position but our first ever chart entry outside of Germany. We weren't surprised to find that we hadn't registered on the UK album chart, but we did scrape in at number 37 on the UK rock chart, a sign that we were starting to get more recognition in our homeland. This was also reflected in the British music press, which had noted our modern reinvention and rewarded us with a lot more coverage and positive reviews than we had got in the past.

A European tour was booked for the following September, preceded by a couple of big festivals in July. It was an exciting time and we couldn't wait to get out and perform our new music. But, before we could do that, we needed to find a new guitarist to provide cover for Nick Midson. Karl had recently produced an EP for a project fronted by a British musician called Pete Morten. They had struck up a friendship and Karl asked if he would be interested in filling in for Nick for our upcoming shows. Pete happily accepted and we now had a full touring band again.

At the end of June we started rehearsing for the upcoming festivals. We had been booked to perform at MetalCamp in Slovenia on 20th July followed by Earthshaker in Germany the following day. They were both large events and it was the perfect way to start our live campaign to promote our new album. We rehearsed instrumentally over the following two weeks, with Mac scheduled to join us from Germany for the final rehearsals a week before the festivals took place.

In between rehearsals I was working with Damian again, recording him performing guest vocals for a progressive rock band based in Chile called Seti. Since leaving Threshold for the second time in 1998, Damian had spent two years playing the lead role in a touring production of the musical *Les Misérables*, recorded with Arjen Anthony Lucassen and toured Europe and South America with former Yes keyboardist Rick Wakeman. We got on really well and it was good to be working together again.

Back at our rehearsal room a week before our MetalCamp and Earthshaker shows, Threshold assembled once more to put the finishing touches on our live performances. Mac was due to arrive by train from Germany, but he was running late and nobody had heard from him. We tried calling a few times but there was no reply, so we assumed that he was probably out of signal range or out of battery. But, all of a sudden, he sent us a short email saying that he wasn't coming over and wanted to get on with his life.

We all stood there in the rehearsal room, shocked and speechless. We tried calling him but he had turned his phone off. We had no idea where he was, what the problem was, whether he would change his mind tomorrow, or what we were supposed to do about our upcoming shows. This was the worst of all possible scenarios and we were absolutely devastated. But after trying to contact him several times over the next couple of days, we eventually had to accept the facts. Mac wasn't coming over and he appeared to have left Threshold.

By chance, Damian had recently told me that, if the opportunity ever arose, he would love to work with us again. Our only conceivable options were to ask him or our other former vocalist Glynn Morgan to cover the two shows, or to cancel them all together. We didn't want to be defeated. We had been through adversity before and we weren't going to let this latest problem be our undoing. Glynn would have been an excellent option, but we had not been in contact with him for years. With only five days until the shows, we needed a swift solution. Could Damian really learn our whole set that quickly? We asked him. He said he would be delighted to come and save the day and accepted the challenge immediately. We were immensely relieved. Although it meant that we would once more be promoting an album with the wrong frontman, at least now we had a way forward.

On the day of the first festival we travelled to London Heathrow Airport to fly to Venice in Italy, from where we would be driven by minibus to the MetalCamp festival site in Tolmin, Slovenia, in time for our performance. It was a tight schedule, but it would be fine as long as nothing went wrong. As we sat in the airport departure lounge, Steve watched idly out of the window as a baggage handler launched a long, black flight case forcefully into the air, landing with a heavy thud on the conveyor belt. He told me that it looked a lot like my flight case. Rain was starting to fall heavily as we boarded the plane and waited to take off. After a while the captain announced that there would be a short delay as the runway was temporarily flooded because of the sudden rainstorm. We waited a little longer.

It was a full three hours before we finally took off from London and flew south towards Italy. When we landed in Venice we were hastily ushered into a minibus to make the 100-mile journey to Tolmin. The driver sped like a man possessed, desperate to get us to the festival in record time while simultaneously calling the stage manager for updates. We were already too late for our time slot, so the band that was scheduled to play after us was told to go on next. Meanwhile we swerved and careered our way towards Tolmin at impossible speeds along the winding, country roads, quite certain that we would crash at any minute. However, the minibus somehow arrived safely and drove straight up towards the back of the stage. We were told that we would have to go on stage immediately, so we unloaded our equipment and started setting up everything as quickly as we could.

It all felt quite unreal. We had just travelled 1,000 miles and now we were about to perform our new set to thousands of fans with no time to warm up, relax or even have a cup of tea! To make matters worse, when I opened one of my flight cases I discovered that my Korg keyboard was broken. Two of the white keys were smashed and a valve inside the casing had broken. Evidently the flight case that Steve had watched being launched into the air in London had been mine. I briefly marvelled at how it was possible for two keys to get broken inside a heavy, padded flight case. Unfortunately, one of the keys was the one I used to trigger various sound effects and samples, so I knew I was in for a tough gig. Some of the guitars were damaged too, but there was no time to think. We hurried onto the stage and started the show.

Unsurprisingly the whole gig went past in an uneasy blur. We were exhausted, shell-shocked and running on adrenaline. Damian had done a miraculous job learning the set in five days, but understandably he wasn't totally sure of some of the lyrics, so he took a few pieces of paper on stage for safety. I quickly reprogrammed my Korg between songs so I could trigger as many of the sound effects as possible without needing to use the broken keys. Some parts such as a reverse 'swooshing' noise in *Pressure* weren't too important, but other moments such as some lengthy drum loop and effects sections in *Fragmentation* and *This Is Your Life* would have left some very awkward pauses. Somehow we got through the set, and left the stage to some gratefully received applause in search of somewhere to wind down, relax and finally have a cup of tea.

The following morning we were up at dawn to fly to Germany for our next show at Earthshaker Festival. The event had a fantastic roster of bands, including headliners Motörhead, who had also topped the bill at MetalCamp the night before, keeping us awake as we tried to get some sleep before our early flight. It had proved quite impossible to sleep during a Motörhead set, but it was far more enjoyable to stay awake and hear them play. Other bands on the Earthshaker bill included Testament, Within Temptation and Masterplan, who until recently had been fronted by our friend Jørn Lande from Ark. Our second show went smoothly, with our new temporary line-up settling in well as we got used to performing together on stage. The following day we headed back to the UK, happy and relieved that we had somehow survived our latest setback and rescued our two shows.

With just over a month to go until our European tour and still no word from Mac, we continued rehearsing with our new temporary line-up. A 14-date tour had been booked with an ambitious four-band package which saw Threshold supported by Communic, Machine Men and Serenity. So, at the end of August, we found ourselves boarding a nightliner once more and heading across the channel towards the continent. While most of our fans were disappointed not to see our new songs performed by the line-up that had recorded the album, it was clear that others were pleased to see Damian fronting the band again. The experience he had gained from *Les Misérables* and touring with Rick Wakeman since his last tenure with the band was noticeable. Gone was the young, slightly unsettled frontman of our 1997 tour. Here was a bold, confident performer who commanded the stage and loved to entertain the crowds.

Our set list for the tour naturally leaned heavily towards our latest album *Dead Reckoning*, alongside a handful of other tracks from our Mac-era albums. We resisted the temptation to perform too many songs from our earlier records as we wanted to present ourselves as a band looking forwards, not backwards. But we couldn't do a tour without including a couple of songs from Damian's previous time with the band, so *Exposed* and *Sanity's End* were included on the set list, much to the delight of the fans who knew our older material.

For a temporary line-up we were doing well, but the whole situation felt very unsettled. Damian had other commitments, such as his solo career and a new band called Headspace with Rick Wakeman's son Adam. We therefore weren't sure about him coming back permanently because of potential conflicts further down the line.

On the other hand, Mac had disappeared and was obviously not coming back. We were also waiting to see if Nick would return from his self-imposed sabbatical, so his replacement Pete Morten's position was also uncertain. Against this backdrop, we didn't feel ready to think about producing a new album yet. But we were really enjoying performing together, so we decided to keep booking shows and put all thoughts of a new studio album on the back burner for the time being.

Chapter 12

The Dust Of The Afterglow

SOME SHOWS GO MORE SMOOTHLY than others. The time we performed with Kamelot and Serenity at the LA2 in September 2007 was not one of those shows.

The day had started well enough. We arrived at the venue in the early afternoon, unloaded our gear in the heavy London rain and made our way to the main hall. But not long after we arrived, everything suddenly went black. There was a mild panic as everyone waited for the lights to come back on, but the storm outside had knocked out the power and the hall stayed completely dark. Slowly, shadows started to appear as crew members reached for their Maglite torches, providing enough illumination for us to find somewhere to sit down while we waited for the power to be restored.

After several hours of darkness it seemed inevitable that the show would have to be cancelled. But suddenly there was a loud buzz as the power finally returned. Everyone cheered and sprang into action, setting up in record time as the doors were kept closed and the fans grew impatient outside. When the doors finally opened, Serenity were already on stage performing their first song. They had travelled all the way from Austria in a camper van to open for Kamelot that night, so their hearts must have sunk as they performed to an almost empty room. However, one by one the fans started to stream in, and before long the venue was full to capacity. By the time Threshold hit the stage, everything was going smoothly and we had a great gig.

But the night's drama wasn't over yet. Half way through Kamelot's opening song, bassist Sean Tibbetts suddenly twisted awkwardly and collapsed on stage. It turned out that he had rather astonishingly broken his leg. He dragged himself off stage as the band continued to play without him, and then even more astonishingly he returned a couple of songs later to complete the show sitting on a bar stool. It was a night to remember for the fans, but for Sean I am sure it was one to forget.

* * *

The next 12 months provided Threshold with a steady stream of festival performances. The first of these was a return to ProgPower USA in Atlanta in October 2007. We had been booked to play a 60-minute set and we were really looking forward to it. After a day off to explore the city and acclimatise ourselves to the time change, we were scheduled to meet backstage an hour before the show. Damian didn't arrive with the rest of the band, so we started setting up our equipment, expecting him to appear at any minute. We finished setting up and our gear was moved onto the stage ready for our performance, but there was still no sign of him. We called the hotel reception desk and the festival shuttle drivers, but nobody knew where he was. As the stage manager signalled for us to start the show, our frontman was nowhere to be seen.

15 minutes later a very hot, flustered Damian came bursting through the door. He hurriedly explained that he had overslept and his alarm hadn't gone off. It was a horrible moment. We had travelled all that way for just one hour on stage, and the first quarter was already lost. We hastily reorganised our set list, rushed onto the stage and started our show. As a result, our performance was a bit rushed too, but somehow we got through it, frustrated but thankful that we had been able to perform most of our set. Damian found himself in more hot water later when he brought a local stripper onto the stage during the all-star jam. ProgPower USA was supposed to be a family-friendly show, so some of the parents in the audience didn't know whose eyes to cover, their children's or their partner's!

Our next two shows were UK festivals, starting with Firefest IV in Nottingham before heading up to Rotherham for The Classic Rock Society's Autumn Rokfest. Damian and Johanne had become popular figures at the Classic Rock Society, being named best vocalist and best drummer a number of times at the Society's annual awards. *Pilot In The Sky Of Dreams* had also just won the award for best song, an honour I was very proud of. That year the festival was very much dominated by Threshold, with performances by Johanne's other band Kyrbgrinder, Pete's other band My Soliloquy and an acoustic set by Damian, before Threshold took to the stage for a headline set at the end of the night. It was a unique and enjoyable evening and a really good way of bringing all of our bands together.

The following month we were in Copenhagen for ProgPower Scandinavia, another offshoot of the flourishing brand. The morning after the show I went for a walk around the city. There was a gentle mist coming off the water that made the whole place glow ethereally in the soft, morning light. By chance I peered through a record store window and saw a display of CD box sets. I wondered what a Threshold box set would look like and what it would contain. I bought a coffee in a local café and thought about it some more. An hour later I was back at the hotel discussing the concept with Karl. It felt like the perfect project to take on until we were ready to start working on a new studio album. We would call our box set *Paradox – The Singles Collection* and it would end up taking more than a year to complete.

Two days after arriving home from Copenhagen I was off to the airport again. Power Quest had decided to record their fourth album *Master Of Illusion* in Italy, where three of the band members were based, so I had been asked to join them at a studio in Vicenza to co-produce it. We spent every waking hour either at the studio or in the local cafés, bars and restaurants. I don't think I have ever eaten so much food in my life, with the Italian contingent seemingly keen for me to experience every culinary delight their country had to offer, from irresistible breakfast pastries to pizzas topped with horse meat.

We worked such long hours that on the seventh day I temporarily lost part of my vision. It was a worrying and frightening experience. My brain stopped processing what I could see on my right-hand side, rendering the whole area with strange black and white triangular shapes instead. I had never experienced anything like it before and had no idea what to do, so I went and sat in a dark room for half an hour with my hands cupped over my eyes until the triangular patterns started to fade away. The following morning I was extremely relieved to find that my vision had returned to normal.

In November our former record label InsideOut released a double CD compilation called *The Ravages Of Time: The Best Of Threshold*, including radio edits of *Slipstream* and *Pilot In The Sky Of Dreams* licensed from Nuclear Blast to make the compilation relevant. For the artwork we dusted off our previously shelved *Pilot In The Sky Of Dreams* cover by Thomas Ewerhard, as although it had not felt quite right for the studio album, it looked a lot more suitable for a 'Best of' compilation. We curated the track list ourselves, looking to include a good number of fan-favourite longer tracks in among the more obvious songs that had been released as singles, videos or promotional tracks. It felt like the compilation drew a line in the sand for where we had got to so far. The journey had been far from smooth, and where we would go next was still uncertain.

At the end of the month, we were back in the Netherlands for our final show of the year, supporting Within Temptation for their homecoming concert at the Beursgebouw in Eindhoven to 8,000 fans. We weren't sure how many of their audience would know our music, but when they started singing along to *Pilot In The Sky Of Dreams* it was clear that many of them were aware of us. It felt overwhelming to hear thousands of people singing one of my songs. There was a lump in my throat and I got a glimpse of how intoxicating that could become for a singer. I was glad that I was just the man in the shadows behind the keyboards. As well as being our new single, Nuclear Blast had also placed the song on the soundtrack album of the movie *In The Name Of The King* starring Jason Statham and Burt Reynolds, so our music was starting to reach a wider audience than ever before.

Our 2007 tour had felt like a triumph over adversity, with Damian thoroughly enjoying the role of returning hero and Pete doing a great job of covering for Nick on second guitar. But while we were relieved to discover that our four-band trek across the continent had not made a loss, it had not made much of a profit either. So, we decided to take matters into our own hands. We cut out the middlemen and for a while I took on the role of booking agent and tour manager.

* * *

I have experienced many loud noises in my lifetime: the piercing scream of feedback in a monitor speaker, the sound of an A380 aircraft powering up on the runway, and the kick drums at a Megadeth concert that were so monumentally loud that they shook my whole body and felt like they would dislodge my heart. But there was also the time I stood next to Johanne for our show on the Sweden Rock Cruise.

It was our first show of 2008 and it took place on board a ferry that sailed from the Swedish capital of Stockholm to Turku on the coast of Finland. Most of the passengers were in high very spirits, having taken full advantage of the low alcohol prices compared to the mainland. The stage was located rather unceremoniously under a staircase and it was extremely small, and as a result I had to stand right next to Johanne's cymbals for our whole set. He certainly knows how to hit them hard; it was one of the longest hours of my life! The sound level was excruciating, and my ears were still ringing on our flight home the following day.

I soon discovered that trying to get six musicians through an airport was no easy task. On any given journey, Johanne would be running late because of delayed or cancelled trains, Karl and Steve would be wandering aimlessly off into the distance, deep in conversation and oblivious to where they should be going, and the ever gregarious Damian would be chatting with any seemingly random stranger that he had met in the coffee shop or check-in queue. Looking back, it's a small miracle that we never missed a flight.

The following month we introduced a new concept to our touring routine, the long weekender. We would drive over to mainland Europe in a van, stay in a central location, and perform two or three shows on consecutive nights, all within a couple of hours' drive of our accommodation. The cost of touring with nightliners was prohibitive, so using them only made sense on major tours to promote a new album. However, hopping into a van meant that we could do more shows in between our main tours. Over the next ten years we would do a lot of long weekenders.

The vehicles we used were called splitter vans. These are essentially long-wheelbase vans divided into three compartments comprising the driver space, the passenger space and the equipment area. The passenger space came in various configurations, sometimes with all of the seats facing forward like a minibus, sometimes with the seats positioned around a central table, and sometimes with a long bench installed across the back that could be used as a bed. Sleeping on the bed was precarious as it was positioned sideways, so if the driver stopped suddenly the sleeper could easily roll off. Along with the band we would normally also take one or two crew members, with Farrah occasionally joining us to sell merchandise at the shows.

The long weekenders could be quite gruelling. I was doing most of the driving and tour managing, so by the end of a long day I would be exhausted and probably not the best company. But they were also great fun, and we had some wonderful times together. Damian was an avid poker player and would often bring a poker set with him, complete with green baize tablecloth and casino chips. Passing through the customs checks between the UK and France, the customs officers would often open the side door of the van to find a poker game in full flow. On one occasion a very stern looking French border officer pulled the side door open to a view that could only be described as a mobile casino. It was pouring with rain and all the border staff looked unimpressed and grim. The officer didn't say a word, but gestured that he wanted to see the pack of cards. The cards were duly handed over and for a moment we thought he was going to confiscate them, but instead he proudly performed a very good card trick! None of us could tell how he did it. We gave him a round of applause and he looked like he might crack a smile, but it never arrived.

As a group of slightly scruffy-looking guys in a van, we would usually get stopped and searched at the customs checkpoint. Occasionally this would involve the van being completely unloaded, so we always had to allow extra time to make sure we didn't miss our ferry. During one such stop the customs officer asked if we would be willing to take part in a training exercise while the van was being searched. Of course, it was impossible to say no without looking uncooperative, so we were lined up along a wall while a new sniffer dog was put through its paces.

It was the cutest puppy, excited by everything, and supposedly able to sniff out large quantities of bank notes. Damian was handed a huge wad of euros and told to stuff them in his sock. The puppy was brought over and told to locate the notes. It was leaping and bounding everywhere, sniffing absolutely everything in rapturous delight while continuously looking up at its handler in hope of a treat. Eventually the handler pulled the puppy unsubtly towards Damian. It had a good sniff and looked up with hopeful eyes, finally earning the dog biscuit it was longing for. Presumably it still had a lot more training to do. Damian had brief hopes of making off with the bank notes in his sock, but unfortunately the officer remembered them before he could make his getaway.

In May we performed our first ever show in Serbia. It was a brand new festival with a new promoter, so to minimise any possible risks I insisted that our flights and hotel rooms were booked in advance by the promoter. It was just as well they were. When we arrived in Belgrade we discovered that the event was in financial trouble. A number of bands had arrived to find there was no money to pay them. Some of them boycotted the show all together, which seemed strange as they were already at the venue and there was nothing else to do. The auditorium was full of fans who had bought tickets, so it seemed counterproductive not to perform for them. We did the show and it lost us money, but at least our flights and hotel rooms had been covered.

Meanwhile, Farrah and I had made the difficult decision to say a final goodbye to our house in the Czech Republic. Our visits to the property had become little more than repair and maintenance trips, and although it was a beautiful place to live, unfortunately we could not foresee ourselves ever moving back there again. We had moved into a house in the village of Shepperton in Surrey, created a recording studio in the spare bedroom and started taking our first tentative steps towards making some new music. It would be a while before we were ready to consider producing a whole album, but it felt good to be recording together again.

Over the summer I was back out with Threshold for more festivals, starting with Minnuendo Fest in the Spanish town of Peralta. Also on the bill was Mick Pointer's 'Script For A Jester's Tour'. Mick had been the original drummer for Marillion, appearing on their 1982 EP *Market Square Heroes* and subsequent debut album *Script For A Jester's Tear* the following year. He had assembled a touring band to celebrate the album's 25th anniversary and I knew most of the musicians quite well. On guitar was Nick Barrett from Pendragon, while bass and keyboard duties were looked after by Shadowland duo Ian Salmon and Mike Varty respectively.

Minnuendo Fest took place in the unusual setting of a Spanish outdoor bull ring. On the day of the show, storm clouds had started to gather, and by the evening the whole area was flooded by torrential rain. We were treated to a spectacular thunder and lightning storm, which filled the sky and rumbled ominously across the whole area. Unfortunately, the sudden deluge of water shorted out most of the festival's electricity supply. Many of the power cables had been run along the floor of the bull ring and were now saturated, shorting out the mixing desk and amplifiers that powered the sound system. The drenched festival goers were crowded expectantly in front of the stage hoping for some music, the bulls were all making discontented noises from their nearby stalls, and nobody knew what to do.

After several hours the festival organisers were still unable to restore the power. It was now after midnight, and neither Mick Pointer's band nor Threshold had played a note. Any equipment that had been powered by the cables on the bull ring floor had stopped working, so the only power left was on the stage itself. Fortunately, Mike Varty had brought a lot of equipment for the show including an on-stage amplifier. After much rewiring, the whole band was plugged into Mike's amplifier and this was connected to the small monitor speakers on the stage. The speakers were turned around to face the audience, and Mick's band performed their set through this temporary set-up. The sound wasn't perfect, and it was a lot quieter than a normal festival, but the fans were rewarded for their patience with a night-time performance of Marillion's *Script For A Jester's Tear*.

After Mick and his band had left the stage, Threshold set up through Mike's amplifier in much the same way, and we performed our full set into the early hours of the morning, pleasantly surprised to find that most of the audience stayed for the whole show despite the lateness of the hour. As the sun started to light up the horizon to mark the dawn of a new day, we finished our two encores, *Sanity's End* and *This Is Your Life*, wearily packed up our instruments and headed back to the hotel for some much-needed sleep. We felt totally elated from the whole experience but utterly exhausted from such a long night.

The following week we were in Milan, Italy, for another outdoor festival. The severe storms had continued to sweep across Central Europe, and as one of the bands started their opening song the late afternoon sky eerily darkened and their sound was augmented by huge rolls of thunder, providing a rather spectacular extra dimension to their show. Fortunately, Threshold escaped relatively unscathed and managed to avoid performing during the torrential rain. Overall, things were going well for us and we were enjoying our season of festivals. We closed out 2008 with further shows in Greece, England, the Netherlands and Switzerland, feeling a lot more like a permanent line-up than we had done the previous summer.

* * *

It wasn't until the following August that we finally completed our *Paradox* box set. Over the last few months everyone from our current line-up had been involved with the project in one way or another. Our former singer Glynn Morgan had also returned for a welcome reunion to record a couple of old songs. The final box set contained eight discs, one to represent each of our studio albums. Each disc featured one of the main singles or promotional tracks from the corresponding album followed by two B-sides, and it was among these B-sides that the real depth of the collection resided.

Before Threshold had signed their first record deal – and prior to me joining the band – they had made three demo tapes between 1989 and 1991. Overall these contained 16 original songs, four of which had eventually been used or adapted for the band's first two studio albums. Many of the remaining songs had been written in a different musical and lyrical style, with titles such as *Rich Bitch* and *Sweet Little Lady* a world away from the dark, progressive leanings of *Wounded Land*. We had subsequently chosen two of the old songs, *Conceal The Face* and *Seventh Angel*, to record acoustically for our *Wireless* album. For the box set we decided to record *Conceal The Face* as a full band arrangement along with another unreleased song called *Shifting Sands*. These took on the role of B-sides for the song *Paradox*, which we also re-recorded especially for the box set.

For the second disc, we unearthed two old songs that had been overlooked at the time, Glynn's *Fist Of Tongues* and my ballad *Half Way Home*. We managed to contact Glynn and he drove down to record new versions of the songs with us. It was great to see him again and it felt as if no time had passed since we had last worked together. Other new recordings on the box set included the previously unreleased *Smile At The Moon*, which had grown out of an old song that I had originally recorded with Farrah. We also revisited the early version of *Long Way Home* featuring Mac's original demo vocals. Mac had not recorded any backing vocals for the demo, so Glynn kindly provided some, marking the only occasion that two of our three frontmen have appeared on the same recording together.

Paradox – The Singles Collection was released as our sixth Direct-to-Fan album in October 2009. To coincide with the release we decided to book another European tour. I wanted my first tour as a booking agent to be something special, so I planned for a video projector and screen to be added to the stage to play the latest music videos from other artists before the show and between bands, and this would also be used by Threshold for video projections during our set. I booked Serenity and Spheric Universe Experience as support bands and scheduled a short, ten-date tour across Europe under the banner of *Essence Of Progression*.

We also modernised our live set-up to include a computer running Pro Tools software. This was the software we used for recording in the studio, and it would revolutionise what we could do on stage. With Johanne playing to a click track, it meant that we could synchronise whatever we wanted to happen during the show. Instead of having to remember hundreds of program changes on my keyboards, the computer could take care of them for me. This was also true for guitars, so if Karl was playing a solo on the opposite side of the stage from his pedal board, he wouldn't have to rush back to change sounds for the next section. Other benefits included playing back sound effects and synchronising to film, so we could have our videos projected onto the screen in perfect time with the band during the show.

However, with great power comes great responsibility. I was in charge of operating our on-stage computer and for a long time I found it very stressful. I remember one show where the audience was so loud that Johanne couldn't hear the click track and lost his timing, so I had to stop Pro Tools and try and restart it again in perfect time as we continued to play. Another time, while we were racing to set up at a festival, the computer refused to configure properly and we were left standing in front of an impatient crowd with no idea how to fix it. It also seemed to make a lot of intermittent buzzing noises at some venues, and it took a couple of years before we discovered that this was due to a faulty power supply. But the benefits mostly outweighed the problems, and the new technology slowly became an integral part of our set-up.

For our *Essence Of Progression* tour we planned a varied set covering most of our studio albums, starting with *Consume To Live* and including as many of our long songs as possible, with *Part Of The Chaos*, *Critical Mass*, *The Art Of Reason* and *Pilot In The Sky Of Dreams* on the set list every night. It made for a great show and went down well with our fans. We filmed our concert at the Boerderij for a possible DVD release, but unfortunately a technical issue meant that none of the vocals were recorded. After the fiasco of *Critical Energy* in the same venue six years earlier, the last thing we wanted to do was release another concert video with overdubbed vocals, so the new DVD never came to pass.

Booking a tour was a lot harder than booking a festival. Finding suitable venues that were available on suitable dates and would pay suitable fees proved to be quite troublesome. But, after a lot of sleepless nights, I finally managed to arrange a full set of shows. The stress continued on the road, as managing the tour by day and performing by night took a lot of effort. One minute I would be organising dinner for the support bands and sorting out contracts with local promoters, and suddenly I would be on stage performing with Threshold, not really focussing on the show because there were too many other things to worry about. But, overall, the tour was a success and I was very relieved that all of the hard work paid off.

Not everything ran smoothly. One of the shows was quite poorly attended and the venue owner refused to pay us our full fee. I was inexperienced at how to deal with this sort of issue, so we lost money that evening. It was one of those clubs that held discos late into the night after the band had finished playing. This is generally unpopular with bands because it results in a tight curfew, so there's always a rush to get packed up and out of the venue as soon as possible, rather than being able to mingle with the fans, sign autographs and have a shower after the show. On this particular evening, the turnaround time between the gig and the disco was so tight that our video technician Jordan was still up a ladder in the middle of the hall taking down the projector when the disco started and hundreds of revellers flooded the dance floor around him, leaving him feeling rather vulnerable. There are some venues that you really look forward to revisiting. Others you vow never to return to again.

* * *

Two weeks later I was supposed to join Damian on stage at the Robin 2 in Bilston. He had assembled a group to play a selection of his solo material and songs by other bands that he had been associated with over the years, and he had asked me to join them to perform a guest solo on *Sanity's End*. Unfortunately, the week before the show I had a bizarre gardening accident that left me unable to play. I was trimming the ivy on my garage wall when I accidentally cut off the tip of my left middle finger. It was only a tiny amount, about two or three millimetres, but it was quite a sight. I remember noticing the blood pumping out in spurts and realising how accurate TV medical dramas were. I also remember calling frantically to Farrah that I had chopped off my finger, an unfortunate choice of words that almost caused her to black out. Thankfully we got the blood flow under control and were eventually able to bandage it, but it would be a few weeks before I could play the keyboards again.

This was one of several hand injuries that I have managed to inflict on myself over the years. I had previously walked through a closed window, resulting in the outside edge of my little finger being sliced off in the falling shards. I had also suffered a deep wound to my right index finger while loading a flight case into the boot of my car after a show, crying out in pain as my finger got sliced between the metal of the case and the car frame. But perhaps my luckiest escape of all was when I was advised by a man with one knee that it was safe to stroke a wild alligator.

The reason that he had one knee was because the other one had been bitten off by an alligator, so it is possible that he wasn't the best person to take advice from. I was on an airboat with Farrah and two other tourists exploring the Everglades. The Florida sun scorched our skin as we skimmed across the water and weaved our way through the narrow waterways between the dark mangrove forests. The one-kneed man was our pilot, and after a while he asked if we wanted to see some alligators. As we made our way towards where they were known to congregate, he thoughtfully recounted the tale of a previous trip when his boat had run out of gas and he and his passengers had been left stranded for several hours, surrounded by dozens of the deadly reptiles. As we started to wonder whether the whole trip might have been a bad idea, we turned a corner and saw our first alligator. It was huge, about four metres long with 70 lethal teeth, and it was coming towards us.

To our immense surprise, the pilot suddenly pulled out a bag of marshmallows and dropped some into the water to coax it to the side of the boat. Then he popped the deadly question: "Who wants to stroke the alligator?"

I looked anxiously around the boat at my fellow passengers and realised that none of them was going to volunteer. So, using impeccable logic, I realised that it would have to be me. I don't think it even occurred to me that it didn't have to be anyone. It was a crazy idea, the sort that could result in the loss of an important part of the body, as the pilot had already proved. Suddenly he somehow grabbed the alligator below the neck, pulled it towards me and told me to stroke the back of its head, assuring me that it wouldn't be able to bite me from such an angle. In something of a trance, I did what I was told and reached forward with my hand. Its leathery neck felt softer than I expected, quite beautiful to the touch. The pilot shouted at Farrah to take a picture, but she was absolutely mortified and by the time her shaking hands had found her camera I had already withdrawn my hand. Thankfully, it was still fully attached to the rest of my body.

* * *

Back home after the *Essence Of Progression* tour, Farrah and I were starting to put some serious thought into what we should do next in terms of music. So far, we had only released two songs and they had got us nowhere. We wondered if we would be better off with a full band focussing on a heavier sound. We had three new songs called *Don't Leave Me Behind*, *Cover Me Now* and *I'm Alive*. The first two of these fell into pop-metal territory and the third leaned more towards a symphonic, progressive style, so we decided that these would provide the blueprint for what we would do next. I had also written a song called *Colophon*, but we couldn't decide if it was a little too progressive for us, so we left it to one side.

Throughout 2010 we continued with our writing sessions and eventually we had ten tracks ready to record. After a lot of thought, we took the decision to release the album ourselves. Although we would very much have liked a record deal, our attempts to get signed so far had been unsuccessful and we knew that at some point we just had to release something. We called the project League Of Lights, imagining our league as a group of luminaries from the music world who would make guest appearances on our recordings, more of a collective than a band. Now all we needed was to decide on which musicians to choose. We agreed from the outset that we would not ask any of my Threshold bandmates. If they got involved it would sound great, but it would just look like League Of Lights was an offshoot of Threshold, and we wanted our new project to have its own identity.

We started thinking about drummers who had made an impression on us. One of my favourite records in recent years had been *Disconnected* by Fates Warning. I had found it in a small record store in the Czech Republic in 2000 and listened to it many times while I was there. The drummer on the album was Mark Zonder and his playing was unique and beautiful. He had also guested on the first Chroma Key record, a project we both loved that was fronted by former Dream Theater keyboard player Kevin Moore. So we decided to get in touch with Mark to see if he was interested. I had never actually met him, having seen Threshold's tour with Fates Warning cancelled back in 1995, so it was a shot in the dark. But, fortunately, he was keen to be involved, so we sent him the songs and he recorded the drums at his studio in California.

For guitars we turned to Ruud Jolie from Within Temptation. Our paths had first crossed in March 1995, when he supported Threshold performing with a band called Hard To Be, and he was an easy choice. Not only was he a very talented guitarist but he was also a thoroughly nice guy. I drove to the Netherlands and stayed at his home for a few enjoyable days while we recorded the guitar parts at his studio. Ruud was an avid Star Wars fan and worked with an organisation called 501st Legion that visited local hospitals dressed as Storm Troopers and other villainous characters to lift the spirits of the patients. He kept a lot of memorabilia in his spare bedroom in the attic, including a life-size replica of bounty hunter Boba Fett. One night I almost jumped out of my skin when I woke up to see the menacing figure watching me from the shadows!

The final piece of our puzzle was bass player Jerry Meehan, the touring bassist for British pop royalty such as Robbie Williams and Bryan Ferry. We had been unable to settle on a bass player and one day Damian had suggested Jerry to me. We were grateful for the recommendation and got in touch. I had originally planned to go to his studio in London to oversee the bass sessions, but when the time came the British railway system was in chaos because of a little snow, so I wasn't able to get there. As a result, Jerry recorded the sessions on his own and he did a fantastic job.

With all of the parts recorded, I finished the mixes in January 2011, and we released the album the following April. It was a low-key affair but we sold a few copies and garnered a handful of good reviews. However, without a record company behind us, it was hard to get much exposure and consequently the album made a loss. Furthermore, writing and producing the album had stopped me from doing other jobs that would have earned some money. Threshold's box set was selling more slowly than we had hoped, and, although we did a few more shows over the spring and summer, it felt like everything was slowing to a stop.

Something was going to have to change soon or we would run into trouble.

Chapter 13

And So We Carry On

THRESHOLD'S TEMPORARY TOURING LINE-UP of Karl, Johanne, Steve, Damian, Pete and me had now been together for almost four years, longer than some of our permanent configurations. Damian and Pete now felt very much a part of our Threshold family, so we decided it was finally time to record a new album together. There was no sign of Mac or Nick returning. Mac had worked on various other projects since his departure from the band, but had not got back in touch with us. Nick had initially missed being in the band and had considered the possibility of coming back the following year, but as more time had passed he had not returned.

In search of a theme for the new album, I had been reading about something called the fatal sequence. This was the idea that empires usually follow a lifecycle, starting with an uprising out of bondage or dependency into a period of freedom and prosperity before eventually becoming complacent and falling back into dependency again. I wasn't particularly interested in studying the history of ancient empires, but I was drawn to the idea of how this cycle could also apply to groups of people or individuals. Presumably during the final stages of the process, the members of the empire still thought they were moving forwards on a relentless march of progress, oblivious to their impending downfall until it was too late. Over the next few months this concept would become woven throughout the lyrics of our new album, and would also provide its title.

Karl and I spent some time discussing how the album should sound. Producing a follow-up to *Dead Reckoning* with Mac in 2008 would have been so easy; we were in our stride and had a well-defined, polished sound and style. However, we knew that wouldn't work in the same way for Damian's vocals. We listened back to *Wounded Land* and *Extinct Instinct*, our previous albums with him, and were reminded of just how much we had evolved over the years. We didn't want to revisit old ground. We needed a fresh approach that would sit comfortably across our early and later work, encompassing both the progressive individuality of our old records and the modern, streamlined sound of our latest one.

Karl sent me his first two demos for the album, an up-tempo track that sounded like the perfect opener and a long, melodic track that sounded like the perfect closer. I worked on the opening song first, drawing on the idea of the fatal sequence to shape the lyrics. I initially called it *March Of Progress*, but we later decided that it was the perfect album title so I changed the song name to *Ashes*.

Karl's second demo was a beautiful ten-minute epic, and I thought it would be interesting if the lyrics somehow told the story of the band, something I had not done before. I remembered reading about how Julius Caesar had crossed the Rubicon river between Italy and Gaul in 49 BC, an event which had led to his rise to dictator of Rome but also a civil war with heavy casualties. I mused that Threshold had never had our Rubicon moment, that elusive event that could have lifted us from being an underground band to superstardom. Whether this was down to our choice of genre, our excessive line-up changes or a combination of other factors I wasn't sure.

But, at the same time, I also wasn't sure if we would have survived the journey. Threshold had always been a fragile entity, a swirling mass of rough edges trying to fit together, and major success would probably have been our undoing. Maybe the very fact that we never had our Rubicon moment was the reason we had survived. And so, the song became *The Rubicon*. Given the song's subject matter, I naturally felt compelled to work our band name into the opening verse, so I wrote the words 'Standing on the Threshold of a dream', and this would later become a good T-shirt slogan.

For the end section of the song I wanted to try something different. I needed eight lines of lyrics, and up to this point we had produced eight albums, so I decided to see if I could somehow use a line from the opening song of each album and build something out of them. It was just the sort of puzzle I enjoyed. It took a while, but I eventually found the lines I wanted, starting with 'Everyone has something more to lose' from *Wounded Land* before ending with 'A penny for the one you thought you'd be' from *Dead Reckoning*. Amazingly, all the lines were roughly the right length and told the story I wanted to tell, so it felt like a fitting way to end the song and the album.

We interspersed our writing sessions with various live shows, including a handful of UK gigs and two more long weekenders in Europe. The last of these took us to Germany where we had been invited to perform at the Night Of The Prog festival in Loreley. Set in an outdoor amphitheatre on a hill overlooking the Rhine Valley, many consider it to be one of the most beautiful venues in Europe. Our journey there concluded with a picturesque ferry ride across the River Rhine before arriving at the venue to the sound of gentle keyboards and meandering flute solos lilting through the air. We were more used to arriving at festivals to the sound of crushing guitars and death metal vocals, so Loreley felt quite surreal and magical in comparison.

By now I had presented three songs for the Threshold album. The first of these was *Colophon*, the track that I had not used for the League Of Lights album because it was too far removed from our sound. It worked really well for Threshold, although I must confess I loved the version with Farrah on vocals. The next song I wrote was *Staring At The Sun*, another progressive track with interweaving rhythms and time signatures. I think I smiled all the way through writing that one. I loved every moment of it, especially the interplay between the instruments and melodies during the verses. The final song was *The Hours*, another track that had originally started as a League Of Lights song. Steve had put forward a few bass and groove ideas, so I used one of his bass riffs to join the second chorus to the middle section, and the song was complete.

I did put forward one further song called *Darkest Hour*. I had written it in 6/8, a time signature that is generally a bad idea for rock music as it can often feel stilted or lifeless. There are notable exceptions of course, such as *The Crow & The Butterfly* by Shinedown or *Kiss From A Rose* by Seal, but sadly *Darkest Hour* was not one of those songs and Karl was right to reject it. It was fair enough; I had previously turned down one of his songs too. Back in 2000 when we were writing *Hypothetical* he had been working on a fast power metal track with Jon, and I had rejected it on the grounds that we weren't a power metal band. Looking back, it may have been rather harsh of me, because it probably sounded a lot more like Threshold than my song *Keep Your Head* which made it onto the album.

Our two newest members Pete and Damian contributed to our latest record too. Pete wrote the songs *Coda* and *Divinity*, and Damian put forward an acoustic track called *That's Why We Came*, which I converted into a full band arrangement for him. Karl later wrote three more pieces of music which would become *Return Of The Thought Police*, *Liberty Complacency Dependency* and *Don't Look Down*, and before we knew it the writing sessions for our new album were complete.

It was then that we received some tragic news. On 3rd August 2011 Mac died from kidney failure following a four-day coma. He had been suffering from some serious health issues during the months prior to his death and had been unable to come back from them. He was only 45 years old; it just didn't seem possible. We were absolutely devastated. All thoughts of our past frustrations suddenly seemed so insignificant. We had lost our old friend. I had always assumed that we would see each other again one day, enjoy a few laughs and reminisce about the old days. But now he was gone. A spark of magic was lost from the world, and it would never be the same again.

* * *

Eventually the long summer drew to a close. Unfortunately, various delays meant that we wouldn't be able to finish recording *March Of Progress* until the following spring. In the meantime I recorded some local artists and mixed an album for a band called The Morning After, whose frontman Sam Ryder would unexpectedly go on to represent the United Kingdom at Eurovision in 2022, coming second with his song *Space Man*. At the same time we also booked a few more Threshold shows but they got cancelled. So, with no further work coming in, I started looking for other music jobs to tide me over. I scanned through the job listings every day in the hope of finding something, but despite applying for dozens of roles I wasn't able to secure any work.

Farrah and I decided to give League Of Lights one more push, so we wrote a new song that we hoped would be the perfect symphonic rock single. It was called *Forever*, and our plan was to make one more round of the record companies in the hope of securing some interest for a new album. We enlisted Mark Zonder to play the drums again, and, as the song lent itself well to being a duet, we approached Glynn Morgan to ask if he would like to make a guest appearance on it. We had got on really well during our reunion in 2008 for the Threshold box set. Farrah and I both loved his voice and we were delighted when he agreed to perform on the track, both as vocalist and guitarist.

We also took the opportunity to organise a League Of Lights concert to test out how our music translated to a live stage. Farrah's Grandmother had been asking us for ages to put on a concert at her local Salvation Army centre. It wasn't exactly what we had in mind, but her enthusiasm eventually won us over. We realised that it would be impractical to bring in all of the musicians who played on the album, so we drafted in local guitarist Aaron Murray alongside bassist Dominic Fiddler and drummer Rob Howe from the Salvation Army band. Glynn agreed to appear as a special guest, marking the first time that we performed together for almost 17 years. We also drew further on the Salvation Army's broad array of musical talent, modifying the arrangements of *I'm Alive* and *Heaven Sent A Star* to accommodate their 40-voice choir and 20-piece brass section.

On the day of the concert we were relieved to find that the seated venue was full. The front row was bravely occupied by Farrah's Grandmother and her friends, and as the band powered through the opening riff of *I'm Alive* there was an urgent flurry of activity as hearing aids were hastily turned down and anxious glances were exchanged. We performed the whole of our debut album, interspersed with *Forever* and a contemporary cover version of *Amazing Grace*. The choir and brass section blended beautifully with the band and the overall result sounded stunning. A couple of weeks later we returned to the venue to film a video of *Forever*, and in July 2012 we released it as our new single. However, although it sounded a lot more commercial than our debut album, we still found ourselves unable to attract any record company interest.

Around the same time I also joined a covers band. One day I was hunting through some online music job advertisements when I found a local band called Supercollider that was looking for a keyboard player. I auditioned by performing *Comfortably Numb* by Pink Floyd and *Hold The Line* by Toto and I got the job on the spot. I was only with them for a few months, but it was great fun. There was something very satisfying about playing tracks like *You Give Love A Bad Name* through a small PA in a local pub to a few dozen drunken revellers. Some nights we were welcomed like gods, as if we really were Bon Jovi, and the crowds cheered almost as if we were playing at Wembley Stadium. However, performing in pubs once a fortnight wasn't enough to pay the bills. I was going to need something more regular than that.

On 24th August 2012, Threshold's new studio album *March Of Progress* was released by Nuclear Blast. It soared into the German national album chart at number 28. This was the moment I had been dreaming of since I had first discovered the chart countdown back in 1979. We had finally made it into the Top 40. Furthermore, we were at number 30 in Switzerland, number 43 in Sweden and had also registered chart positions in Austria, the Netherlands and France. It was truly a monumental moment. Our reputation was stronger than ever, we had delivered a critically acclaimed album and Nuclear Blast had done an amazing job of promoting it.

But instead of staying up all night celebrating, I was having sleepless nights from worry. I knew that royalties would eventually come, but they would take more than a year to arrive and I was out of money. So, what should have been one of the most wonderful moments of my life was tainted with disappointment. Threshold was finally a Top 40 band, but in order to survive I was going to have to get another job.

With no opportunities coming from my regular searches of the music job listings, I eventually faced the inevitable. I would have to consider returning to my former job as an acoustics consultant. Don't get me wrong, I knew there was nothing wrong with having a regular job. I had worked in acoustics for 11 years after I left university, but the thought of going backwards and giving up on my dream felt like a crushing defeat. I had worked so hard to make a living from music, but it hadn't been enough.

I searched the job listings once again, this time looking in the acoustics section. I found a role that seemed suitable and applied for the job. One advertisement, one interview and one job offer. It was all horribly easy. I know it can be really hard to find a job, so I understand how fortunate I was. It's just that I didn't want to do it. And so, as the fireworks and celebrations marked the coming of another new year with the promise of fresh starts and new opportunities, in January 2013 I started my new job, feeling thoroughly wretched and defeated.

Shortly before I accepted the role, I had received a call from Dec Burke asking if I would like to join a new band. Dec had previously been a member of the British rock band Frost* and had been working with former Pain Of Salvation bassist Simon Andersson on a new project. He sent me a demo of a song called *Now* and I was hooked on the spot. It was powerful, melodic and totally mesmerising. Although the project would not provide an eleventh hour reprieve from my return to a day job, it proved to be a very welcome distraction. After a few name changes we settled on AudioPlastik and released an album called *In The Head Of A Maniac*. Dec and Simon had already recorded most of the material when I joined, so my contribution was limited, adding a few keyboards and backing vocals and helping out with the mix. But it's an album that I am tremendously fond of to this day.

March Of Progress, on the other hand, is an album that I would rather forget. I have never understood it when artists make negative comments about their own work, as it is bound to be someone's favourite album and those sorts of remarks can taint a record forever. So, to be clear, I do consider *March Of Progress* to be a very good album. It's just that, for me, it will always be associated with stopping being a full-time musician. The two things were inextricably linked, so it's not an album that I would ever choose to listen to.

However, I would have to hear the songs many times that year, as we rather appropriately started our *March Of Progress* tour on the first day of March in London. I had stopped booking Threshold shows following the cancellation of our 2012 dates and the start of my new job, so the tour was booked by a European agency instead. It was a longer tour than usual, taking in eight countries over 19 dates, including a return to places we didn't often visit such as Austria, Poland and Slovenia.

I found it very hard jumping from my job to being a touring musician again, and I must confess that most of the tour went past in a depressed sort of haze. We were still having a lot of technical problems with our on-stage computer, which was now starting to give me bad dreams. One evening when we walked onto the stage for a show in Switzerland, we discovered that it had stopped working all together. By some miracle one of the venue's technicians had a suitable replacement, so we were able to load everything onto that and perform our show after a rather long delay. But by that point I couldn't really bear it anymore. I hated the tour, not just because of the technical problems, but also because I knew it would soon be over and I would have to go back to my job again.

The tour visited quite a few venues we hadn't been to before, and some were more successful than others. The Orto Bar in Slovenia was so small that there was physically no space for our opening band Cryptex, so they dreamed up the creative solution of performing acoustically outside the venue as fans were walking in. At another club we arrived to find the hall contained two stages, the main one and a small makeshift one. Although we were contracted to play on the main stage, we were shocked to be told that, unless we paid a lot of money, we would have to use the small one instead. The tour accounts could not cover such an unexpected cost, so later that night the large crowd struggled to see us because the stage was so low, while the main one stood dark and empty beside us. It was a ludicrous situation and we have never thought of going back.

Our set list for the tour naturally leaned heavily towards material from our new album, but we opened and closed the shows with two of our biggest songs, *Mission Profile* and *Slipstream*. We also managed to fit in a few older tracks such as *Angels*, which we had not played for ten years, along with *Part Of The Chaos*, *Long Way Home* and *Light And Space*. Over the summer we played a number of festivals, including Celebrat8 in the UK, a return to Rock Hard in Germany and a long-awaited appearance at Sweden Rock. We also returned to Loreley, this time for Metalfest, so the lilting flute solos that had serenaded our previous arrival at the amphitheatre were long gone and replaced by the more familiar strains of death metal again.

Our final festival of the summer was called Ciao Luca Festival. Set in the picturesque grounds of Gradisca d'Isonzo Castle in north-eastern Italy, it had been organised to commemorate the tragic death of a local boy called Luca. It was touching to see so many locals come out to support the event. Our flight home wasn't until the following evening, so the morning after the festival we dropped our equipment at Venice Airport and caught a water taxi to Venice. Farrah had come along for the trip and we enjoyed a perfect day, complete with a romantic gondola ride for two through the city's idyllic canals.

Venice had provided some much-needed respite, but back home I was very unhappy and constantly worn out. My commute to work was long and the job was tiring, so I would get home every night feeling shattered and downcast. I just hated doing it, and every moment of every day I longed for it to be over. And every moment of every day Farrah was my rock, providing unconditional love and support, however low I got. It must have been really hard on her too, and I wouldn't have got through it without her.

* * *

He cried up to the heavens:
"This wasn't my design.
There must have been an error,
There must have been some grave mistake"

The words filled my thoughts as I travelled to my next appointment on the London Underground. The air was hot and stale and I was exhausted from carrying heavy noise monitoring equipment down endless flights of stairs and along overcrowded platforms. And, as is so often the way for me, the words formed into a song. I continued with my thoughts.

> *And struggling every second*
> *Was pointless and sublime;*
> *Wherein he found his character,*
> *Wherein he found he couldn't break*

It certainly wasn't how I was feeling, but maybe there was some purpose in what I was going through. I wrote the words down in a notebook. I wasn't sure they scanned quite as smoothly as other lyrics I had written, but there was something to them. Three years later they would form the chorus of *Lost In Translation*, but I still had a few more moments to live through before I could complete the whole song.

After I had been in the job for almost a year, I was head-hunted by another company. Their office was closer to home, so it would mean less time commuting and hopefully a slight improvement in my overall mood. I accepted the job over a coffee without even doing an interview. That turned out to be a bad idea. After two days at my new workplace I realised that I had no idea how to do the job. It was a senior role in a specialist area and I just didn't have the right experience for it. How this had not come up before I joined was beyond me, but now I was in trouble. On the third day I surrendered and gave up. I told the manager not to pay me for the two days I had done and we would call it quits. I hadn't done anything useful anyway; I was totally out of my depth. The manager was shocked and angry, but he understood, and I trust he carried out a rather more thorough interview for my replacement.

As I took the train home, I slumped down with my head in my hands. I had never felt so crushed or humbled, overwhelmed by life's demands. I had no hope and no plan. If you know the song *Lost In Translation* you will probably recognise those words too. It may sound a lot like a first-world problem from the outside, but for me it was a very dark moment. I was totally lost and had no idea what to do.

Fortunately, salvation would eventually come in the form of a text message from an old colleague at my previous job. John was also a former professional musician who had found it necessary to move into another line of work, and one day he got in touch to ask how I was doing in my new job. I briefly wondered whether to do the usual British thing, keep a stiff upper lip and tell him everything was fine. That's probably what I would have done in the old days. But I was different now, I felt broken and defeated. There was no point showing bravado, no more battles to be won. So, I confessed that I had taken a wrong turn and didn't know what to do next. I told him there was no need to keep it a secret; I had no pride left to protect.

A couple of weeks later I got a call from the company. They had secured a new contract close to where I lived but they didn't have enough staff to do the work. Fortunately John had mentioned my dilemma, so they wondered if I would consider going back to work for them on a part-time freelance basis. It was fantastic news and I couldn't believe my good fortune. I could so easily have told John that everything was fine, but somehow by owning up to my failure I had been offered a way out. I gratefully accepted the job offer.

Since going back to work I had seriously thought about giving up music for good. But throughout my time in London I continued to write down my thoughts and ideas whenever I had them. And after a while I found that I had quite a lot of material. Maybe there was one more album left in me after all.

Chapter 14

A Faded Photograph

As Karl started to send me instrumentals for what would become our tenth studio album, I was pleased to find that I had already written most of the lyrics. Some of the ideas I had been working on were unfinished and would find their way onto our next album, but there were four well-developed sets of lyrics that seemed to fit Karl's demos perfectly. I had also written three songs of my own, so it was a nice surprise to discover that much of the work for our new record had already been done.

The album initially had a working title of *The Lost Road* before going through various iterations such as *Subliminal Freeways* and *Oblivion Highway* until we eventually settled on *For The Journey*. The songs were mostly about going through the journey of life, with themes such as learning to let go, forgiving those who've hurt you along the way and struggling through the hard times. They were themes that were close to my heart and *Lost In Your Memory* felt particularly poignant, drawn from what I had been through over the past year. The line 'every day is a testament to all the things you've done, and all you've overcome' was a reminder to keep going whatever comes your way.

The album opener *Watchtower On The Moon* was an acknowledgement that you never know what's coming next, there are no early warning systems for the future. The lyrics fell perfectly into place in Karl's music, even down to the smallest detail. After the second chorus Karl had written a short refrain on the bass guitar: three phrases of seven notes, six notes and six more notes. I wanted a lyric to sit directly over these phrases, so I looked in my notebook and there was one unused set of words left: 'There is always bad to find, so push it from your mind, and let it all unwind' – three phrases of seven syllables, six syllables and six more syllables. It couldn't have worked better.

I had also started to go beyond writing about specific topics to compose some story songs. I wondered what would happen if you actually could see what was coming next, and what the implications would be for a man who saw through time. However, while that particular song would not be complete for a couple more years, the lyrics for another story song were already finished. *The Box* was a tale about technology coming to a primitive community for the first time. The way I had structured the story meant that the song would need to be quite long, with an opening prelude that was repeated at the end with modified words to tell the end of the story. Coincidentally, when Karl sent me his longest instrumental it had just the right structure, so the lyrics slotted in without too much adjustment. After the album came out, I was asked many times about what was in the box, but I mostly tried to keep it a mystery. I've always preferred people to draw their own conclusions about our songs.

Pete had written another great track called *Siren Sky*, which would become our album closer, and we now had an hour's worth of music ready to record. Johanne had put forward an old Kyrbgrinder song called *I Wish I Could* that he had previously released in 2010. As it wasn't exclusively a Threshold track, we didn't want to include it as part of the main running order, so it was chosen as the bonus track instead. Steve hadn't come forward with anything this time, and while Damian had originally intended to contribute something, he had unfortunately lost the phone where he had recorded his demo, so the idea was lost forever.

Unsure of how we wanted our new album cover to look, we started trawling the internet in search of potential artists and artwork. It's a fairly joyless way to find a cover, rather like hunting for a rare LP in a large second-hand record store where nothing has been put in alphabetical order and you don't even know if they've got a copy in stock. But eventually our working title of *The Lost Road* led us to a Polish artist called Leszek Bujnowski, who had created some artwork with the same name. His work was dark and beautiful, and although his lost road design was not what we were looking for, another of his creations was perfect. We got in touch and he was very happy for it to be used as our album cover.

While we were waiting for the album to come out, we headed off to Germany and the Netherlands for another long weekender. We had rehearsed one of our new songs *Turned To Dust* and were considering the possibility of previewing it at the shows, thinking it might be a nice surprise for our fans.

However, Damian wisely pointed out that it would result in most people's first experience of the song being a low-quality mobile phone recording uploaded to YouTube. So we decided to hold it back until the album was released, instead opting to refresh the set by bringing back a few older songs and performing *Liberty Complacency Dependency* for the first time.

Back home I finished mixing the AudioPlastik album with Simon Andersson and recorded Damian's vocals for the second Headspace album at Thin Ice Studios. Damian and I also had the pleasure of donning our finest suits and attending the 2014 Progressive Music Awards at the Underglobe in London, as Threshold had been nominated for the 'Band/Artist of the Year' category. In the end we were fairly beaten by Dream Theater, but it was an enjoyable evening, capped by a very humorous speech by British comedian Bill Bailey as he handed Peter Gabriel the well-deserved award for 'Prog God'.

For The Journey was released on 19th September 2014, two years after *March Of Progress*. We were pleased to discover that it had achieved similar chart positions to its predecessor, including our debut Top 20 entry in Switzerland and a respectable number 33 in both Germany and Finland. We even made a small impression at home, not only entering the UK album chart at a lowly number 116, but also achieving the highest new entry in the rock chart at number 3. The only albums above us were by Slash and Foo Fighters, so we were proud to be in such good company.

We toured the album a few weeks later, starting with Maximum Rock Festival in Romania before boarding a nightliner once more for a 19-date trek around Europe. Our support bands for the tour were Overtures and The Silent Wedding, although during our trip we would also be joined by more guests along the way. Progressive rock veterans Caravan performed with us for one night in the Netherlands, Tygers Of Pan Tang joined us for a show in Germany, and US heavy metallers Lizzy Borden were with us in Italy, complete with full stage make-up and fake blood. It was a very unlikely billing but our fans didn't seem to mind. Our shows on the tour typically started with *Slipstream* and ended with *The Box*, with a nod to our early days in the shape of *Part Of The Chaos* or the occasional rare outing of *Siege Of Baghdad*.

By the time we reached Slovakia, we had spent almost three weeks together in close quarters, and tempers were beginning to fray. We were all rather exhausted after a 500-mile drive from Italy, and the Slovakian capital

Bratislava would be our seventh successive show without a day off. The concert itself went well enough; there was a good-sized crowd and they really enjoyed the show. But, as we were getting ready to leave, there was a totally unnecessary altercation between two members of the group. Unfortunately, it would affect the atmosphere for the rest of the tour. In fact, the ramifications would continue well beyond the tour, and the camaraderie that we had developed since coming together as a temporary line-up back in 2007 would be lost forever.

The following January we flew to the US for one of the best festival experiences I have ever known. We had been booked to perform at 70000 Tons Of Metal, an annual five-day heavy metal festival that took place on a large cruise liner. Every year the ship hosted 60 bands and 3,000 fans for a journey from Fort Lauderdale in Florida to a Caribbean island and back, with each band performing two shows. So, essentially, we were on a five-day Caribbean cruise and we were getting paid to be there. The overall line-up was a lot heavier in style than Threshold, with bands like Annihilator, Arch Enemy and Cannibal Corpse on the bill. As far as I know we were the only progressive band on board, but the fans seemed happy for us to be there and so were we.

The mood in the band was no longer hostile but some friendships had noticeably cooled. As a result, most of us spent the five days doing our own thing. Damian spent a lot of time in the casino, his poker skills coming to the fore as he impressively managed to be runner-up in the ship's poker championship. Pete could often be found on the pool deck soaking in one of the hot tubs located around the main outdoor stage, and the rest of us just took the opportunity to relax and unwind. Johanne was rather taken with the vast food hall on Deck 11 of the ship; it was always buzzing with activity and he spent most of his time there. One morning I recorded the sound of the ship's elevator saying the words 'Deck 11' on my phone. I still have the recording and whenever I play it back to Johanne his eyes light up!

The ship had four stages of various sizes, from the small Sphinx Lounge to the impressive outdoor area that was billed as 'the biggest open air stage to sail the seas'. Each band was allocated two stages, performing one set on the way to the Caribbean and one on the way back to Florida. On the way out we played in the Sphinx Lounge. The stage was slightly too small for a six-piece band, so I had to set up my keyboards to the side, but nobody seemed to mind. For the return trip we were allocated the much larger Platinum Theatre and we had a fantastic show there. We varied our two sets a little, playing our biggest songs like *Mission Profile*, *Pilot In The Sky Of Dreams* and *Ashes* both times for fans who hadn't attended both shows, but with a few different tracks in each set for those who saw us twice.

After two days at sea we arrived in Jamaica for a day on the island. I had been pre-booked onto a trip to a local waterpark, so I headed off with some fellow passengers including my old friend ZP Theart, who had now left DragonForce and was there performing with Tank. We had a great day swimming with dolphins and climbing waterfalls before heading back to the ship for the return journey. That evening I met a fan who hadn't been quite so fortunate. He had disembarked in the morning and found a local taxi to drive him to a tourist spot. However, the driver had taken him to a desolate location in the middle of nowhere and demanded $1,000 to take him back. He had managed to escape from the car and ran away, and spent most of the day hiking back to where the ship was docked. When he finally arrived at the port, exhausted, sunburned and dehydrated, he reported the incident to the local police, who just rolled their eyes and said: "Oh yeah, we know who that was." I was very glad that I hadn't gone off on my own.

The cruise was a perfect place for songwriting. With several free hours between shows and signing sessions, I spent a lot of time sitting on a secluded side-deck with a notebook and pen, soaking in the sun and composing songs. The story that I had started writing for our last album about someone who saw into the future was still unfinished. But now, with countless hours ahead of me on the cruise ship, I had the perfect opportunity to work on it. I had been pondering what would happen if someone got a prophecy about their future and whether their actions would subsequently affect the outcome. The result was *The Man Who Saw Through Time*, a song that would eventually make its way onto our next album.

Over the summer we drove to mainland Europe for another long weekender, followed by shows at Headbangers Open Air and Neuborn Open Air in Germany. When we got home, we found out that two of our songs from *For The Journey* were going to be featured on a video game called *Metal Hammer: Roadkill*. Having been such keen video gamers in our younger days we were absolutely delighted. Meanwhile we had also been working on a new live double album called *European Journey*, compiled from various shows that we had recorded during our 2014 tour. It was released in November and we were amazed to see it enter the UK rock chart at number 22, a totally unexpected achievement for a concert recording. However, we didn't realise that it would turn out to be our final release with our current line-up.

*　*　*

To promote our new live album, we returned to Europe for another tour which we called *The Journey Continues*, where we performed the whole of *For The Journey* from start to finish along with a few perennial fan favourites. It was the first time we had ever played one of our albums in its entirety and it went down really well. Our support bands for the 11-date tour were fellow Brits Damnation Angels and French progressive metallers Spheric Universe Experience, who had previously opened for us during our 2009 tour. Having seen Serenity progress from opening band to main support in 2009, it was nice to offer the same opportunity to our friends from France and it turned out to be a really good package.

Our tour crew included David Sievers looking after front of house sound and tour management, and Toby Schwietering looking after the stage. They had both worked for us before and they were our dream team, great guys to have on the road and the epitome of German efficiency. David had first worked with us on our *Critical Mass* tour in 2002, and always indulged us by using the same two songs to assess the sound system, *I Will Remember* by Toto and *The Hounds Of Winter* by Sting. Over time the songs have become synonymous with being on tour, and every time I hear them I am instantly transported back to setting up my keyboards on a dark wooden stage, a cup of fresh coffee on my riser, musicians and technicians buzzing around me, lights flashing and smoke machines being tested, untangling cables which I was sure were not tangled when I put them away the night before, and preparing my work space for the night ahead.

Every year David would bring more and more elaborate equipment with him, and by 2016 he was recording most of our shows on a multi-track recorder. Each day, after the now obligatory Toto and Sting tracks, he would play back the recording of our previous show through the sound system and fine tune our sound before we had even finished setting up. We had performed together for 22 years but we had never been able to hear what we sounded like from an audience perspective, so it was fascinating to wander into the main hall and listen to him working on our sound. The recordings would also prove to be very useful later in the tour.

On the day of our seventh show I went for a long, scenic walk by the river in the snow-covered Swiss town of Aarau. When I got back to the tour bus I wasn't feeling too well and couldn't get myself warm. I thought I had probably just got a chill, so I climbed into my bunk and slept for a while, and when I woke up I felt a little better. However, that night as we performed our set I started to feel dizzy. As the evening wore on I found it hard to keep standing, and by the end of our set my head was pounding painfully and I could barely concentrate or keep my eyes open. As we came off stage before our encores, I reluctantly told the band that I wouldn't be able to continue and we had to cancel our remaining songs.

I went straight to bed and slept through the night while we travelled to our next show in Aschaffenburg. The following morning I felt worse, so I was checked into a local hotel while the band decided what to do. I was in no fit state to go on stage that evening, so I asked David if it would be possible to load a recording of one of my previous performances into Pro Tools. As our whole show was synchronised to the computer, the performance would be perfectly in time, barring any mistakes I had made during the earlier show. In principle it was possible, so David and Karl spent the afternoon sorting out all of the technical details so they could do the show without me.

That night as I lay in bed in Aschaffenburg, our stage technician Toby took my place on stage and operated the computer. It was the first time I had ever missed a Threshold show, but it wouldn't be the last. It turned out that I had a bad case of the flu and, as a result, I also missed the following night's performance in Essen. Farrah was really worried about me and considered driving over from the UK to take me home. But thankfully I started to feel better and was able to return to the stage, feeling rather weak and shaky, for our last two shows in Zoetermeer and London. Meanwhile, Steve had picked up a nasty infection and also felt pretty rough, so we both finished the tour feeling like the walking dead.

***

In 2016 the publishing company that was responsible for collecting our songwriter royalties went into administration, taking most of our *For The Journey* profits with them. Royalties from songwriting, or publishing as it is more commonly known, had always taken a long time to arrive. A portion of money from the music sales was paid by the record company to a collection agency in Germany, who passed it onto a collection agency in the UK, who in turn passed it on to a publishing company, who finally passed it on to the artists who wrote the songs. Each company would hold on to the money for several months, benefitting from the interest it earned as well as taking a cut. As a result, it could sometimes take up to two years to arrive, with the final amount noticeably smaller than the amount that was originally paid into the system. Presumably it was set up this way to protect songwriters from unscrupulous record companies who didn't want to pay out, but in reality it just meant that a whole lot of other people could take a cut.

We had been with the same publishing company for our whole career, although it had changed names and owners over the years. Every three months we would receive a convoluted statement that was supposed to show how much money we had earned from each song. However, none of the numbers ever made sense, with inconsistent sales data and unspecified deductions. The only consistent thing about them was that the total balance always seemed to be a lot smaller than it ought to be. The arrival of a statement would often be followed by several hours of spreadsheet calculations to try and work out what had gone wrong. We would invariably present our findings to the publishing company and they would make all the right noises and promise to look into it. But none of their investigations ever produced any results, so we would just give up and hope the next statement corrected the errors. But, of course, it never did.

It sounds rather naïve looking back, but we had no experience of other publishing companies, and because the royalties arrived via such a circuitous route it was impossible to know where the money was getting lost. We weren't successful enough to afford lawyers or move to a major publishing house. After the collapse of the company, we moved to our record label's in-house publishing company instead, and when our royalties started to arrive it was a total revelation. The amount was a lot more than we had ever received from our original publishing company. It was only then that we understood how much we must have been losing for all of those years. I can't even tell you how let down and angry we felt. We had trusted those guys for our whole career, and it's possible they had been defrauding us the whole time.

Chapter 15

The Moon Goes Round The World

In July 2016 Threshold signed a new contract with Nuclear Blast and we officially announced that we were writing our eleventh studio album. In contrast to our former publishing company, Nuclear Blast had been a pleasure to work with since we had first signed with them ten years earlier. We had fulfilled our three studio album contract with them, albeit taking a little longer than we thought we would, and along the way they had also reissued our whole back catalogue on CD and vinyl along with a double live album. It had been a fruitful partnership so far and we were very happy for it to continue.

That month we headed over to mainland Europe for two festivals, the excellently named Bang Your Head in Germany and Masters Of Rock in the Czech Republic. The Czech festival was one of the largest events in the country and took place near the Slovakian border in Vizovice, roughly 180 miles east of my old house in Nové Hrady. The stage was huge and my keyboards were set up quite a long way back, so my view was limited and I was a lot less aware of the crowd than usual. It wasn't until afterwards when I saw photographs of the event that I realised just how large it had been, with a sold-out crowd of 25,000 people watching our performance. It was a fantastic homecoming to the country that I had fallen in love with so many years before.

Back in the UK my writing sessions were going well. The first song I finished was called *Stars And Satellites*. The chorus was another of those 'floor of heaven' moments, and for a while I was worried about finishing the rest of the song in case I couldn't make it match up to the chorus. The words were from the perspective of someone watching over you, guiding you and managing your journey, and I thought that the combination of the lyrics, melody and chords felt quite potent. I wanted to go further and deeper than a normal song structure, so I spent a while layering up sound effects and generating a robotic voice using some old speech synthesis software to create an interlude half way through the song. I was pleased with the results, so I followed through the sound effect concepts into my next two songs.

Next up was *The Man Who Saw Through Time*. I had made a lot of progress on the 70000 Tons Of Metal cruise and most of the song was now finished, but once again I wanted to go further by introducing other concepts and elements. I was contemplating how I could musically portray the idea of travelling into the future when I noticed that the song title's initials TMWSTT were also the initials of various days of the week. So, I loaded up the speech synthesis software once more and got it to say the words Thursday, Monday, Wednesday, Saturday, Thursday, Tuesday. I gradually sped up the words until the speech became so fast that it was unintelligible, layered some other sounds around it and eventually I had an introduction to the song which felt like the man in the story was accelerating into the future. At the end of the track I applied the same effect in reverse, slowing down the words to bring the man back to a stop.

I wrote one more song while I was waiting for Karl to present his first demos for the album. I sat at the piano one night and composed a short track called *Swallowed*. It was in a major key and only a couple of minutes long, so I didn't really think about it as a Threshold track at first. It was only later when I started looking at the possibility of the album having a concept running through it that I added the second half, a reprise and conclusion to the slow section from *Stars And Satellites* followed by one of Karl's trademark solos. I also repeated the idea from *The Man Who Saw Through Time* of looping sound effects to create a hypnotic bridge between sections, and now I felt like I had a trilogy of songs that worked together and were starting to tell a story. But before going any further I wanted to know what Karl was working on.

Karl initially presented two demos that would become *Small Dark Lines* and *Snowblind*. I thought they both sounded phenomenal and sat listening to them over and over as I slowly crafted melodies for them. I took a slightly different approach than usual and was careful not to write any lyrics at first, as I just wanted the melodies to be the perfect shape: rising, falling, accelerating and slowing to bring the right amount of tension and release. I later wrote a lot of the lyrics on holiday in Cornwall over the summer. Farrah will readily attest to the fact that I am sometimes not the most sociable companion on holiday. Often we'll go for long walks along the rugged Cornish coastline and

I'll get so lost in my thoughts that I forget to talk to her. It's possible that's one of the reasons she took up photography, so that she would have something to do while I was writing songs. I honestly do mean to be there in the moment with her, but as soon as a phrase or melody gets stuck in my head I often stop noticing what's going on around me.

On one particular walk I was working on *Snowblind*. We had left the holiday cottage to go for a stroll and were just planning to make a quick circuit around the area before dinner. Unfortunately, the heavens opened and we got absolutely soaked. We tried to find a short cut back to the cottage, but we got totally lost and ended up taking a much longer route home, getting more drenched by the minute. Throughout the walk I had the pre-chorus of *Snowblind* looping around in my head, and by the time we got home I had settled on the melody and found just the right lyrics: 'it's not impossible, it's not debatable; sooner or later you'll get lost in a storm'. The words were very much the product of what had just happened to us, but they fitted the story of the song perfectly.

When Karl sent me the music for what would become *The Shire (Part 2)*, I remember sitting in my studio, closing my eyes and pressing play for the first time. As the music reached the one minute mark I started singing along softly, not knowing yet whether I was listening to a gentle chorus or another part of the verse. I found a melody that flowed really well and got a small shiver of anticipation. The music carried on until the two and a half minute mark, at which point it paused briefly. During that split second I remember hoping that the whole band would just crash in at that moment and play a powerful version of the chords I had just sung along to earlier. I thought that would make such a great chorus. To my total delight, that was exactly what Karl had done. I punched the air in excitement. This was going to sound huge!

By now I was starting to develop a concept for the album. The lyrics so far were painting a picture of someone trying to find their place in the world, with the unexpected backdrop of pastoral life in rural England. I wanted the story to have a double meaning, so I thought it would be interesting to turn it into an analogy for how a country evolves to fit in with the nations around it. At the time, the UK had just started the controversial process of leaving the European Union. I thought of it as a divorce between British Prime Minister David Cameron and German Chancellor Angela Merkel: Cameron playing the role of a philanderer who couldn't settle down or commit to the relationship, and Merkel as the woman scorned. I don't know how this could possibly have become an idea for a song, but one day Farrah and I were out walking on Box Hill in Surrey and I started writing along those lines. Farrah took out her camera; it was going to be a long afternoon. The song became *State Of Independence*.

The next demo that Karl sent me was a long one: ten minutes of epic chords and winding progressive passages, melancholic and uplifting, one of his finest pieces of work. I looked through my lyric book to see if I had anything suitable. My unused lines from 2013 about wanting to cry up to the heavens seemed to fit the chorus. And the story of my fateful train journey home from my short-lived job in 2014, slumped down with my head in my hands, worked well for the verse. I wondered if this could be the moment to incorporate all I had been through into a song. I wasn't too sure I wanted to immortalise one of my darkest moments and share it with the world. However, it would work really well for the album's developing storyline, so I decided to go with it. I called the song *Lost In Translation*. Maybe someone would identify with my experience and find comfort in knowing they weren't alone.

* * *

Now that it was becoming evident that we had a concept album on our hands, we decided to take it one step further and make it a double album. Karl and I already had eight songs and we hadn't even received any demos from the others yet, so we were confident we would have more than enough material. I had mapped out the rough storyline and discussed it with the rest of the band. Damian was more focussed on his solo career at the time, so he had decided not to put anything forward. He had just performed at two huge CarFest events in the UK and was getting exposure on BBC Radio 2, so that was understandably his priority. Johanne had a song in mind, but, as it was about a fighter pilot in the war, we couldn't find a way to make it fit into the storyline. We asked if he minded keeping it for a future album and he kindly acquiesced. Pete and Steve were keen to be involved, so we worked out how their potential contributions could fit into the overall concept. They both started work on their compositions and we looked forward to hearing the results.

In October we drove to Baarlo in the Netherlands to headline ProgPower Europe for the fourth time. The atmosphere in the band was uneasy. It felt as though some of the relationships had never fully recovered from the fracas that took place after our show in Bratislava two years earlier. That night in Baarlo we sat down for drinks and tried to plan out some studio dates so that we could start recording our new album. However, Damian seemed unsettled and wouldn't commit to anything. The following week we found out why. He dropped into the studio to see Karl and told him he wanted to leave the band.

Karl called immediately to tell me the news. To be honest it didn't feel like a total surprise, there had been a definite feeling of change in the air for quite some time now. We considered our options and realised straight away that there was only one possible replacement, our former vocalist Glynn Morgan. Since our reunion in 2008 I had worked with him a number of times for League Of Lights and other projects that he had in the pipeline. His voice sounded as good as ever and the idea of him coming back to Threshold was rather compelling. Damian had kindly suggested a few vocalists who he thought would be good replacements for him, but we only had one person on our shortlist.

However, later that month Damian called to say he was having second thoughts. It was all rather unexpected, he had just done some shows supporting former Spandau Ballet singer Tony Hadley, so we thought his solo career was blossoming. But we cautiously welcomed him back and scheduled some dates at the studio to record his vocals. However, at the recording sessions that followed he often seemed distracted. Sometimes he wouldn't feel like singing and other times he didn't show up at all. It seemed as though his heart was somewhere else.

Meanwhile, Karl and I completed a couple more songs for the album. Steve put forward a track that sounded promising: a dark, technical piece that would slot in nicely. Unfortunately, Pete's contribution didn't fare so well. He had written some great songs for the band in the past and his composition *Coda* had become a fan-favourite during our live shows, but his new offering just didn't feel like a Threshold song. Karl and I discussed the problem at length. We felt really uncomfortable but we knew that we would have to turn it down. We had both rejected tracks by each other in the past, but turning down someone else's work felt rather awkward and unkind.

As January came around, we flew to Switzerland to perform at Ice Rock Festival. This rather unique event took place in a huge open barn surrounded by beautiful snowy countryside, with a large hot tub unexpectedly situated in the middle of the crowd. It was incredibly cold on stage which made it quite difficult to perform, and before the show most of us wore gloves until the very last minute. But Damian was going to make the show memorable for a different reason.

As we started *Pilot In The Sky Of Dreams* he made his way through the audience and jumped fully-clothed into the hot tub. He looked iconic as he rose out the water, steam rising all around him in the cold night air as he performed the song and the crowd cheered him on. It was Damian at his finest; Threshold wasn't the headline band that night, but he had produced the moment that most people would be talking about the following morning. He performed the rest of the show dripping wet and must have been absolutely freezing.

However, off stage the atmosphere in the band was even colder. Most of the guys kept to themselves and it was becoming increasingly apparent that nobody wanted to continue with our current line-up. Our temporary formation that had come together ten years earlier for our *Dead Reckoning* shows looked like it was coming to an end, and it would only be a matter of time before something changed. First Pete left and then Damian was gone too.

Over the days and months that followed, there were rumours of conflicting accounts of our line-up change in the press and on social media. I was approached to do a couple of interviews but I turned them down. The whole episode had become very stressful and I was wary of making matters worse. As far as I was concerned the band had naturally reached a point of no return, and the thought of getting embroiled in a public debate over the finer details of our break-up was enough to stop me sleeping at night. We had all been good friends and, above all, I hoped that would continue. But, at that moment in time, the only way for Threshold to move forward was to go our separate ways, and hope that eventually time would honour its promise to heal all wounds.

* * *

Following the demise of his band Mindfeed at the end of the '90s, Glynn Morgan had mostly remained under the radar. After releasing two albums on InsideOut, he recorded a couple of three-track demos for a possible third album, with Judas Priest's Ian Hill assisting on production, but unfortunately communication broke down with the label and he found that his heart was no longer in it. For a while he teamed up with a former bandmate, GZR guitarist Pedro Howse, and over the next couple of years they wrote several songs together, but despite some airplay on national radio the project eventually stalled.

Glynn had briefly reunited with Threshold for the *Paradox* box set in 2008, and, following his guest appearance on the League Of Lights single *Forever*, he went on to write and record songs with Mark Zonder and Shadow Gallery's Gary Wehrkamp. However, nothing was ever released, and he found himself increasingly disappointed that none of his projects had worked out. So, when I called to ask if he would be interested in coming back to Threshold, he was over the moon. He was very positive about our new material, and told us that of all the albums he could have returned to the band for, this was the perfect one. We scheduled some vocal sessions for later that month and he started learning the songs.

Meanwhile, Karl and I had written a couple of tracks as possible replacements for Pete's song in the storyline, and we ended up using both of them. *Subliminal Freeways* was crafted around some of the unused parts from my *Stars And Satellites* writing sessions, and *Superior Machine* was an old-school Threshold song that could have comfortably appeared on one of our early albums. We also wrote a few possible segues to sit between the tracks, including a gentle reprise of *Snowblind* and a dark poem spoken by the speech synthesis software over a backdrop of sinister sound effects. But ultimately there was only space in the running order for one of them, a short piano piece based on a melody from the opening track that would eventually become *The Shire (Part 3)*.

We had decided to call the album *Legends Of The Shires*. Part of the lyrical concept was to tell the story of a nation, but those words didn't sound particularly evocative, so we opted for *Legends Of The Shires* as a more creative way of saying much the same thing. By coincidence, I noticed that all of the song titles began with the letters L, O, T or S – the acronym of *Legends Of The Shires*. I know this doesn't sound like it could possibly be a coincidence, but it honestly was. Early on in the writing I had noticed that most of the song titles began with S or T, and I thought at the time that it was rather odd. But once I had written *Lost In Translation*, there was now an L and the oddness was gone. Sometime later Steve told me he was ready to present his song for the album, so I asked him what it was called. He told me it was *On The Edge*. There was our O. You really couldn't make it up.

Over the following two months we recorded *Legends Of The Shires* at Thin Ice and my home studio. Karl played all of the guitars as he had done for *Dead Reckoning* 11 years earlier. We would leave the decision about a second guitarist for another day. Glynn recorded the vocals over two long weekends at my place. Meanwhile, Karl invited our former bassist Jon Jeary to record some guest vocals on *The Shire (Part 3)*. The two had kept in touch over the years and Jon had followed our progress with interest. Having been Threshold's frontman during the early years as well as singing on *Eat The Unicorn* in 1997, it was great to have him back to make a cameo appearance.

For the cover design we wanted to portray a mysterious world where you could imagine the story slowly unfolding. We reviewed the artists from our previous albums but none of them seemed to be producing the sort of work we were looking for, so we started the rather monotonous task of trawling the internet for artwork once again. Eventually we struck gold with a piece by Russian artist Elena Dudina portraying a lush, intriguing landscape that was half way between fantasy and reality. It was exactly what we were looking for, and it would later go on to be shortlisted in the 'Best Album Cover' category at the Progressive Music Awards.

When the album was finished, we produced an edited version of *Small Dark Lines* and filmed a video for it with a British company called Sitcom Soldiers. They had come up with the concept of people painting lines on their bodies to represent their regrets and then symbolically washing them away. We loved the idea and the video came out really well. One fan flew over especially from Sweden to be involved, and with her striking red hair she became one of the key visual elements of the video. Unfortunately for our actors, the water that was used to wash the paint off was freezing cold, so any expressions of elation on the faces of those involved were closely followed by genuine expressions of shock!

We had originally slated *Small Dark Lines* to be our opening single to precede the release of the album. However, the video was not going to be ready for Nuclear Blast's promotion schedule, so they asked us to choose another song to come out first. We went through every track on the record to try and decide the best option, but in the end there was only one choice. It would be a bold move to release a ten-minute song, but it would be the perfect statement to announce our return. Our first single would be *Lost In Translation*.

Legends Of The Shires was released on 8th September 2017 and its success exceeded all of our expectations. We achieved our highest ever position in the German chart at number 13, with Switzerland close behind at number 14. All my life I had dreamed of getting in the Top 40, and now we were in the Top 20 in two countries. It was an amazing feeling. We had stuck at it through thick and thin and we were still going strong. We even broke into the UK Top 100, something we thought we would never do. The album was also getting great reviews, and although some people understandably missed the voice that had fronted the band for the last ten years, most were hugely receptive towards Glynn and hailed it as a triumphant return.

The following month we started rehearsing for our first Threshold shows with Glynn for more than two decades, for a run of dates that would take us to 18 countries over the next couple of years. We took the decision to remain as a five-piece. Our line-up felt stable and positive again, so we weren't in a rush to upset the balance by introducing someone else to the fold. So, instead of having a dedicated second guitarist, it was decided that Glynn would play some extra guitar parts on stage where they were most needed. He was more than up to the job, having been both singer and guitarist in his own band Mindfeed. In fact, he once told us that when he had first started out in music all he wanted to do was play guitar.

There was always something comfortable and reassuring about turning up for rehearsals: seeing old friends again after a long time apart, setting up equipment that had been hibernating in its black, dusty flight cases, and hearing the familiar strains of drums being set up, guitars being tuned and microphones being tested. Gone were the days of practising through loud sound systems in cold, damp halls. Nowadays we rehearsed in the comfort of the studio, with everyone hearing each other through in-ear monitors. Our guitar amplifiers had long since been replaced by modelling software, so the only actual sound in the studio was from our unamplified voices and the onslaught of drums coming from the live room.

Our tour was booked to start on 28th November, but before that we had three pre-shows in Greece, Wales and England. At our show in Athens we were supported by local band The Silent Wedding from our previous tour. Returning to the stage with Glynn was like going back in time, especially when we performed *Sunseeker* and *Innocent* from our first album with him. It was as if no time had passed at all, and he sounded even better than he had in 1995. Half way through the set when he sang *Mission Profile* there were moments when he sounded so similar to Mac that it was quite eerie. But it was the new material where he shone the brightest, and closing our set with *Lost In Translation* and *Small Dark Lines* made for a powerful end to a very successful first show together. We returned to the UK to headline the second stage at HRH Prog followed by a club show in Manchester. Next up was our European tour and we couldn't wait to get going.

On the day of my 50th birthday, I boarded a nightliner outside Thin Ice Studios in Surrey with Karl, Glynn, Johanne and Steve and we travelled off towards mainland Europe for the tour. The thought of turning 50 had always loomed like an unpleasant milestone, so spending it on a tour bus heading off to do something that I loved was the perfect antidote. I was sorry not to spend the whole day with Farrah, but being on tour softened the blow of no longer being in my forties. I certainly didn't feel that old, and, in many ways, I now felt more comfortable in myself than I ever had. For years I had been constantly striving to get somewhere, to climb that elusive ladder and reach the top. The pressure had often felt unbearable and every setback had always hit me hard. But now I just felt blessed to be there, touring an album that I was proud of with a group of good friends. For the first time since I could remember, I felt totally relaxed on tour and I savoured every moment.

Our support bands for the trek were Damnation Angels, who had opened for us the previous year, and Dutch progressive rockers Day Six. They had previously supported us during one of our long weekenders in 2011, so it was nice to give them the opportunity to do a whole tour. We kept our set fairly consistent for the shows, opening with *Slipstream* before launching into half a dozen *Legends* songs interspersed with older fan favourites. I was particularly happy to be on stage again in Aschaffenburg and Essen, having missed both venues the previous year with flu. We finished the tour with a triumphant return to the O2 Islington Academy in London. Our first tour as a five-piece had been a success; and we had only just begun.

Chapter 16

Greater Stories Still

2018 GOT OFF TO A PERFECT START. Threshold had been invited to return to the glorious 70000 Tons Of Metal festival. This time the cruise liner would be sailing from Florida to the Turks & Caicos Islands for a five-day trip of winter sunshine accompanied by the sound of bands such as Exodus, Meshuggah and Sepultura. We flew into Miami International Airport and were greeted by a wonderful wall of humid holiday heat as we stepped off the plane and acclimatised ourselves to the early evening light. Eventually we found a taxi driver who was willing to drive us and our oversized luggage 30 miles north up the I-95 to Fort Lauderdale where we would spend the night before boarding the ship the following morning.

This time we spent a lot more time together than on our previous cruise, savouring the delights of the Deck 11 food hall together and enjoying the performances of the other bands. Glynn was invited to be a guest judge for the cruise's belly flop contest, an event which had to be seen to be believed. Our two shows went down well with the broad-minded audience, who seemed just as happy to see us as they were to watch some of the heavier death metal acts on board. I managed to get a bit more writing done on the secluded side-deck where I had written *The Man Who Saw Through Time*, but mostly I just relaxed, sunbathed and soaked in the whole experience.

Meanwhile, following the completion of *Legends Of The Shires*, Farrah and I had started writing more League Of Lights songs again. Our new material was less guitar-focussed than before, and saw us leaning more towards our original roots as a pop-rock duo. Over the following year we would continue writing until our second album was finally ready to record. I had also co-written a song with Power Quest founder Steve Williams. It would become the title track of their comeback album *The Sixth Dimension* and featured guest vocals by former Nightwish singer Anette Olzon. I had never co-written with other bands before, apart from occasionally helping out during vocal sessions, and I found it really enjoyable. Steve and I had become good friends over the years, and it was always a pleasure to work with him.

Threshold's next shows saw the band flying back to the United States for the Rites Of Spring Festival, or RoSfest as it was more commonly known. The festival took place in Pennsylvania and had been running since 2004, welcoming familiar names such as our fellow countrymen Jadis, Arena and Pendragon over the years. Up until now our only shows on US soil had been our two visits to ProgPower USA in Atlanta, so it felt good to add another American venue to our list. We had previously tried to tour the US supporting Edguy in 2007, but unfortunately the finances had not worked out, so our plans had fallen through, and since then the opportunity had not returned.

We asked our booking agent to see if he could find us any other shows while we were over for RoSfest, and he came back with two nights in Canada. We had never played there before so we were delighted. We only had a small following there as far as we were aware, so the shows would not have been viable if we had flown over especially for them. But as we were going to be on the continent already for RoSfest, they had now become possible.

The trip involved a lot of time in the air, with six flights in seven days, so it was exhausting but fun. With Johanne's aversion to flying, it wasn't the best itinerary for him, but Glynn thoughtfully kept him amused by winding him up mercilessly every time there was turbulence or any sort of problem with the aircraft. The shows in Canada were small but the audiences were very welcoming, especially at the notorious Foufounes Électriques club in Montreal. The venue had previously hosted bands such as Nirvana, Green Day and Queens Of The Stone Age, and although we only had a small crowd, they made us feel like we were The Beatles. Many of them had been waiting to see us for 25 years and never thought they would get the chance, so they gave us a heroes' welcome and made us feel like we were playing to a capacity crowd.

The following day we took two flights to reach Baltimore and were driven to Gettysburg, where we had a couple of days to explore the area before our performance at RoSfest on Saturday night. It was a great place to visit if you were interested in the US Civil War, as it was the location of the Battle of Gettysburg and the Gettysburg Address by former President Abraham Lincoln. There seemed to be a constant flow of people walking around dressed up in period costumes, and every other shop sold Civil War memorabilia. Glynn was fascinated and booked onto a guided tour immediately.

Farrah had come along for the trip and we spent much of our time walking around the historic battlefield or searching for vegetables. The food available in American restaurants and diners was rather different to the food we prepared at home, and finding somewhere that offered a healthy selection of steamed vegetables to accompany our meal proved surprisingly difficult. We eventually found a diner near the venue that had broccoli on the menu. Farrah immediately ordered a portion and was slightly taken aback to discover it was served in sweetened condensed milk. The following night we had an excellent show, and after two more flights we were back in London, jetlagged and aching but very satisfied with our week in North America.

In July we headed back to Europe for another long weekender. Our first destination was Loreley where we had been invited back to the Night Of The Prog festival. I don't recall any lilting flute solos accompanying our arrival this time, but it was a welcome return to one of our favourite venues.

The following day we headed north for a club show at the Hypothalamus in Rheine, which after four visits in four years was starting to feel like a second home. The night got off to an awful start though. It had been agreed that the stage curtains would be kept closed until our intro music started, and then slowly opened as the music played. It turned out to be a terrible idea. One of the curtains got stuck, so all the audience could see was some furiously flapping fabric as the local crew tried desperately to free it. As our intro reached its climax and the band was about to start, we had to make a last-second decision to stop until the crew could fix the problem. We left the stage and restarted the show a few minutes later, this time with the curtains fully open. It was all rather embarrassing, but the audience were enjoying themselves and we had a good laugh with them.

In August, Farrah and I took a very welcome holiday in Switzerland. I had visited the country many times over the years with Threshold, but never long enough to explore or really get to know the place. We stayed in Saas Fee, a popular ski resort in the winter but also stunning in the summer. We enjoyed long walks on the surrounding mountains, overawed by the breath-taking scenery with its snow-covered peaks, rolling forests and occasional low clouds that swirled majestically through the village. During most of our walks I remembered to talk to Farrah, but I must confess the scenery was so inspiring that I couldn't help composing one song along the way!

My writing process hasn't changed much over the years. I normally start with a simple melody or hook, and then slowly build up the chords, rhythms and other parts until I have a full composition going around my head. Once they've looped around enough times I usually remember them for years. Occasionally I prefer to sit at a piano if I am working on more complex chord sequences such as the opening verses of *Pilot In The Sky Of Dreams* or *The Man Who Saw Through Time*, as the richness of the piano often provides inspiration all of its own. But, for the most part, I'm happy working in my head, slowly honing my ideas until they are ready to record. The only exception is writing lyrics, which for some reason don't stay in my memory in the same way, so I usually have to write those down.

A week after we returned from Switzerland, I was back in Europe on the other side of the Swiss border in Italy. Threshold had two more shows, starting with the 2Days Prog+1 Festival in Veruno followed by Rock On Fest in the Hungarian capital of Budapest. Both events took place outdoors under perfect blue summer skies, so our trip felt more like a holiday than a working weekend. It was the last time we would be playing some of our older tracks for a while, as the following month we would be doing something a little different.

* * *

It was late in the afternoon when the sleek, black nightliner slowed gracefully to a halt below the trees outside Thin Ice. Autumn was setting in and there was a slight chill in the air. It was a scene we had witnessed many times before, but the passing years had done nothing to dampen our sense of anticipation and excitement as we prepared to board the bus once more.

Following the popularity of our 2016 tour where we had performed the whole of *For The Journey* from start to finish, we had decided to repeat the idea for *Legends Of The Shires*. Many of our fans had been urging us to do it, and, because it was a concept album, it felt even better suited to touring this way than our previous album. So, we loaded up the nightliner and started our familiar journey to mainland Europe once more.

It was the perfect tour. Throughout my 25 years of touring with the band, promoting 11 studio albums alongside 12 different musicians, I had experienced a lot of highs and lows, amazing successes and monumental mistakes. But October 2018 was the moment where it all came together. No dramas, no disasters, just five guys and countless fans converging with one common purpose – to celebrate and enjoy our music together.

We released another Direct-to-Fan album *Two-Zero-One-Seven* to coincide with the start of the tour. It was a live album recorded over several nights during the previous year. David had recorded quite a few shows during the tour, and while most of the album was taken from one of the German shows, it was useful to be able to drop in the occasional moment from another night if there were any problems. With the recent resurgence in the popularity of vinyl we decided to make *Two-Zero-One-Seven* available on both CD and LP, something we never thought would be possible for a Direct-to-Fan release. We opted not to produce a further live album from our 2018 tour, partly because it was so soon after *Two-Zero-One-Seven* and partly because it would have sounded so similar to the studio album. But I suspect David kept a few live recordings on a hard disk somewhere, so it's possible those could come out one day.

I had decided to take a GoPro camera with me and film a tour diary as a personal memento. I had owned the camera for a few years now and often used it to film holidays with Farrah, but I had never taken it on tour before. However, this time I wanted to document our whole trip. After the tour I edited the footage down to a five-minute video, cut to the soundtrack of *The Hounds Of Winter* by Sting. The music fitted the film beautifully, a song about growing old and looking back nostalgically at memories of the past. A while later we would end up releasing a modified version of the film as an official tour diary, with the soundtrack changed to one of Threshold's songs to avoid any copyright issues. But, whichever version I watch, it's become a cherished memory of a wonderful tour.

＊＊＊

By the beginning of 2019, Farrah and I had finished recording our second League Of Lights album, opting to record as a duo as we thought it suited our new sound better. By April I had finished the mixes but I wasn't totally happy with them. By coincidence, that month I was offered the opportunity to spend a week in a studio with Manny Marroquin. Manny is one of the top mixers in the world, a winner of ten Grammy awards who has worked with everyone from Bruno Mars to Linkin Park, so the thought of learning from him was too good to turn down. Unfortunately, it would mean delaying our album a little longer, but if I could learn how to sprinkle some Manny Marroquin gold dust on our music, it would be worth the wait.

Meanwhile, Threshold performed a couple of shows in the UK before flying out for some concerts in Estonia, Finland and Norway. These started with a small club show in the picturesque Estonian capital of Tallinn before we headed north the following morning for a two-hour ferry crossing to Helsinki. Despite reaching the Top 40 in Finland with *For The Journey*, we had never performed in the country before, so we were curious to see what sort of reception we would get. What greeted us was far beyond our expectations. It turned out there had been a lot of excitement and anticipation for our first concert there, and it was one of the best club shows we have ever performed.

The next day we flew to Norway, another country we had never visited before. We had been booked to perform for two consecutive nights at a rock festival just outside Oslo, with a mixed set list for the first night followed by a full performance of *Legends Of The Shires* for the second one. The accommodation was rather special, with the whole band sharing a log cabin in the woods overlooking the sea. It was a beautiful place and we found ourselves falling in love with yet another country. Our new album was opening up more territories for us than ever before.

With the second League Of Lights album almost finished, Farrah and I commissioned Polish company Grupa 13 to produce a video for our opening single *Kings And Queens*. I had originally contacted them in 2017 about the possibility of making a video for Threshold's *Small Dark Lines*. They had pitched a great idea, but it had been too elaborate for our budget, so we had opted for a local British company instead. Grupa 13 developed a great storyboard for *Kings And Queens*, so we hired some outfits from the National Theatre in London and organised our trip. Unfortunately, the owner of the venue they had hired received a better offer at the last minute and cancelled our booking, so there were a few anxious moments while another venue was sourced and the storyboard was modified. We landed on our feet though, as the replacement venue was simply stunning: an old, dilapidated palace a few miles from the Czech border set in some beautiful grounds. The resulting video was beautiful and really brought the song to life.

A month later I found myself in a studio in the idyllic south of France with the legendary Manny Marroquin. The week that followed would be one of the most rewarding and fulfilling moments of my career. Manny was insanely talented, knowledgeable and helpful. Sometimes when people reach the top of their profession they can become unapproachable or condescending, but Manny was the complete opposite. Over the seven days that followed I learned so much about how to craft a mix, looking at both the technical aspects and their emotional impact in ways I had never thought of before. What he taught me would end up affecting my whole approach to putting together a song. I spent the two weeks that followed updating the League Of Lights mixes, applying some of the lessons I had learned in France. As a result, the mixes sounded a lot better than they had before.

Threshold travelled back across the Atlantic the following month for the third time in two years, with two more shows in Canada and a return to ProgPower USA in Atlanta. This was our third visit to the festival, each time with a different vocalist. I spent much of my time glued to the computer promoting the release of *Kings And Queens*, which came out the day before our show. The song was also featured on the ProgPower USA CD that was given out to attendees of the festival, so there was a good buzz around the release. As a result, I didn't find much time to go outside, apart from catching a bit of much appreciated sunshine beside the hotel pool and going out for lunch with Glynn for an unfeasibly large sandwich. The whole band also enjoyed a very fine meal together with some of the festival's sponsors whose donations help bring so many artists to the event in return for VIP access to the venue and backstage areas.

The launch of *Kings And Queens* went well, with the video soon overtaking *Forever* for our highest number of plays. The numbers were nowhere near Threshold's level, but for a self-release it seemed like a good start. Our album *In The In Between* followed at the end of the month. It was largely overlooked by the major music press, but earned some positive reviews in some of the more niche outlets. We had put most of our focus on finishing the album and a lot less on promoting it. I was so used to Nuclear Blast taking care of all the details for Threshold that I hadn't given much thought to employing anyone to get the record out to a wider audience. As good as it felt to have total control over everything there was no substitute for having a good team of experts around you.

We had also not planned any live shows. The album was too far removed from the progressive metal world that I had been a part of for so long, so we didn't really have a starting point for getting support slots or festival appearances. We did take part in one show, although not performing our own material, when we appeared as special guests at a Power Quest concert in London to celebrate the anniversary of their album *Neverworld*. The show also commemorated the life of their late bassist Paul Finnie, who had sadly passed away earlier that year. It was a special evening and we joined the band on stage to perform a couple of their songs. But presenting our own music live was another detail that we had largely overlooked.

In October Threshold travelled back to Europe for our final shows of the year. We flew to France for Ready For Prog festival, coincidentally sharing the bill with our 1999 tour supports Pain Of Salvation and Eldritch, before driving to Spain for shows in Madrid and Barcelona. As we arrived at the venue in Barcelona everything looked eerily familiar. We started loading our gear out of the van and into the small, dimly lit venue. It slowly dawned on Karl, Johanne and me that this was the same club that we had played at on that fateful night in 1997, when Damian had thrown a monitor off the stage and walked out half way through the show. The venue's name had changed, but it was definitely the same place. Back then the local promoter had told us we would never play in the city again. It had only taken us 22 years to prove him wrong.

Farrah and I ended the year with a holiday in New Zealand, a country we had wanted to visit for a long time. After a couple of days recovering from the long journey, we made the most of our time there, exploring as much of the South Island as possible. It was absolutely idyllic – sailing on Milford Sound, hiking around Mount Cook, whale watching in Kaikoura, taking a helicopter ride up to Franz Josef Glacier and swimming with wild dolphins in the open sea – it was the perfect way to unwind and close out a busy year. 2019 had been very much dominated by international travel, jetting off to different countries almost every month. I had flown around the world, visited so many beautiful places I had never seen before, and experienced so many new things.

Nobody knew how abruptly all of that was about to come to a halt.

Chapter 17

Stopped By Unrelenting Forces

IN JANUARY 2020, TWO CASES OF a virus called Covid-19 were reported in the UK. The global pandemic that followed would go on to profoundly affect the lives of countless people around the world. However, in those early moments we were totally unaware of what was to come and were mostly concerned about how it would affect our touring plans. By March, several countries across Europe had started to close their borders, so we had to postpone our upcoming Threshold shows until the end of the summer. A few weeks later we also had to announce the cancellation of our first ever Australian tour. It was hugely disappointing, but clearly the virus wasn't going away any time soon.

Our plans for League Of Lights were affected too. We had hired a PR company to promote our new single *On A Night Like This*, but our flagship interviews on BBC Radio and London Live TV both had to be cancelled as nobody was allowed to visit the studios. All live shows were also off the table, including our plans for a showcase in London and a performance at Winter's End Festival. We had prepared a great set for the festival, including a guest appearance from Glynn to perform duets of *Forever* and Threshold's *State Of Independence*. But as one door closed another one opened, and a few months later we would unexpectedly find ourselves on the bill for one of the only European festivals to go ahead in 2020.

At the end of March we released an EP of extended League Of Lights mixes, appropriately called *Extended Light*. Growing up in the 1980s I had fallen in love with 12" singles that featured longer mixes of my favourite songs. So often they would transcend the original versions by allowing the music to breathe, exploring elements of the production more deeply or introducing new ideas to carry the songs in a different direction. The team at the ZTT record label were the kings of the 12" remix, and I still love listening to their work for bands such as Frankie Goes To Hollywood and Propaganda. So, in the spirit of the format, I produced extended remixes of three songs from our album *In The In Between*, letting the music unfold and expand in ways that weren't possible on the shorter versions of the songs. I was aware that it was always going to be a niche release, but hopefully it would resonate with others like me who loved the 12" concept.

With the whole country going into lockdown to try and reduce the spread of the virus, and all avenues to promote *In The In Between* seemingly closed off, we decided to make the best of the situation by starting another League Of Lights album. It would be the perfect project to work on together while we weren't allowed to go anywhere. We already had two songs on the way, so those became our starting point.

I had written the first one the previous year and it had come at a rather inopportune time. We had got up early to drive to Cornwall and we were just packing the last few things into the car. We wanted to get away as early as possible to beat the traffic. However, I had woken up with some new words and music in my head and they wouldn't go away, so I found myself totally distracted from the job at hand. In the end I rushed to the piano to record a quick demo in the hope of putting the song out of my mind and concentrating on our holiday. However, by the time we went for our first walk along the coast the following morning, the song was almost complete. It was called *Twenty Twenty One* and it alluded to how much life would change between 2020 and 2021, a concept that would resonate strongly the following year.

The other song we had on the way was called *Modern Living*. It was the first track I had written after my week in the studio with Manny Marroquin, one that I had started as a production exercise to try out some of the principles I had learned from him in France. With a more focussed pallet of sounds than our previous album and plenty of space for Farrah's vocals, it would also help to define how our new album would sound.

At the same time, we decided to make a short documentary about one of our older songs. Farrah had written the lyrics for *Scarlet Thread* after discovering some family history. It turned out she shared a birthday with her Great Great Grandmother Laura, born 99 years before her. Laura was an Austrian Jew who was murdered along with her husband in a Nazi death camp. Farrah's Grandmother had been saved by being sent by train from Prague to the UK on the Kindertransport set up by Sir Nicholas Winton just before World War 2 broke out in 1939. Farrah felt a strong connection to Laura and we produced a short film to tell the story. We had originally planned to travel to Europe and work with a film director there, but because of the lockdown restrictions this became impossible, so we produced it at home instead.

In the absence of any live shows, festival organisers started setting up virtual online events where musicians would film themselves performing at home. The quality of the results varied wildly from one act to the next, with some artists producing highly polished professional videos while others sat in front of a phone camera with an acoustic guitar. Throughout the course of the year, Farrah and I performed at three of these online events, and our living room temporarily became our stage.

Our living room is rather small, so to make enough space to film our performances we had to remove half of the sofa and a coffee table. That left us with a background that was far from aesthetically pleasing, a plain white wall with an unattractive radiator spanning its whole length. So we decided to go the Hollywood route, and we bought a large green screen to cover the wall. This meant we would be able to superimpose whatever backgrounds or videos we wanted onto the screen during post-production. With a combination of our video for *Kings And Queens* and a few other clips, the results turned out well and we really enjoyed putting them together.

By the time we filmed our performance for our third virtual show, a charity event called Unlock Festival to raise money for The Prince's Trust, our results were looking quite professional. In fact, it turned out we had gone a bit too far, as we were subsequently asked if we could remove the videos and just show the room instead to fit in better with the other performers. This was of course impossible, as removing the videos would just show us standing in front of a green background. So, to solve the problem, we downloaded a picture of a moody looking living room with black walls and black fireplace, and superimposed that as our background instead. It looked good and satisfied everyone apart from Farrah's Mum, who was mortified that her friends would think her daughter lived in a house with black walls!

Throughout the spring and summer we settled into a daily routine of writing, recording and taking walks by the River Thames where we would discuss our progress. Every three or four weeks we had another song recorded and mixed, and by the middle of summer our third League Of Lights album was almost complete. By taking the dark pop of *Modern Living* and the rock-tinged *Twenty Twenty One* as the parameters for our sound, the result was more focussed and concise than *In The In Between*. It also helped that our new album had taken just six months to make, compared to our previous effort which had been produced over many years and sounded more like an anthology as a result.

We were due to drive to Cornwall for a holiday on 14th August, and as the day rapidly approached we realised that we might just have our album finished before we left. It was a tight deadline, but on 13th August I mixed our final track *Echoes Of A Dream*, featuring elements of every song on the record woven through it. Of all the compositions on the album, this one took the longest to complete. With some final tweaks I had also contrived for the album to have a length of 20 minutes and 21 seconds on each side of vinyl, a totally unnecessary but nonetheless satisfying detail, given that the album would be released in 2021 and contained a song of the same name. As we drove down to Cornwall the following day, we listened to our finished album in the car for the first time, rocking in our seats and smiling all the way there.

Meanwhile, Karl had started writing some new Threshold music, and by the time the League Of Lights album was complete he had sent me three new demos. As always, they sounded powerful, complex and totally compelling. I had told Farrah that I was planning to take some time off before getting started on another album, but I took Karl's demos to Cornwall anyway so that I could get to know them. The following morning Farrah woke up to find me sitting on the sofa, coffee and pen in hand, where I had been fully immersed in writing lyrics for the past two hours. She looked at me with a raised eyebrow. "What happened to taking some time off?" she asked. "I had a good night's sleep," I replied. "I'm ready now." Farrah rolled her eyes; it was going to be another quiet holiday!

* * *

As Covid-19 continued to spread across the globe, Threshold's European shows, which had been postponed from April to September, had all now been cancelled apart from Artrock Festival in Germany. The festival's organiser, Uwe Treitinger, was deeply passionate about the event and was determined for it to go ahead, even if it meant having to settle for a much smaller, socially distanced audience. However, one of our band members was anxious about the thought of travelling through crowded airports, potentially catching the virus and passing it onto vulnerable relatives, so we withdrew from the festival along with many other bands that had similar concerns.

With Uwe's roster shrinking by the day, I contacted him to ask if he would like League Of Lights to appear instead. If we had to categorise our album *In The In Between*, we would have called it art rock, so appearing at a festival called Artrock seemed like a good fit. It turned out that Uwe had been impressed by our video for *Kings And Queens*, so he decided to add us to the bill. Now all we needed was a live band!

We had already chosen a drummer, namely Threshold's live sound engineer David Sievers. Over the years we had become close friends, and it had become a regular part of our Threshold touring routine to seek out the best local café each morning to catch up over a latte or two. David had started out as a drummer, and over one of our coffees we had discussed the possibility of him playing with League Of Lights at some point in the future. It would be difficult logistically as he lived in Switzerland, but we all hoped we could make it happen.

We had originally lined up a local bassist and guitarist to join us for the cancelled Winter's End Festival, but they were both reluctant to travel because of the virus, so we had to look elsewhere. The other half of Threshold's 'dream team' road crew was Toby Schwietering. He was also an accomplished bassist who had previously worked in Nashville performing in a country band. The thought of having our dream team on stage with us was too good an opportunity to miss, so I got in touch and he accepted on the spot. For guitar we approached Ruud Jolie who had played on our debut album. He also accepted and we now had an incredible line-up for our League Of Lights live band.

We arranged to convene in Germany a couple of days before the festival to rehearse together. With travel restrictions becoming tighter across Europe by the day, we had no certainty at all that we would all get to the rehearsals, let alone perform at the festival. Shortly before Farrah and I were due to drive to Germany in the splitter van that would become our tour vehicle, all road travel through France was banned so it became impossible to get there. We hastily cancelled our cross-channel ferry and van bookings, replacing them with flight tickets and a rental van for collection in Germany instead. Meanwhile, large regions of Switzerland and the Netherlands had travel bans imposed on them too, but by some miracle they weren't the regions where David and Ruud lived. So, against all the odds, we finally found ourselves in a rehearsal room in Germany arranged by Toby.

Our new band hit it off straight away. As David obviously couldn't be our sound engineer as well as our drummer, he had brought along a Swiss engineer called Asi Furrer, and over the course of the next two days the six of us rehearsed and fine-tuned our sound until it was time to head to the festival. The live band line-up really brought our songs to life, and it was a very enjoyable couple of days. For some reason there were some life-sized cardboard replicas of Mr Bean and Princess Leia at the rehearsal room, and at one point we heard a loud scream of horror when Farrah went to the restroom and discovered Mr Bean was in the cubicle with her! The cardboard Princess Leia had also found her way into the men's restroom but none of the guys seemed to mind.

As we prepared to drive to Reichenbach for the festival, Toby discovered that his daughter had been sent home from school to self-isolate. For a heart-stopping moment we thought Toby would have to stay at home too, but thankfully the Covid-19 rules still allowed him to leave the house. Several hours and one speeding ticket later, we finally arrived in Reichenbach, exhausted and apprehensive, with no real certainty that the festival would actually be going ahead. The roster of bands was very different to the line-up that had originally been announced, with many bands pulling out during the weeks leading up to the event. We were scheduled to appear between the Polish progressive rock band Retrospective and English rhythm and blues legends The Animals, best known for their 1964 chart topper *The House Of The Rising Sun*. It was a very eclectic bill.

At 8pm on Friday 18th September, the house lights in the Neuberinhaus dimmed and we took to the stage for our first League Of Lights show for eight years. It was actually happening. The band locked together beautifully as we ran through a selection of songs from our first two albums, along with a cover of Farrah's favourite Threshold song *Avalon*. We closed the show with our 2012 single *Forever*, with Farrah covering all of the vocal parts in the absence of Glynn Morgan, who had guested on the original recording. The audience gave us a rousing reception, and although it was strange playing to a socially-distanced crowd, we got used to it very quickly and it ended up feeling just like a normal show. I loved every moment and it felt really special to be performing our songs with such good friends and musicians.

As soon as we arrived back in the UK, we started preparing for the release of our next League Of Lights single. We had been in touch with the organisers of the London New Year's Eve fireworks, and it looked like there could be a small possibility that the closing lines of our new song *Twenty Twenty One* would be used as part of the soundtrack. It was a massive opportunity, so we chose this as the first single from our new album and prepared to release it in December. Travel restrictions had now stopped most of Europe in its tracks, but Sweden was still open, so we arranged to film a video with a company based in Gothenburg called Revolver, best known for their work with Within Temptation, In Flames and Europe.

A few days before our flight we were crestfallen to discover that the London fireworks had been cancelled to stop crowds gathering in London and spreading the virus. However, we decided to proceed with the single anyway, and over the next few days we enjoyed a pleasant stay in Gothenburg, slightly unnerved by seeing so many people not wearing face masks in stark contrast to what was happening in the UK. A few weeks later Sweden closed its borders too, so we felt very grateful to have been able to film a video at all.

It later turned out that a cut-down version of the London fireworks went ahead after all, but it was themed as a tribute to the UK's National Health Service and our song wasn't included. On New Year's Eve we sat down in our living room to watch the whole display, secretly holding onto a glimmer of hope that our song might burst forth from our television at any moment. However, it was not to be, and as the final firework faded into the first night sky of 2021, we said a slightly wistful "Happy New Year" to each other and went to bed feeling rather deflated.

2020 had been a strange, unpredictable year. I know that many people struggled during lockdown, and I count myself fortunate that I enjoyed staying at home. It probably helped that I am naturally quite introvert, but I was quite content to hibernate from the outside world for a while, spend more time with Farrah and make more music. Our year had been filled with both excitement and disappointment, but, despite those last few moments, we knew we had enjoyed a pretty good 12 months.

Chapter 18

Don't Know What The Future Brings

As 2021 rolled into view, progress on our twelfth Threshold album was going well. I had finished working on Karl's three demos and these were now called *Hall Of Echoes*, *Complex* and *Defence Condition*. At just under 11 minutes, *Defence Condition* was our longest composition together and took the most time to finish. The song's coda reminded me of the end of *Voyager II*, but while Karl and Jon had opted not to add lyrics to that part of the song, I wanted to introduce some words to the end of *Defence Condition* to complement the heavy, brooding music. It would be the darkest section on the album, and I originally thought it would sit half way through the running order. However, we eventually chose it as the closing track as it provided the perfect crescendo to the record, albeit a rather dark and sinister one.

While Johanne and Steve opted not to put anything forward for the album, Glynn had been busy writing and presented three songs in the form of *Run*, *King Of Nothing* and *Let It Burn*. This would be the first new material he had written for Threshold since 1994, so Karl and I were curious to hear what he would bring. Glynn had always been a strong songwriter and *Innocent* remains one of the best songs in our catalogue. His new demos sounded excellent, and we agreed to record all of them, with *Let It Burn* offering some compelling new textures to our sound and *King Of Nothing* standing out as a strong contender for a possible single.

I had also put forward four songs of my own. For *Silenced* and *Haunted* I imagined it was 20 years ago and I was writing more songs for *Hypothetical*, *Critical Mass* or *Subsurface*. Those were the albums where I felt I had really found my feet writing for Threshold, having relied more heavily on composing ballads up until that point. It was then that I had discovered my own voice as a progressive metal songwriter, Mac had found his place in our sound and Thomas Ewerhard had designed some of our best covers. It was a wonderful era and it felt magical to imagine that I was back there once again. In a rush of nostalgia I wove the titles of our two old sound check songs *I Will Remember* and *The Hounds Of Winter* into the words of *Haunted*, songs that I will always associate with being on tour with the band.

The Domino Effect gave me a chance to spread my wings and write another long song. It always feels like there is more room to breathe and explore when you're writing a song that clocks in around the ten-minute mark, coming up with ideas and concepts that wouldn't usually work in a shorter piece. Unlike my previous long compositions, I wrote *The Domino Effect* to be more of a rhapsody comprising three distinct parts woven together before resolving back to one final chorus, and at one point the song was going to be called *The Domino Effect (Parts 1-3)*. The second part of the song gave me the opportunity to sit at the piano and compose some more intricate, gentle chord sequences, something that I have always loved to do, to provide some contrast to the heaviness of the album around it.

Lost Along The Way consisted of music that I had composed on holiday in 2018 surrounded by the Swiss mountains in Saas Fee, lyrics I had written in a Munich park a couple of months later during the Threshold tour, and a chord progression that I had first recorded as a small boy growing up in the small, picturesque village of Newton Ferrers, using two portable cassette recorders with the drum parts played on cardboard boxes. I had originally thought of *Lost Along The Way* as a title track for a possible solo album. I imagined that it would mostly consist of various songs that actually had got lost along the way, featuring new recordings of unreleased tracks that I had written over the years for various projects. However, after I played the demo to Karl he was keen for us to record it, so it became a Threshold song instead.

By now we had a pretty good feel for how our album was going to sound. If *Legends* had a darker, moodier older brother, this would be it. Earlier in the writing process we had considered calling the album *The Fall Of The Shires* and making it a sequel to our *Legends* story. Back in 2018 I had drafted a storyline and opening song for a possible sequel, and most of our new compositions more or less fitted the story. So, I started focussing more closely on the concept, completing the opening song *The Fall (Part 1)* and writing a companion track *The Fall (Part 2)* to close the album, using elements from *Legends* to connect the two records together. However, although the idea seemed popular at first, opinions changed and we eventually opted to make a shorter, non-conceptual album instead. The sequel idea was therefore dropped, and the new songs were left on the cutting room floor.

Although I was initially disappointed, I knew that we had a strong album regardless of whether it was a sequel or not. It bore a darker narrative than *Legends Of the Shires* and was more of a collection of cautionary tales than a concept album. There was a political commentary woven through it that reminded me a little of *Subsurface*, covering topics such as propaganda, censorship and corruption. But there was also a positive message of staying true to yourself, trusting your heart and not being swept away by the events going on around you.

Early in 2021 my Dad's health took a turn for the worse, and over the course of the year I ended up moving in with him for long periods of time to look after him. Sadly, my parents had separated several years earlier and had eventually got divorced. Our old family home Steps Cottage had been sold to be knocked down and replaced with a more modern property. I felt like a sailor who had woken up one morning to find the ship's anchor was missing. Growing up with two parents in a family home was something I had always taken for granted. There was an unspoken security in knowing there was always a home base, a safe harbour to return to whenever you needed one. It took me a long time to come to terms with our family breaking up. Dad had eventually moved to Hampshire, still by the sea but a lot closer to me and Farrah. He had always been fiercely independent but now he needed some extra help, so, if there was a silver lining, it was the opportunity to spend more time with him.

Now 90 years old, Dad's memory was not what it once had been, but he still enjoyed recounting tales of his younger years. For a while his favourite story was of a 70-mile trek he had taken through British Columbia with three friends in 1957. The 11-day expedition had taken them from the treacherous rapids of the Stein River to the snow-covered summit of Gott Mountain, crashing their home-made raft and losing most of their supplies along the way. It was a memorable trip and Dad recounted the story many times, but I never tired of hearing it. He had also documented the whole adventure along with a selection of old photographs, so I took the opportunity of converting everything into a hardback book for him using an online printing company. I have recorded a lot of albums over the years, but that book is one of my proudest creations. With Dad needing a lot more sleep than me, it was also during my time at his house that I wrote most of this book.

With the new Threshold album now fully written, it was time to focus on the release of the third League Of Lights album, which we had decided to call *Dreamers Don't Come Down*. The phrase was taken from the song *Dreamers* and was about pursuing dreams and never giving up, a concept that had resonated strongly with us during the making of the record.

Having done so little to promote *In The In Between*, we learned from our mistakes and assembled a good team to help us manage and promote our new record. We commissioned videos for three more singles, opting for an anime video for *Modern Living*, a lyric video for *The Collector* and a live action production for *Persephone* which was filmed in North Macedonia. We would have loved to fly over and appear in it ourselves, but travel restrictions meant that we had to stay at home, so the video was more of a concept piece depicting a woman pursued by death across the beautiful North Macedonian landscape.

Dreamers Don't Come Down was released in March 2021 and earned some positive national coverage in *Prog*, *Classic Pop* and *Fireworks* magazines, as well as some long-awaited airplay on the BBC courtesy of the late DJ Janice Long. We considered releasing more singles as we felt that songs like *Ghosts*, *I Still Remember*, *Dreamers*, *With You* and *North Of The Sun* all had radio potential. However, there is a law of diminishing returns and it felt as though four singles were enough, so we drew the line after *Persephone*. We were immensely proud of our new record and had loved every moment of putting it together. Out of all our albums, *Dreamers Don't Come Down* felt the closest to what we had set out to achieve when we had recorded songs like *Summer* and *Bring It On* 20 years earlier when we were just starting out on our musical journey together.

* * *

As the summer approached, Covid-19 restrictions started to relax across the UK. Thin Ice Studios opened its doors again, so we were finally able to start recording the new Threshold album. Karl took charge of the drum and guitar sessions while I looked after vocals, bass and keyboards. It was great to be able to see everyone again after almost two years apart, and the recording sessions were some of the most enjoyable ones we have ever done.

One day I was in the control room at Thin Ice recording Glynn's vocals when I thought I saw a reflection of Damian's silhouette in the studio window. Damian had recently joined Arena and had come to the studio for a band meeting. I had not seen him since his controversial departure from Threshold four years earlier. "This could be interesting," I thought to myself. I took a deep breath, stopped the session and we headed outside to say hello.

"Mr Wilson!" I called out with a big smile.

Thankfully, he returned the smile and everything was fine. We all breathed a sigh of relief. Whatever water had needed to pass under the bridge had obviously now passed. I introduced him to Glynn, as astonishingly they had never met, despite all of the times they had replaced each other as Threshold's vocalist over the years. We joked and chatted for a little while, then I took a photo of the historic meeting and we went our separate ways again. And a heavy weight quietly lifted from my shoulders.

After numerous failed attempts by everyone to come up with an album title, I was working at my computer one morning compiling the final vocals when the phrase *Dividing Lines* popped out at me from one of Glynn's songs. I hadn't particularly been looking for an album title at that moment, but there it was and it sounded just right. I put the idea forward and it was met with approval, so our twelfth studio album finally had a name.

During the process of making *Dividing Lines* we also reissued some of our old Direct-to-Fan CDs that had been out of print for a while. This gave us the opportunity of extending *Surface To Stage* to a double CD by adding three tracks that had been left off the original release to fit onto a single disc. We also reissued our *Paradox* collection as a double CD, something we had meant to do for a long time, sacrificing some of the beauty of the original eight-disc box set for the practicality of not having to change discs every three songs.

Over the summer I returned to Cornwall with Farrah for our usual holiday. With no Threshold or League Of Lights songs to be composed, I briefly considered a fortnight without writing. But the feeling didn't last too long. The following morning I woke up before Farrah, and I couldn't stop myself. I slipped into the kitchen to make a pot of coffee as the sun rose, illuminating the rugged Cornish cliffs outside and the deep blue Atlantic Ocean beyond them. And once again I was inspired to write.

The decision to drop the sequel concept of *The Fall Of The Shires* had left me with a feeling of unfinished business. I had a storyline, an opening and closing song, the dark poem spoken by the speech synthesis software that was left over from the original *Legends* sessions, a few other parts that I had written in the meantime and a strong desire to see the concept through. So, over the course of the following two weeks, I mapped out my original story across eight chapters and continued writing. By the end of our holiday, I had written the lyrics and most of the music for an album of eight songs that would fit comfortably onto a single LP, telling the story in a more concise and focussed way than the Threshold record would have done.

Over the next few months I started putting together some demos, and before long I had a rough recording of the whole album. I also realised that I had storylines for two further sequels, so I was slightly relieved that Threshold had opted not to follow what could have become a very long road. I loved what I had produced, but it was purely a private undertaking, and I had no intention of pursuing it further. I even thought of an obscure name for the project to emphasis the point. It would be called Oblivion Protocol, a combination of two previously unused Threshold titles. If the project had a mission statement it was to go absolutely nowhere and to be heard by no one.

Meanwhile, after going nowhere for two years, Threshold was finally back on the road again to play two UK shows. We had previously been booked to perform at two HRH Prog Festival shows in Sheffield and London in 2020, where half of the roster would perform in one city on the first night and then swap to the other city the following night. The shows had been postponed due to Covid-19 and rescheduled for September 2021, but, with government restrictions constantly changing, nobody knew if they would go ahead. So to be back on tour again with Threshold was something of a surprise.

The festivals had been sold out for months, although it was uncertain how many fans would want to venture out because of the virus. As it turned out, the shows were well attended and we were pleased to discover that there were a good many Threshold fans at both venues to cheer us on. As is often the case at progressive rock festivals, we were the heaviest band on the bill. We were scheduled to perform between 1970s progressive rockers Atomic Rooster and headliners The Enid, who we had previously supported 25 years ago for Glynn's final show of his first tenure with Threshold. For our set we had originally intended to introduce some songs we hadn't played for a while such as *Devoted*, *Turn On Tune In* and *This Is Your Life*, but with two years off and no warm-up shows we opted to play it safe and built our set list around songs we had been performing regularly before the pandemic started.

As we took to the stage on Saturday night at the O2 Academy in Sheffield to start our opening song *Long Way Home*, conflicting thoughts and emotions filled my head and heart as I looked down at my keyboards and out into the crowd. For so long these keyboards, stands, racks, pedals and cables had felt like home, wherever we travelled in the world, standing next to Johanne as the rest of the band prowled across the stage in front of us. And it was wonderful to be home again. But, at the same time, I knew this was more of a temporary reprieve than a triumphant return, a small break in the clouds that allowed us to bask in the heat of the stage lights for a brief moment before returning to the darkness and uncertainty of the days and months to come.

There were thankfully very few signs of rust in our performance as we powered through our set, closing with *Lost In Translation* and *Small Dark Lines* before heading backstage, filled with a combination of euphoria and relief at a job well done. The following night we did it all over again at the glorious Shepherd's Bush Empire in London, and then suddenly it was all over.

"That was wonderful," said Johanne, as he tried hopelessly to peel off his sweat-soaked T-shirt after the show. "When can we do it again?" But nobody knew the answer.

Back at Thin Ice Studios, Karl broke the news that the property which housed the studio was being sold, so this would be the last album we recorded there. This came as quite a shock. I thought back to all the times I had worked at Thin Ice, the bands I had met, the lifelong friends I had made, and all the wonderful music that had been produced within those walls over the last quarter of a century. It would be hard to say goodbye. Over the winter we completed the album and submitted our work to Nuclear Blast in January 2022. It had been over 18 months since Karl had sent me his first demos to set the ball rolling for what would eventually become *Dividing Lines*, and it would be several more months before it was released. But we had finally completed our twelfth album and we were very proud of what we had produced.

With the Threshold album finally delivered, I found my thoughts returning to Oblivion Protocol. While I had originally only written and recorded it for my own personal satisfaction, I started to wonder if it was something I could release as a solo project, a spin-off story to *Legends* along the lines of all the Star Wars offshoots that have been made over the years. I mentioned the idea to Karl and Glynn and they gave me their blessing. Karl also kindly recorded a guitar solo for the opening song.

I discussed the project with some old friends at Atomic Fire Records, a label founded by former members of Nuclear Blast. Before long I was sending them the demos. I started to consider who else to involve in the project. It was wonderful to have Karl performing on the opening track, but I knew that Oblivion Protocol required its own identity rather than drawing further on members of Threshold. I started to dream up a wish list of musicians to form my perfect line-up. To my surprise, they all said yes.

So let me introduce you to the band...

On guitar I'm delighted to welcome Within Temptation guitarist and occasional League Of Lights collaborator Ruud Jolie. On bass is my former AudioPlastik bandmate Simon Andersson, also known for his work with Swedish progressive metallers Darkwater and a former member of Pain Of Salvation. And on drums is Darby Todd, the touring drummer for Devin Townsend, who lives just around the corner from me and almost auditioned for Threshold back in 1997. So that just leaves me to take on the roles of vocalist, keyboard player and producer.

On 19th July 2022 the UK recorded temperatures of over 40 °C for the very first time. There was a spate of fires across London and railway tracks buckled in the heat. It was the hottest weather that I had ever experienced, and by mid-afternoon my studio was so sweltering that it was almost unusable. At this very moment I found myself signing a record contract for Oblivion Protocol. I can't think of a more suitable day to sign with a company called Atomic Fire.

I had no idea when I started writing this book that it would conclude with me becoming the frontman of a band. I thought that I was quite content behind the keyboards, working in the background and staying out of the spotlight. I find myself filled with wonder, excitement and gratitude that something like this could happen. There have been times when I've thought of giving up, when I've felt so weighed down that I couldn't see a way forward. But somehow life has continued to surprise me in ways that I never thought possible. It has also made me realise that I'll have to reconsider my views on just being the man in the shadows.

But before I fully immerse myself in Oblivion Protocol there is a Threshold album to release.

Writing and producing *Dividing Lines* was only the start of the album's story. What follows is a schedule of singles, videos, promotional meetings, interviews, quotes, social media campaigns, website updates, signing sessions, paperwork and all the other jobs that take place behind the scenes to successfully launch an album. It's all part of the process, part of being in a band, part of doing what we love. We have also just agreed with Nuclear Blast to remix and remaster our early albums *Wounded Land*, *Extinct Instinct* and *Clone*, along with a fully restored recording of our unreleased London concert from 1999. So, I'm really looking forward to immersing myself in those old recordings once more.

I hope everyone will enjoy *Dividing Lines* as much as we do. We'll be watching closely as those early reviews come in, sharing that potent mix of anticipation, anxiety and, hopefully, joy as everyone hears the album for the first time and puts their thoughts into words. A while ago someone told me that they were looking forward to our new album and casually added: "Of course, it won't be as good as *Legends*!" But *Dividing Lines* has its own personality, a different atmosphere for a different time. I hope that our songs will continue to connect with those that listen to them and become part of the soundtrack of their lives. It's an honour that we don't take lightly. It can be a long road from composing the first lines of an album to releasing the final product, but it's always a road worth travelling. And I'm already looking forward to the next one.

***

Looking back now, it's hard to believe that I've been in Threshold for well over half of my life, a band that I thought I was just doing a couple of studio sessions for in the winter of 1992. We have come a long way since that first *Wounded Land* rehearsal in the damp, neglected Longcross village hall. We have travelled the world, released a large catalogue of music and even fulfilled my childhood dream of getting in the charts along the way. At 54 years old I still feel as young and creative as ever, with a heart full of hope and a head full of dreams. And I still have time to be many things.

> Maybe a painter, a guide, a clerk, a maker
> Or maybe a writer...

But, as long as I can choose, I will always choose music.

Acknowledgements

THIS BOOK WOULD NOT HAVE BEEN possible without so many people.

Firstly, I have to thank Farrah, love of my life, best friend and soulmate for her support and encouragement throughout this journey. I wrote this book over a period of more than a year and she has cheered me on through every moment, despite the endless hours I was lost in my thoughts or glued to my computer.

I must also thank all of my brothers who have been in Threshold past and present – Karl Groom, Damian Wilson, Jon Jeary, Nick Midson, Tony Grinham, Glynn Morgan, Nick Harradence, Jay Micciche, Mark Heaney, Johanne James, Steve Anderson, Pete Morten and the late Andrew 'Mac' McDermott. It has been a privilege to work with you all.

And without wishing to turn this into a prolonged awards acceptance speech, I really have to thank the countless people at Nuclear Blast, Atomic Fire, InsideOut, Giant Electric Pea, all the promoters, agents, tour crew, venue staff, support bands, journalists, bus drivers (well, most of them!), all the musicians and friends I've met and worked with along the way; my family for their love and support, Nick Shilton at Kingmaker for his 'if not now when' attitude, Professor Geoff Parks for his eagle proofreading eyes, and most importantly our loyal fans for loving our music, coming to our shows and cheering us on. You make me feel truly blessed.

I hope I have not offended anyone with my imperfect memories of the past. I have tried to be as accurate as possible, but I appreciate that history can have many versions. Either way I hope you have enjoyed joining me for the journey.

Thank you all.

Rich

Photography Acknowledgements

THE AUTHOR WOULD LIKE TO THANK the following sincerely for their kind permission to use their photographs in this book as follows:

- Tom Barnes for (1) front cover and (2) "I don't remember what the joke was…"

- Fudge Smith for (1) "Early Threshold photo session…"; (2) "Another early Threshold photo session…" and (3) montage photo #5.

- Nigel Crane for (1) "We started recording…"; (2) "Photo shoot for Threshold's fourth album…"; (3) "Impromptu photo shoot…"; (4) "Performing at London Astoria 2…"; (5) "Another shot from our LA2 show…"; (6) "At Thin Ice Studios in Virginia Water…"; (7) Official photo shoot for Threshold's *Critical Mass* album…" and (8) montage photo #6.

- Sy "Wooks" Seddon for (1) "Mac soaking in the atmosphere…" and (2) "On stage in Weert…"

- Axel Jusseit for (1) "Hard rocking on the Rock Hard stage…" and (2) "Relaxing behind the stage…"

- Ron Marzok for (1,2) "Additional photo shoot on location…" and (3-8) "Outdoor photo shoot on a cold winter day…"

- Julian Small for (1) "First official photo shoot of our new temporary line-up…" and (2) "Drinks at the Wheatsheaf Hotel…"

- Farrah West for (1) "Relaxing in the Netherlands…"; (2) "The last night…"; (3-6) "Back on stage for Threshold's only shows of 2021…"; (7) montage photo #4 and (8) inside back cover.

- Robert Burress for (1) "With Farrah…"; (2,3) "*March Of Progress* photo shoot…"; (4) "Back at Wisley Airfield…"; (5) "Photo shoot with Farrah…" and (6) "Threshold photo shoot for *Dividing Lines*…"

- Steve Anderson for (1) "Reviewing the mixes…" and (2) montage photo #8.

- Leon van Hulst for (1) "Lining up for our traditional end-of-show bow..." and (2) "Sharing a joke..."

- Hans-W. Rock for (1) "Pulling shapes..."; (2) "An impromptu sit down..." and (3) "Filming the audience..."

- Daniela Adelfinger for "Pouting through the smoke..."

- Leroy Ludovic for "Trying to look cool..."

- Nicole Schade for (1-4) "The guys rocking out at the Markthalle..."

- Astrid De Ronde for (1) "With our crew and support bands..." and (2) montage photo #1.

- Mix With The Masters for "A master class..."

- Dariusz Szermanowicz for "On set with Farrah..."

- Chris Meany for "Farrah on stage with Power Quest..."

- Joel Barrios (Norrsken Photography and Design) for "Our third visit to ProgPower USA..."

- Frank Landzettel (Mr ProgBook) for "League Of Lights at Artrock Festival..."

- Andreas Tittmann for "Another shot of Artrock Festival..."

- John Tucker for (1,2) montage photos #9 and #11.

- Johanne James for montage photo #13.

The photographs "Mercy Train..." and "Looking young and moody..." were taken by the late Malcolm Robertson.

The author and publisher have been unable to trace the photographers of (1) "All dressed up..."; (2) "Emergency Exit..."; (3) "Hanging out backstage..."; (4-7) "Long-haired lads on tour..."; (8) "Photo shoot for Threshold's third album..."; (9) "On 13th June 1998..."; (10) The tour bus casino..."; (11) "Outside Thin Ice Studios..."; (12) "A stage-eye view..."; (13) "Outside Oslo Airport..." and (14) montage photo #7.

All other photographs are copyright of the author.